W9-BNC-145

Never Name the Dead

Never Name the Dead

A Novel

D. M. ROWELL
Koyh Mi O Boy Dah

NEW YORK

Published in the United States by Crooked Lane Books, an imprint of The Quick Brown Fox & Company LLC.

Crooked Lane Books and its logo are trademarks of The Quick Brown Fox & Company LLC.

Library of Congress Catalog-in-Publication data available upon request.

ISBN (hardcover): 978-1-63910-127-6
ISBN (ebook): 978-1-63910-128-3

Cover design by Kara Klontz

Printed in the United States.

www.crookedlanebooks.com

Crooked Lane Books
34 West 27th St., 10th Floor
New York, NY 10001

First Edition: November 2022

10 9 8 7 6 5 4 3 2 1

For All My Relations

Prologue

A storm brewed outside and inside the cluttered workroom. Two men stood, long hook nose to long hook nose, rocking unsteadily on their old legs. James Sawpole stepped back, shook his head and snorted, "*Mawbane!* You dishonor the Kiowa Tribe, your family."

Wilson Crow shuffled backward and dropped onto the threadbare couch. He cleared his throat before pushing out, "It's better this way. Others will—"

James cut in, "You choke on your lies! You've done that since you were a boy. We all knew a lie was coming when you had to clear its way."

Wilson struggled to rise from the low-slung couch. Once righted, he pleaded, "You don't understand . . . it's my property—"

"Enough." James reached past Wilson to open a cedar spirit box sitting on a table by the couch. "My granddaughter is coming from California." He pulled out a pouch of cedar and a sage bundle. "You need to cleanse yourself, right yourself, find balance. You will see how shameful—"

"Don't lecture me, James. I have done what is necessary for my family." Wilson turned and watched as James retrieved his eagle-feather prayer fan before closing the box.

A buffalo jawbone club lay on the coffee-ringed table beside the spirit box. The dawn's first light fell on a table lamp with a Kiowa camp scene painted around its shade. For James, everything was a canvas.

James moved to his handmade easel desk. "My granddaughter arrives today. We will speak to the Tribal Council."

Wilson took a halting step. "Does she know?"

Shaking his head with disgust, James dropped into his desk chair, rocked the desk, splashing gray water from a multicolor speckled jar holding his well-used paintbrushes. "You've heard nothing."

Standing above James, Wilson looked about the room. His eyes settled on the buffalo jawbone club. "James, you're leaving me no choice."

James turned his chair to the desk. "There is no more to say." Signaling the end, James turned his back on Wilson.

Chapter One

This really was not a good time for me to leave.

But Grandpa had called. His message, "Granddaughter, *Bow anh tah geah daw. Aim hay ah,* I have a bad feeling—come now," worried me, but it had been Grandpa's voice that tugged at me. He sounded . . . wrong . . . out of balance.

Since then, I had not been able to reach him. I'd left a message telling him I had the earliest flight out. I was coming.

I didn't want to, but I was coming.

I swung the messenger bag over my shoulder. Thought a moment, then dropped the bag and unzipped the center compartment. I found the pocket hidden within and touched the supple leather of my medicine bundle. All these years away from the Reservation, our traditions; yet I kept the bundle close to me as if it held the medicine necessary to enrich my spirit, as my traditional Kiowa grandfather insisted.

I shook my head: enough stalling. I needed to catch a flight to Oklahoma.

During my ride to the San Jose International Airport, I left the necessary messages to keep production moving forward at the agency for the few days I would be away. After six months of careful research, strategy, and development, everything was in place for the announcement of my client's initial public offering, or IPO. Richard was taking his privately owned company public, and my agency was creating the story and images that would define it. We were down to reviews and executive rehearsals for the big day's announcements. I would be back before the final rehearsal for the big event. I told Richard the agency had everything handled. I would be gone two days, three max. Back as soon as possible.

Now, I paced from one end of Lawton–Fort Sill Regional Airport to the other. The airport was too small for me to work off my rising anxiety. I spun around to face the baggage area again. I'd left Grandpa a message that I would be on this flight, the only daily arrival. When I'd gotten off the plane, I'd left another voice message that I had arrived, and I'd called again just a few minutes ago. He wasn't answering his phone or returning my calls. I had expected Grandpa to be here, waiting for me. My worries mounted. This was not like him.

His summons had spurred me into immediate action. Grandpa sounded off—not like himself. I wanted to get here, help him, and get back to my Silicon Valley agency. Work needed me. I glanced at the digital clock above the baggage conveyor. An hour already wasted, waiting. Things were not going according to plan.

The annoying rattles and buzz of the baggage room AC continued as it struggled to keep the humidity and heat outside. I looked through the sliding glass doors, the small airport's only public entrance and exit. Where was he?

Back to pacing. I tugged my rolling suitcase behind me one short length of the airport to the other, my phone grasped tightly in my free hand while my eyes scanned the few gathered to greet or leave. Not much of a crowd. Mostly military personnel, with country folks scattered here and there. To one corner I noticed a man in a dress shirt and tie in an intense conversation with a small Kiowa woman. His yellow tie with, yes, matching yellow cowboy boots stood out in the sea of military green and faded jeans. Obviously, this guy was someone playing at cowboy.

My eyes returned to the digital display of the outside temperature and time, claiming it was a hundred and two degrees outside. That seemed impossible—it was only ten o'clock in the morning. But this was late June in Lawton, Oklahoma.

There by the luggage conveyor, I spotted the back of an elderly Kiowa man, his braids, more gray than black, hanging down below his collar. I waved and called out, "Hey, Grandpa."

Before the man turned fully around, I knew he wasn't my grandfather. I tossed a "Sorry—wrong grandpa" toward him and moved away, letting a slight smile slip out as I wondered how many other "grandpas" had turned with my call.

The hiss of the automatic doors opening pulled my eyes to the front of the airport. A solid, fifty-something Kiowa woman marched in. Her head swiveled, making her silver disk earrings swing as she looked quickly around the airport. She caught sight of me and headed in my direction.

Chapter Two

The woman looked faintly familiar. She had the typical look of the older Kiowa women that I had grown up with: one dark braid with threads of gray, pulled back tight as if to center a long straight nose on a scowling face. She aimed her scowl at me as she strode over. The woman announced, "You're James Sawpole's granddaughter." Before I could say yes, she continued, "I see you still got that curly hair."

The old jab was a direct hit. *I was different.* I had been born with naturally curly hair amid a reservation full of people with stereotypical straight Indian hair. Even in my family, I'd been the only one born with this wild hair. My curly hair branded me a mixed breed to the tribes while my high cheekbones and long hook nose marked me Indian to *Hanpokos,* the non-Indians.

Despite the jab, I smiled. My grandfather had called my hair "buffalo hair" to make me feel special rather than an outsider in my family and tribe.

I dropped my messenger bag from my shoulder. "Yes, James Sawpole is my grandfather. Have we met?" I took in her going-to-town clothes—dark slacks topped with a matching blouse and a Pendleton blanket–style blazer. The silver of her handmade earrings reflected the bright colors of her jacket.

She faced me, but her eyes scanned the area, searching. She seemed anxious, looking for something, someone. Then she did something very un-Kiowa: she did not formally introduce herself, reciting her ancestors, so that I could then reply, noting our cross points through the generations. She simply launched into "You may remember, I'm Anna ManyHorse. I am a legislator for the Kiowa Tribe. Your grandpa and I were supposed to meet early this morning. He made it sound urgent, but didn't show up. James mentioned he planned on being at your flight. I thought I would catch him here." Anna continued scanning nearby faces. "I need to talk with him."

Grandpa's words echoed in my mind: "*Bow anh tah geah daw. Aim ah.* I have a bad feeling."

Anna's eyes settled on me. In typical Kiowa fashion, she waited for me to consider what she had said. I didn't have a response. Grandpa hadn't left any other message, and I couldn't reach him. But maybe Anna had some answers.

"My grandfather's not here. Why were you meeting? Do you know what he—"

A shrill voice rang out, "Is he here? Where is he?"

The screeching voice came from a small, colorful Kiowa woman, about the same age as Anna but decked out in a clash of a floral pink top and an orange blossoms jacket topping plum-colored pants. She pushed in alongside Anna. The woman placed her hands on her hips and aggressively leaned forward—at me. "Well, where is he? Just like him to call a meeting and not show. He's always been full of himself." Her dark, shoulder-length hair bounced.

Before I could respond to the small woman, Anna faced her, lifted her left palm up while making a quick horizontal swiping motion with her right hand across the upturned palm—the Plains Indian sign language "stop now" motion. One I was very familiar with from my childhood.

Anna followed the motion with "*Ohdayhah*—enough. James is a Tribal Elder, our sacred story keeper. I was talking with his granddaughter before you interrupted—"

I heard a low harrumph behind me. It came from the man that I had thought was Grandpa earlier. He seemed to know the two women. "Anna, what are you doing here?"

Before Anna could answer, the smaller woman announced, "Anna's on important business." She wiggled as she declared, "Tribe business."

At that comment, I remembered I had met Anna years ago with my grandfather. She was one of the few in the Kiowa Nation government that Grandpa liked and, more importantly, respected.

The man that I had mistaken for my grandfather cracked a smile at Anna and the small woman. "Tribe business at the airport? You all runnin' off?" He laughed at his joke. No one joined.

Up close, I recognized the older man: Wilson. I couldn't remember his last name or family connections. He had been a tribe legislator years ago. Grandpa had known Wilson since their shared childhood, yet Grandpa had never voted for or endorsed Wilson.

Anna scowled at the two intruders and turned back to me. "As I said, I'm Anna." She shifted to include the others. "This is Nita Yee, an admin at the Kiowa Tribal Complex, and you may know Wilson Crow."

Crow . . . My eyes shifted from Anna to Wilson Crow. I knew someone named Crow. Nita moved closer to Wilson, and under her breath, barely audible, she hissed, "Just stop!" Wilson scowled and shifted away from her.

Anna went on, not noticing the exchange, "Wilson, you are no longer on the Kiowa Tribal Council or a legislator; why *I* am here is none of your concern."

"More than hers," Wilson used his chin to point at Nita Yee. "She's never been a legislator. Just a lifetime hanger-on, always got a job at the tribe, don't you, Nita?" Wilson smiled with no humor at the small woman.

Before Nita could respond, Anna demanded, "And you, why are you here?"

Wilson coughed, cleared his throat, and muttered, "Guess same as you. Lookin' for James."

Nita scowled at Wilson while Anna glared at them both. All three seemed to have forgotten me. I stayed silent standing to the side. No one seemed happy to see the other. Even though I had been gone for years, I knew this display of hostility was wrong. Kiowas usually behaved better than this—in public, anyway.

Grandpa would be embarrassed for them. Where was he? I thumbed the "Redial" button on my phone, and this time the call went straight to voicemail. I let the others hear Grandpa's recorded greeting. At the beep, I responded, "Grandpa, I'm still here at the airport. There are a few others looking for you too. Give me a call. I'm worried." I hit the "End" button and faced the three.

Nita shook her head, "Well, isn't that just like James? Can't be bothered."

Anna gave her a stern look, seemed to want to say something, but squeezed her lips together.

Wilson's eyes focused on something over Anna's shoulder. Almost in a daze he muttered, "Things are happening. *Bow anh tah geah daw.*"

Hair bristled up my neck, I shivered in the heat. *"Bow anh tah geah daw. I have a bad feeling."* It's what Grandpa had said in his message. The last thing I had heard from him.

A dread hit me. I turned to Wilson. "Mr. Crow . . . Wilson, is my grandfather all right?"

Anna and Nita leaned in.

Wilson cleared his throat. "He . . . yeah . . ."

Anna reached toward Wilson. "You talked to James this morning?"

Wilson stepped back. "He said his granddaughter was coming in." Wilson's eyes slid across Anna to me. "Time's wasting. We gotta go."

Wilson stooped, took my roller suitcase with my messenger bag on top and marched out of the airport. The door hissed behind him. Wilson didn't look back.

I watched him rolling my bags out to the parking lot. I turned back to Anna and Nita. Both remained in place, staring at where Wilson had been.

Grandpa's words, *"Bow anh tah geah daw. I have a bad feeling,"* drummed through my head and sent a chill up my neck.

Was Grandpa in danger?

I was wasting time here. I needed information from Wilson. Now. He couldn't leave without me.

"Sorry. I have to . . ." I trailed off.

I nodded to the two women, turned, and chased Wilson, my suitcases, and—I hoped—answers.

Chapter Three

I caught up with Wilson as he slung my messenger bag into a faded blue 1963 Chevy pickup truck that looked like it still did chores on a working farm. My roller case followed the messenger bag, sliding across a long bench seat. Wilson grunted, grabbed the steering wheel, and pulled himself up into the old truck. I opened the passenger door and jumped inside as the truck's engine coughed to life.

Wilson jammed the floor stick shift into reverse, which shoved my suitcase and messenger bag farther down the bench seat and pushed me tight into the metal door. I started a futile search for a seat belt. "Grandfather . . . Wilson, right? I think we met when I was younger." We both jostled forward as Wilson found and engaged first gear.

Sweat collected and dropped down my forehead as I waited for a reply. I tried again to get a conversation started. "Did my grandpa send you for me?" My question met silence. Fishing for a response, I muttered, "Strange, with all the family around . . ."

Wilson bit. "I told James I was headed to town. No sense wasting good rubber."

I looked around my suitcase at the driver of the old pickup. Wilson had the typical look of a full-blood Kiowa elder. Long hook nose, braids more gray than black, and the Kiowa long earlobes—cursed with growing longer and longer as we aged. I was in fear of my earlobes eventually sitting on my shoulders at the rate they were stretching.

Since I had Wilson talking, I threw another question at him, the one that mattered: "Is my grandfather all right?"

Wilson cleared his throat again, kept his eyes on the road. "We was talkin' early this morning about some frackin' problems around the Slick Hills. We was discussin' what to do after them oil boys wouldn't listen to James." Wilson stole a look my way.

I leaned toward him. "Oil boys? Fracking? Is Grandpa having problems with wildcatters out in his back pastures?"

Much of the backcountry pasture lands were miles from the nearest house. Anything could happen out in that solitude. It could be days, maybe weeks before unwanted activities would be discovered.

"Your granddaddy will have to tell you about it, but it's not good." Wilson slammed the truck into third gear. It bucked forward, and this shook a bit more out of Wilson. "They're messin' with the spring. That hurts everyone farmin' down river." He nodded his head in agreement with his statement. "But I ain't got nothin' to say—you'll have to talk to your granddaddy 'bout them oil boys messin' with him." His lips smacked close.

That's where he left it—*"Them oil boys messin' with him."* My mood shifted; I started getting mad at "them oil boys."

We bounced down the road, heat building and silence growing. Stereotype though it may be, it was true of my tribe—my family: the stoic, silent Indian lives. I returned Wilson's silence. I was tired of trying to get more out of him. Why didn't Grandpa explain what was going on? My nagging worry over my grandpa had evolved to frustration. I wasn't sure who to be most irritated with: Grandpa, Wilson, or "them oil boys." The old truck's AC blew hot air about. I sweated and brooded while watching the town go past.

In the ten years since I had last been in Lawton, a lot had changed. Lawton had started as an early U.S. Cavalry town on the fringes of Fort Sill, built during the 1860s Indian wars. The small town thrived and died, depending on the Fort's roller-coaster existence. For the last dozen years, Lawton and Fort Sill had been riding a rapid upswing.

Lawton now sported two Walmart Supercenters and too many restaurant chains to count, catering to the always-on-the-go military families. Cars streamed here and there; people went from one air-conditioned location to another. No one ventured outside in the mounting heat and humidity. Even the blackbirds stayed put, lined up on the wires above. They hunched forward with wings partially open in hopes of capturing a wayward puff of cool air. I swear I could see small black tongues hanging out of beaks as we drove by.

As a kid, we only came into town for our twice-a-month grocery shopping trips or to go to the Lawton Indian Hospital on one of the family's numerous emergency room runs. I started treks to the hospital as soon as I could move on my own. Stitches were my specialty. At one point, I counted over a hundred, half of them accomplished in one spectacular summer of horse racing.

At twelve, I was the perfect size and weight to race grandpa's prized quarter horse. Sundays were race day. After a few good showings at the pasture race track, I got rides for the day's other nine races. I was paid five dollars a race, double if we placed, twenty for second, and a pocket-burning fifty for first place. At the very least, I went home with forty-five dollars every Sunday, and on a few occasions I pocketed over a hundred dollars. The memory still brought a smile to my face.

A vibration in my front pocket brought me back to reality. Wilson leaned forward to look at me around the suitcase barrier. "I got a quick stop. Is that you, or a new sound in my Bess?"

I pulled the phone from my pocket and waved it where I thought Wilson could see it. I leaned forward to be heard around the suitcase wall. "Stop where you need to. I'll take care of some business." I waved the phone again.

He replied with a grunt and shoved the case back at me, securing it in barrier position.

In search of privacy, I turned toward the passenger door as I answered the call. "This is Mae."

"Mae, you've picked a fine time to leave me," a voice sang from the phone. I smiled, mentally seeing Bernie, my five-foot-tall office manager. She kept things running as smooth as an assembly line. Like a feral cat, she had showed up one day and never left; she'd insisted I needed her—and she was right.

I lowered my voice. "Hey, Bernie, doing okay. I'm headed to my grandfather's house now." I couldn't see Wilson, but I felt his ears perk up.

"You never explained what was going on. Why are you there and not here? Especially now."

"My grandpa called." I knew she wanted more than that. She didn't understand how I could leave the agency with

Richard's company IPO event so close. I added, "Bernie, it's a big thing that my grandfather *called*. He is very traditional."

I bounced and slid forward on the seat as the truck bucked over a driveway lip. My messenger bag flipped into the footwell. I reached down into it—more like a cavern in these old trucks—to retrieve the bag. I could see Wilson's faded denim-clad legs down to his work-worn cowboy boots.

Bernie pushed for more. "What does that mean?"

"Calling me, using the phone, means this is serious." I pulled myself back up into the seat. I nodded in silent agreement with myself: I had thought it was serious and had dropped everything to be here. Yet where was my grandfather?

I tried to keep the worry out of my voice. "It may have something to do with fracking." Sweat rolled down my long nose.

She replied, "What the frick do you have to do with fracking?"

Wilson drove down a single lane in a large parking lot facing the backs of several businesses. I'd lost track of where we were. The town had changed so much since my last visit.

"Bernie, what do you need?"

I heard a sharp intake of breath; she wasn't used to me being abrupt with her. Bernie became all business. "Just wanted to let you know Richard is placated. We're doing a run-through this afternoon. The only problem is Thomas. He's looking over the artwork after Marcus has already given directions. It's getting ugly and I don't mean the art."

I felt my shoulders tighten at the sound of my business partner's name. A partnership with Thomas had been a mistake. Originally, he funded the agency's start-up while I brought in the clients. It had seemed like a good match . . . then.

Wilson made an abrupt right, nosed the pickup truck up tight to a seven-foot stucco wall. I watched his brown work-worn hand shove the long stick shift into neutral, turn the key, then remove and pocket it. Wilson muttered, "Right back. Don't go nowhere." The old metal door slammed close.

"*Hey, Mae*, you hear me?"

Bernie's voice pulled me back to our conversation. I focused. "Bernie, yes. Okay, do this. Leave Thomas there at the office. The crew know to do *only* what Marcus has directed. You—no, Marcus—take the latest version to Richard, do the run-through at Richard's office. He will love the personal attention from the creative director."

I could hear Bernie tapping away on the keyboard. "Yeah, that works with everyone's schedules. Got it." The keyboard sound stopped. "Did you get the printouts of each presentation?"

Her topic shift threw me for a moment. I had to think back. "Yep, I took them along with the pile of mail on my desk. Haven't gone through them, but I'll get to it." I remembered a couple of oversized envelopes in the batch I had jammed into my messenger bag. I liked to review speech and visuals in hard copy, side by side. Unconsciously, I patted the bag. Everything I needed to keep Richard's IPO press event on track was in my messenger bag. "I'll go through it all as soon as I get a chance."

Bernie pushed at me. "Is everything all right?"

I paused a moment, then spilled. "I'm sorry. Things are confusing here. I haven't seen my grandfather yet. There was a weird scene at the airport, and I don't really know the guy I'm riding with . . ."

Looking around, I realized that to the front of me was the stucco wall; to my right, too close to allow the truck's passenger door to open, sat a garbage dumpster; and on my left was a suitcase barrier blocking access to the driver's door. I was trapped in this rapidly heating metal cab. The passenger door had no crank to roll the window down. I used my fingers on the exposed sprocket. The window stayed in place. Sweat beaded on my forehead.

"Mae, you're in a truck with someone you don't know?"

Drops rolled off my forehead. "It's not like that—he knows my grandpa." I shifted around in my seat, pushed and displaced the suitcase, giving myself an extra inch or two of breathing room. The suitcase was wedged tight against the floor stick shift. There seemed to be less air available.

It felt like the heat had increased inside the metal cab ten degrees since Wilson had left. Sweat trickled down between my breasts. Panic rose. I didn't like being trapped in small places. I needed to breathe moving air.

I cut Bernie off. "I really have to go. I know you've got this. Just keep Thomas out of it." I shoved the phone into my pocket.

I knew it was pointless, but I tried to open my door. Not even a puff of air came through the inch-wide opening. I leaned forward; my shirt clung to my now sweat-soaked back. I tried to control rising panic.

The truck engine and its AC was off, both windows closed, my door blocked and unable to be opened, and my own suitcase formed a fourth wall in this oven. I couldn't stay inside the cab much longer. The heat continued to rise. I needed to get out.

I turned to examine the suitcase barrier. The stick shift blocked any attempt at crawling to the driver side from the floor well. There wasn't enough room between the top of the case and the truck's ceiling to go over the suitcase. Pushing the bag toward the driver's door and reaching around to the door handle looked most promising. If I could get the driver's door open, I could push the suitcase out the door and escape this furnace.

I shoved the suitcase; it didn't move. I pushed harder—nothing. The suitcase was wedged between the seat back, the steering wheel, and the stick shift. Its soft top would give, if I could shove hard enough. Sweat rolled down my nose as I moved into position. I needed to get to the driver's door handle.

I wedged my back against the door, placed my feet on the side of my suitcase, and pushed. It moved, shifted, and stopped. I slid forward, reached around the case for the door handle—still too far away. I put my shoulder into the case and shoved. It released like a popped cork for about four inches, then hit the metal door. I fell forward with the case, jarring my jaw on the side of the stopped case.

The heat made it hard to breathe. I shook my head to clear it—I had to focus on the door handle. I maneuvered around the case, stretched and reached for the door handle. My fingers brushed the warm metal. Escape remained just out of reach.

Determined, I heaved forward, gaining less than an inch, but enough to finger the handle and pull it down. A loud clunk announced my freedom. I didn't waste any time, I shoved the suitcase out the truck door ahead of me, rolled it to the front of the truck, then stepped away to breathe.

The still air felt cool on my soaked back and front. I tried to take a deep breath but was blocked by air so thick and heavy it was impossible to suck it in quickly. Still, it felt good to be free of the hot truck.

What was Wilson thinking, leaving me trapped in the truck's cab in this heat? I stomped back to the truck's open door, reached in for my messenger bag, and dragged it out. Where was he? Just what I wanted to do—chase down another missing Indian.

I slung my messenger bag over a shoulder and headed to the back of the truck. We were parked at the end of a single lane coming down the middle of a block of businesses back doors. I wasn't sure which side of the block Wilson had walked along or what door he might be behind.

Halfway down the lane, a van idled outside an open back door. I headed in that direction, in pursuit of Wilson and, in truth, air conditioning. I needed to cool down physically and emotionally.

As I got closer to the van, I slowed. Over the engine, I could hear snatches of raised voices.

". . . has it, get it back . . ."

Then, a lower, barely audible, "Gera . . . arranged."

I was pretty sure the lower voice was Wilson's, but the exchange sounded tense. I hung back, not wanting to interrupt. Yet I was curious as to whom Wilson was talking with. I peered under the idling van to see a pair of well-worn cowboy boots toe to toe with a set of new work boots.

I angled wide, staying out of sight. I was sure the old cowboy boots were Wilson's, but wanted to see who belonged to the new work boots. As I moved closer, I made out Wilson's low clipped tones. "Don't worry about James—"

That brought me up.

James. My grandpa.

Something was wrong.

Wilson's comments propelled me forward at the same time the wearer of the new work boots turned from Wilson with a whine loud enough for all to hear, "Grandpa, I need it now." I stopped in place, stared at a face I had last seen with peach fuzz but that now sported a ragged, mountain man–inspired beard.

At twelve, after I had sent him home bleeding and crying, his mother had erupted from their house shouting obscenities. One insult she hurled at me I had never heard before: *lesbian*. I didn't know what the word meant, but there was truth in the sound of it.

Last thing I'd expected was to run into the man who had married my first love.

Chapter Four

I stood rooted to the spot, eyes locked with Buck Crow's. My body broke out in a cold sweat. I was unable to look away from him.

He was still solid, with a full chest and ripped arms. In high school Buck had been a star pitcher. He had spent hours boasting about that, lifting weights, and bulking his body up. By then, he had learned he needed muscles to back up his bullying ways.

In our senior year, Buck was named homecoming king; and my Georgie, queen. After that, she started seeing Buck as a convenient cover for her conservative parents. I refused to continue our by then two-year secret relationship behind the guise of her dating Buck. It all came to a head in a sensational senior prom exposure that kept the gossips drumming for months. In the end, Georgie stayed, dated Buck, and married him straight out of high school. I left for UC Berkeley and never looked back.

Buck broke the freeze. "What the fu—" His eyes slid toward Wilson as he remembered his grandfather's presence, and he stopped short. Neither of us moved. We were twelve again, facing off. At that age we had been evenly matched in body size; my advantage had been righteous anger and a stubborn refusal to admit defeat at all costs.

After discovering an old bike chain, Buck had decided it was fun to use it as a whip on the younger kids, always the smallest ones. When I found my younger brother with link-style welts across his upper arms, I went blind with rage. I had Buck on the ground, landing a solid punch to his nose before I was pulled from him. Being beaten up by a girl was embarrassing, but it was his tears that shamed him—and his mother—the most.

Wilson burst between us, causing Buck and me to break our stare-down. I faced Wilson. "You were talking about James Sawpole, my grandpa. What is going on?"

Wilson glared at me. I knew I had broken one of our tribe's unspoken taboos: Do not be direct, especially to an elder. It is considered rude to question an individual directly—they will share when ready—but I had no time for such foolishness. "Wilson, where is my grandpa?"

I was pushed backward as Buck shoved forward between us and spoke: "Don't speak to my grandfather like that." Buck puffed up to his full five feet nine inches.

I straightened myself, stood tall, and faced Buck. "Get out of the way. I am talking to Wilson."

Buck's face distorted with anger; his eyes burned into me. I ignored him, moved to the side, and looked directly at his grandfather. "Wilson, what is—"

Before I could finish, Buck again shifted to face me. He seemed to increase in size, inflated with hate and anger. I refused to cower as he towered over me, spitting rage. "You little dyke, you haven't changed a bit! You need a good man to teach you to behave." A spark of malicious glee came into his dark eyes. "I got Georgie trained real good now." Through his bushy beard, his lips curled into a smile.

I refused to react. My face remained closed. I forced it to. But I wanted to beat him with my clenched fists.

I grew up tough from necessity, not just from living on a working family ranch with a wildlife refuge for a backyard but also as an Indian surrounded by many who hated us simply for being who and what we are. I learned early to stand my ground and often to back my stance up with my fists. Once I arrived in Silicon Valley, I traded the fists for the art of persuasion, building a thriving communications agency. Now, back in Oklahoma for less than two hours, I was back to fists.

Before I could launch into Buck, Wilson pushed in. "Enough, Buck. Kiowas don't think that way. It must be your mother's Apache blood polluting your mind lately."

Buck grabbed Wilson's age-bent shoulder, held it tight. "Never Kiowa enough for you, old man. Well, I am all you got, and don't forget it." Buck squeezed and Wilson grimaced but made no sound. Then Buck released his grandfather with a cold grin. "It's nearly noon now, Grandpa. I need it by four. And I don't mean Indian time. Do. Not. Be. Late."

Buck stomped over to the van, got in, slammed the door and squealed out of the parking area. I watched, too stunned to react.

A man in a yellow tie leaned out of a back door and peered over at us. Others, drawn by the squealing tires, stuck heads and shoulders out back doors to watch Wilson walk toward his truck. Face forward, Wilson marched past the prying eyes.

I watched all this, yet felt detached from it as my mind slowly tried to process what was going on. Questions repeated on a constant loop: Had something happened to Grandpa? What did Buck have to do with it? Did this have anything to do with fracking on Indian land? Where was Grandpa? Buck . . . Grandpa . . . Georgie?

I pulled at my hair. *Oh, Georgie!*

Enough. I had to stop the spin.

Adrenaline tremors shook my hands. I clenched them tightly to stop the shaking. I took a deep breath, then released it and my fists. I slung my messenger bag toward my back and went after Wilson. He knew something. If I couldn't get him to talk, at least he was a ride to Grandpa's house. Where I should get answers.

I reached Wilson as he opened the truck's door. His tender shoulder caused him to wince. Seeing this ignited my anger at Buck. The bully had injured his grandfather. I forced it down—again—and tried to speak with a calming voice. "Grandfather, are you hurt?"

Wilson ignored me. Impulsively, I stepped forward, halting his progress into the truck. "Wilson, what is happening?"

He answered with a flat stare. His eyes were dead orbs.

I tried again, "Is my grandpa okay?"

Wilson snorted and reached past me for the oversized steering wheel. "You want a ride to your grandpa's? 'Cause I'm leavin'."

I knew he had avoided answering my questions—and probably would be silent the whole way to my grandfather's house. But rides out to the backcountry were hard to get.

I gave in. "*Haw*, yes, I would appreciate a ride."

Wilson let a slight smile slip. It was gone before I was sure I saw it.

I looked around for my roller case. I had left it by the truck's door after my earlier escape from the overheated truck cab. Wilson must have moved it. I looked back at him. "Wilson, did you see my suitcase?"

He used the steering wheel to pull himself into the truck. He winced and rubbed his shoulder as he settled into the seat. He grunted, "*Hawnay*, no." Without another word, Wilson pulled out a phone and directed his full attention to its small screen.

I glanced toward the few heads still sticking outside back doors and called back to Wilson. "I'm going to check to see if anyone noticed my case."

His head came up from the phone. "Sure, you do that." Suddenly helpful, Wilson leaned forward with a sneer that was offered as a smile. "Here, give me your green bag. It's too hot to carry that around."

A clump of sweat-soaked, dark curls flopped over my eye. "No. I'm much more comfortable keeping it with me." I pushed the wet mass off my forehead and turned toward the back doors in time to watch the last one close.

There was no answer at the first door I tried. The next one was a Quick Copy Center. The kids working barely looked up from their phones when I tried to ask if they had seen my roller case. They saw nothing, heard less, and barely spoke anything.

The next door wasn't fully closed. Its dead bolt was extended, keeping the door from seating. Cool air seeped through the crack. It lured me in. I pushed the door as I stepped into a cool office. The chilled air felt wonderful. I took a moment to indulge before calling out, "Hello! Anyone here?"

No one answered, but I could hear low murmurs ahead. I stood a moment longer, soaking up the AC, before moving forward toward curtains that separated a back office from the store front. The curtains muffled an ongoing conversation. One of the voices sounded familiar. I stayed silent but edged forward.

A woman's raised voice came clearly through the curtain: "All I want to know is if any Kiowa has requested testing."

It sounded like Anna from the airport, the legislator who had been going to meet with Grandpa this morning. On tiptoes, I moved closer to the canvas curtains and leaned toward a small opening.

A gruff voice answered, "Anna, I'm not getting in the middle of this."

Anna! It must be the Kiowa legislator.

I couldn't see anything through the curtain opening. I inched closer to the crack. The rough canvas material tickled the tip of my long nose.

"I just—"

Gruff Voice cut Anna off. "If you have water you want me to sample and analyze, let me know. Otherwise, I have work to tend to."

An itching sensation developed deep in my nose. An explosion was building. I pinched my nose, held my breath. The itch continued. I couldn't risk staying in place any longer. I eased back and escaped out the back door.

I stepped away from the door, rubbing my itchy nose and thinking. It had to be Anna, the Kiowa legislator, that Gruff Voice was talking with. Way too much of a coincidence to be anyone else. Though I wish I had been able to confirm it.

I hesitated a moment before I turned back to the door and knocked loudly. This time a wiry, lean man in his mid-thirties opened the door. "Yes?"

I smiled into his slightly whiskered face. "Sorry to disturb you. I left a black roller case out here. Any chance you saw it?"

The man answered at the same time as he moved to close the door. "Naw, I've been up front with a customer. Sorry."

He was the owner of the gruff voice.

I gave him my most winning smile. "Customer? What type of business do you have?"

Gruff Voice returned my smile but didn't open the door any further. "I do pretty specialized work." He turned his faded blue eyes on me. "I don't think you would be needing my services."

I amped up my smile. "Now I've got to know. What do you do?"

The door opened a bit. Gruff Voice leaned toward me. "I'm a water quality inspector. I sample and test the quality of . . . well . . . water." His eyes smiled at the end.

I leaned forward. "It does sound specialized. I'm surprised you have enough customers to have an office here."

I was flirting, working him. It was the easiest way to get the information I wanted. And I was never going to see this guy again. Sometimes it paid to play the girlie part.

Gruff Voice pulled the door toward him. "Oh yeah. I'm real busy." The door opened wider. "Fracking has been really good for my business."

I moved a bit closer. "How?"

"All the regulatory hurdles have been relaxed. Any one dealing with oil and fracking needs me." With this, he opened the door wide. He had the look of a man who preferred being outdoors. His jeans appeared worn and faded from use, and the same with his plaid shirt.

I stole a glance toward Wilson's truck. He hadn't left yet.

I gave Gruff Voice an encouraging nod. That's all he needed to continue, "I've been dealing with individuals, tribes, the feds, and oil people." He hung a thumb from a front pocket. "Business is good."

I leaned forward. "Tribes? Why would tribes need you?"

"Tribes are fighting over fracking." Gruff Voice rubbed his whiskered chin. "It sure brings in the money for some. But oil guys can really mess up local water and the environment."

I didn't have to fake interest. Gruff Voice had my full attention.

He hitched his jeans up. "I was just talking to one of the high-ups in a local tribe." The man's eyes focused on my obvious Kiowa nose and high cheekbones.

Before I could confirm it had been Anna, a buzzer from the front of the business sounded.

Gruff Voice looked over his shoulder and back to me. "Hey, I'm Roy. Come by the front later, and we'll go have a drink."

"I'm just here for a short visit. But I will keep your offer in mind." I gave him a final smile. My cheeks ached. Smiling was hard work.

The buzzer sounded again. Roy smiled before he closed the door.

I wandered toward the next door, reviewed what Roy had told me. He tested water for individuals and tribes, *and* he had just been talking to a tribe official. Had to be Anna. What was she after? Did it have anything to do with Grandpa and fracking? Was that why Grandpa wanted to meet this morning and why he was being urgently sought at the airport?

I gave a sideways glance toward Wilson's truck. It looked like Wilson was on the phone with someone. Good. That gave me more time. I moved to the next office.

I knocked on a door marked "TribalVision Gallery." A young woman cracked open the door and peeked out at me. I could feel cool air escaping. I leaned toward it. "I'm sorry to bother you, but I lost my black roller case. Any chance you saw it out here?"

The door opened enough for me to see she was blonde. She looked up the parking lot. "Well, Gerald had one, but I'm sure it was his." In the distance Wilson's old truck engine coughed into life.

The blonde opened the door wider and stepped out to look up and down the block. "I don't know where he went." Sweat beaded on her forehead. She wiped it away and turned to rush—as well as anyone in four-inch heels could—back to the cool inside before she could melt. She called back at me, "Maybe he's in the office."

I took this as an invitation and followed. Chills raced down my back when I stepped from the humid heat outside to the icy cool inside. Soothing Native flute music played softly in the background as I went down a hallway lined with watercolor paintings from the artists that defined Early American Indian easel paintings: Woody Crumbo and the Kiowa Six: Lois Smoky, Stephen Mopope, Spencer Asah, James Auchiah, Monroe Tsatoke, and Jack Hokeah. The hallway led to a solid, golden oak double door. The blonde woman disappeared inside. I followed, slowly. It was hard to leave the incredible art.

As I entered the office, a coveted C. E. Rowell watercolor caught my eye. It was a simple, yet striking painting of a Kiowa *Koitsenko*, or Wild Dog Warrior, one of the ten bravest warriors in the Kiowa tribe. Only *Koitsenko* warriors used a leather sash and society lance, to stake themselves to the ground and the people they protected. In the painting the young *Koitsenko* faced a mounted Ute warrior. The Kiowa warrior stood with one end of the sash around his neck and the other end driven through by the lance into the ground. The artist, with simple lines and primary colors, brought a moment in history alive.

The painting held me. It took a few moments before I noticed a tall case directly beneath the vivid painting. Involuntarily, I sucked in a breath. In the case stood an original beaded and ragged-feathered *Koitsenko* sash and lance. I stepped closer to peer in. This set had obviously survived many battles on the open Plains.

I could not believe my eyes. There had only been ten *Koitsenko* sash and lance sets ever created. Each was handed down from warrior to warrior through the generations. Only two remained in the tribe, and both were cherished family artifacts. I couldn't believe either family would allow their original *Koitsenko* sash and lance set to be captured and displayed this way.

The blonde's voice pulled me away from the display. "Well, Gerald's not here—or any suitcase."

It was hard, but I looked over at her. "I really appreciate your help. Do you—"

Before I could continue to question her about the *Koitsenko* sash and lance, a flash of silver caught my eye. A clear shadow box stood on the corner of a massive mahogany desk. Two four-inch silver disks with wood centers peeking from their edges were suspended within the box.

As if pulled by a magnetic force, I moved closer, to be sure. The disks were 1801 Jefferson peace medals. The side profile of Thomas Jefferson shone on one side, and on the other, in high relief, were two clasped hands, one an Indian's and the other, a soldier's, both centered under the legend "Peace and Friendship." The shadow box was built to hold three medal disks. Room for one more remained.

I stood staring. "Those are amazing."

"Oh, you really shouldn't be in here." The assistant danced over to the medals. "Those are priceless. One-of-a-kind kinda thing." She straightened her tight business jacket.

I moved in for a closer look. The medals' wood centers were crumbled and worn from age.

Preening a bit, she continued as if reciting, "Lewis and Clark had over eighty-nine peace medals when they started their expedition; but only three four-inch disks. They gave those largest three peace medals to significant Native American chiefs during their expedition." In an aside, she clarified, "You know, the Lewis and Clark Expedition. Sometimes you just have to say it all together to understand, you know, *the Lewis and Clark Expedition.* Anyways . . ." She tossed her blonde locks back. "This is the first time all three large peace medals will be together since Thomas Jefferson presented them to Lewis and Clark before the start of their historical expedition."

I eyed the empty spot.

She picked up a cloth and rubbed at a nonexistent smudge on the glass case. "All three are going out to one of our more select collectors. Gerald's just waiting for the last medal to get here."

My head jerked up. The assistant continued working on the glass. It was good she was absorbed with wiping the glass case.

I did not want her to see the impact her words had on me. I knew there was no way anyone would ever get that third Jefferson peace medal. It had been presented to the Kiowa Nation in 1802.

I forced my face into a false smile. "How did Gerald get the medals?"

She stopped wiping the glass to chill me with her words and smile. "Oh, Gerald has his ways." She wiggled and practically squealed, "He is just so good at what he does."

I shivered. She was edging toward too much information.

The blonde gave the case a last wipe and glanced at her watch. "It's getting late. You really shouldn't be in here when Gerald returns."

Before the blonde walked me out of the room, I reached to the edge of the desk and grabbed a business card. Back in the hallway, we were greeted by a consistent honking that drowned out the soothing sound of the flute music.

I slid my hand into a front pocket of my messenger bag, pulled out my card, and handed it to the blonde assistant. "Please ask Gerald to call me. Perhaps he saw my black case. I really would like to talk with him."

She didn't bother looking at my card. "Yes, I'll give it to him . . . when he gets back." Almost to herself she added, "Should be soon. That package absolutely has to go out today."

She opened the back door and responded to an excessively long honk with a glare first out at the parking lot, then back onto me. "Can you get that to stop?" Not waiting for a reply, she slammed the door behind me.

Wilson had pulled up along the building. I could see him mouthing, "Come on," through the truck's windshield.

I walked slowly toward him, thinking. I knew that this Gerald guy would be waiting a long time for the third Jefferson peace medal. There was no way that package was going out today—or ever—with all three peace medals. Lewis and Clark had presented that third peace medal to a Kiowa chief on the day of our first contact with *Hanpoko*, Americans. With the gift of the medal came a sealed-by-breath promise of everlasting friendship and peace between the United States and our People. The peace medal had been a prized possession, worn only at the most prestigious of times. It had been lovingly handed down in the chief's family for generations, until it had been lost.

I knew where that medal was. I was with my grandfather when the Jefferson peace medal had been returned to our tribe.

It had been lost since 1863, when Chief Yellow Wolf traveled to Washington, DC, to meet with President Abraham Lincoln during the height of the Civil War. Lincoln wanted the Kiowas to side with the North. The Kiowas just wanted to be left in peace. Yellow Wolf wore the Jefferson peace medal on the long train ride to Washington, in hopes that the invading government would recall their promise of a forever peace with the Kiowas. Unfortunately, Yellow Wolf died of pneumonia in Washington and never returned from the trip. It was said that the prized Jefferson peace medal had been buried with Yellow Wolf, until it had been discovered in a private collection.

I remembered the soothing, resin-rich, sweet smell of cedar burning to dispel negative spirits while listening to drummers beat the steady heartbeat of the Tribe as the representative from Washington, DC, had walked into the Kiowa Complex. My grandfather stood in the center of our Tribe's Great Seal, tiled into the floor of the Complex, the Tribe's chairman to his right and a spirit woman to his left. While refusing to be in the Tribe's government, Grandpa nonetheless was a recognized Tribal Elder, a Kiowa of distinction, our sacred story keeper.

I remember Grandpa receiving the Jefferson peace medal for the Tribe that day. He wrapped it in red, our spirit color, cleansed it and presented it to the Kiowa Museum for all Kiowas to be able to see the emblem of first contact. The four-inch disk that forever changed the way of the world for the Kiowas.

Walking back to Wilson's truck, I realized the water quality office and TribalVision's back doors were located where Buck had been parked with his van. Buck had said he wanted *it*. Was the "it" the Kiowa's Jefferson peace medal—or a quality report on illegal fracking?

Chapter Five

I looked out the old truck's large windshield: the sky roiled in reds, purples, grays, and near blacks as the oppressive heat pressed down across the open farm lands. A thunderstorm brewed. It matched my boiling emotions.

My mind churned with increasingly dark thoughts. What was going on with Buck and Wilson and the Jefferson peace medals and fracking? How did Grandpa fit into this mess?

My mind kept going to and retreating from believing Wilson had purposely left me trapped in his truck's cab to bake in the day's rapidly growing heat. I side-eyed Wilson. That wasn't possible, was it? Why would he hurt me?

Headed out of Lawton, the truck bounced over railroad tracks that separated a cattle pasture from a neglected neighborhood. Wooden fences struggled to stay upright. Downed fence sections provided peeks into dirt-patched backyards. Barefoot kids played in clouds of red dust. The low-income neighborhood surrounded the Indian Hospital.

Buck's words—*"I got Georgie trained real good now"*—haunted me. I couldn't shake the glee in his eyes. It made my stomach clench.

Georgie had been full of joy in high school. She—*we*—had big dreams together. Until we didn't. I had spent the last ten years purposely, religiously trying *not* to think of Georgie. Yet she entered my thoughts consistently.

I became a serial dater. After a few dates or the first sign of a woman getting serious, I moved on. None kept my interest on all levels, in or out of bed.

I sighed. After all these years, I still loved Georgie.

I had been lovestruck at first sight in a shared algebra class. Georgie was new to the school and a rarity as a non-Indian. Her wavy, golden hair stood out in our school of dark manes.

I was in my typical slouch in the back row, while Georgie sat up straight and attentive in a desk up front. She turned to look at me as the teacher called my name. She smiled, our eyes locked, and lightning struck. I don't remember anything about the day, except that the gold of her hair matched the flecks in her eyes.

I rested my head on the side window, looked at nothing. Thoughts whirled.

For a year, we grew close, first as friends over homework and after-school sports. I stayed silent on the depth of my feelings. I watched and listened as she went out with this or that guy. I never said a word on how I felt. I just couldn't. It was Georgie who poured her heart out to me first, after sparks developed between me and another girl. It was Georgie who kissed me first. It was Georgie I loved first . . . and, it seemed, forever.

A sigh escaped. Wilson glared across the seat at me. I turned away, dove deeper into my memories.

Georgie led and I happily followed. Until I couldn't. I felt no shame or embarrassment in loving her. It was natural. Though the game she wanted to play, using Buck, cheapened our love. I wanted her to leave for Cal with me, as we had planned.

The truck bumped onto the highway ramp. Wilson accelerated to forty miles per hour. The truck seemed to rear and buck in response. *Buck* . . .

That Georgia had stayed and made a life with Buck confused me. Not that he was a man, but that he was so not a partner for her. Georgie and Buck married soon after high school, and she followed him into his failed dreams of baseball fame. She had not gone on to college—she'd replaced her dreams with his demands.

I shook my head, tried to shake free of Georgie. Memories of her did me no good. I was able to escape them working nonstop at the agency, but here, Georgie lived.

My eyes drifted to the pasture. Cows gathered in groups, crowding rare shade in the open field. A whiff of manure circulated in the warm cab. Wilson slid a lever up. A fan deep in the dashboard increased its speed. The truck slowed. Hot air blew in my face. It offered no relief.

Without my suitcase serving as a wall barrier, I was able to look at Wilson. He clutched the steering wheel, staring forward as we headed down Interstate 44, toward Oklahoma City, at the breakneck speed of forty-five miles per hour. At this pace, I could clearly see the Cavalry-era cobblestone walls of Fort Sill's horse corral and the close-cropped grass of the fort's polo field. Yes, a polo field in Indian Territory.

Wilson had remained silent since my return to the truck. Maybe he would talk now. I faced him. "Wilson, what did you mean when you told Buck not to worry about James—my grandpa?"

Wilson tightened his grip on the steering wheel but said nothing. I let the silence build as he exited the interstate for Highway 58 toward Medicine Park. We were slowly getting closer to Grandpa's house. Wilson shifted in the seat but still said nothing.

I hesitated in questioning Wilson further. It went against Kiowa customs to be direct. It was assumed that if another wanted you to know something, they would share the information. It was rude to pry. Yet I wanted . . . *needed* information. Grandpa had given me none.

I reviewed Wilson's profile. It was obvious that he had no intention to speak. His jaw was set, reminding me of early photos I had seen of the Old Ones. Forced to be photographed, they had sat rigid, jaws locked with silent anger.

My phone buzzed, startling us both. I quickly pulled it from my pocket. Without looking at the screen I responded, "This is Mae."

"Hey, Mae" rang out in the cab. *Marcus.* My creative director's tone hit a false note.

I pressed the phone tighter to my right ear, "Marcus, how did the review go?"

Marcus sounded guarded with his reply. "We're headed there now."

I felt a rush of anger. This "we" had better not include Thomas. I did not want my business partner near this client, especially now. Once a private company planned a public offering, the company, executives, and all associated with it fell under numerous securities laws. Richard's company was under an SEC-mandated quiet period. Everyone associated with the company must not speak about the company—anywhere.

We had a special exception working with the executives on the public announcements, but the fewer people exposed to the company's secrets, the better. Thomas was *not* someone I wanted hearing such high-level information.

Our partnership had seemed to work at first, but then Thomas decided he didn't need to be in the office every day. That led to never in the office and our first of several costly late penalties on operations costs. Then as suddenly as Thomas had stopped showing up at the office, he started appearing unannounced at client meetings. Existing clients tended to ignore him, as he added no value to our discussions, but new clients were scared away.

Now I tried not to let my anger leak into my voice. "Did you say, '*We're* headed there?' Who is the 'we'?"

"Thomas and I are going to Richard's office now."

I felt an eruption coming. I lowered my voice. "Marcus, turn the car around. Take Thomas back to the agency. And give Thomas the phone. *Now.*"

I could not have Thomas near this client. Richard was already having pre-IPO jitters.

Marcus said nothing, but I could hear the phone being transferred and a faint question from Thomas, "What are you doing?" And then a louder "Why are you having Marcus return to the agency?"

When I get angry, I don't get shrill; my voice gets low, measured, and direct. I squeezed each word out through clenched jaws. "Thomas, you are not going to see my client. You are not doing anything but returning to your office and doing your work." I added, "We've lost the last two clients you were near, and we cannot afford to lose this one."

Thomas tried to interrupt. "Well, you're not here—"

I barreled on. "*Now hear me clearly.* Stay out of my projects and away from my clients. Go near them, interfere with Marcus any further, and you will regret it."

This was met with silence, then a dead line.

I returned the phone to my pocket and took a long, deep breath, letting it out slowly, trying to control myself from immediately turning to spew my pent-up frustration at the silent Wilson.

Not trusting myself to even look at him, I turned to the side window. The usual placid Lake Lawtonka was dark and churning with whitecaps. Mount Scott towered over the lake, its top hidden with swirling black clouds.

The Kiowas called Mount Scott *K'Hop'Ale*, the Big Old Mountain. In our legends, it is said that the last of the free-range buffalo knew that they had lost the war for territory with the invading white settlers. The day of buffaloes roaming across the Great Plains was over. After the last of the great herd gathered, it was decided that the herd would save those left for another day. A young Kiowa woman, up early getting water, watched as the morning mist parted and the last of the great buffalo herd walked into a garden paradise within *K'Hop'Ale*. There the herd remains until the world is once again brought into balance.

Just what I needed—balance. I had to get back to the agency before my balancing act there toppled.

Making an annoying throat-clearing sound, Wilson finally spoke. "We'll stop up ahead at McClung's. I'll get some gas, a bite, and we'll move on along. Be there in just a bit."

I couldn't believe this; three miles away from my grandpa's house, and I was being stalled again. "Wilson, I really want to go on to my grandfather's house. It feels like you're keeping me from Grandpa." I couldn't hold my frustration in. "What is going on here?"

Wheels crunched across gravel as Wilson turned the truck toward the single-pump gas station at the old McClung's trading post. McClung's had started as a two-room, cobblestone trading post in 1909—one of the few stores in Indian country that served Indians, the only one that had allowed Indians entry through the front door. It quickly grew into the area's grocery store; bait shop; gas station; and, after a wood-siding addition, local diner. McClung's and its three-point intersection were the closest thing to a town square in the backcountry of the old reservation land.

The diner's front windows were lined with locals.

Wilson ignored me. He glanced at his phone and then up again, to steer toward the pump.

"Wilson, I'm going to walk from here."

I could cut across a couple of cow pastures to reach the tree-lined Canyon Creek. From there, I could follow the creek and its shade to the back of Grandpa's house. I had walked it almost daily as a kid. Decisive, I repeated, "I am walking from here."

I slipped my messenger bag's strap over my neck and held the bag tight at my side. My computer and the notes for Richard's IPO were inside. I needed to keep my bag with me.

Wilson stared straight ahead as he maneuvered the truck alongside the pump. "Nah, your grandpa wouldn't want me to leave you here. It's gonna storm real soon."

I reached for the door handle and pulled upward, anxious to exit. Wilson heard the clunk of the door release. He reached and grabbed the strap on my messenger bag. My head was jerked toward him while my legs tried to move away.

Wilson pulled hard on the strap. "You go ahead and walk. I'll drop off the bag."

Without thinking, I grabbed the handle on top of the messenger bag and twist-pulled it back to me. Wilson flinched as the strap was wrenched out of his grasp. At the same time, I pushed the door open and propelled myself out of the truck. I slipped on the gravel, fell to the ground, ripping my jeans at the knee. Gravel bit into my knee and palms, drawing beads of blood.

Wilson leaned across the seat to glare at me. "Get back in here."

I rose from the ground, returned the glare and—louder than I'd intended—let out: "Wilson, that's it. I've had enough. Leave. Me. Alone." I slammed the truck door with a satisfying metallic bang and turned to see several noses pressed to the diner's front window. Immediately, I lowered my head.

Wilson must have recognized that we had become the early lunch crowd's entertainment. He revved the engine and pulled forward, spitting gravel back at me. The truck settled into a parking slot facing toward the road. Wilson shifted in the seat to look back at the pump. I could see his eyes scanning for me. I kept moving away from him toward the store. Last thing I wanted was to get trapped with Wilson again.

I felt the stares from the faces pressed to the diner's window. This was going to be big news. I could hear the drums beating already. I kept my face turned away. Maybe no one would recognize me.

Growing up in what had been the Kiowa–Comanche–Apache Reservation was worse than a small town. Here, not only did everyone know everyone else, but most likely we were also related—which everyone assumed granted them all rights to be in your business. Odds were good that someone I was related to had a nose pressed to that window.

I turned my back to the diner and walked toward the wood-framed screen door of the cobblestone store. Not looking back, I grabbed the metal knob, pulled, and went into the dimly lit store. I wanted to get away from Wilson and really didn't want to see any family or friends. My parents didn't know I was here. They would be crushed to learn I was in town and hadn't said a word to them. They would not understand that this wasn't a visit. I wasn't sure what it was. But I didn't plan on staying long. I needed to get back to work. I had to get back to my agency.

I could hide out in the store for ten minutes or so, wait out Wilson, then head across the cow pastures to reach my grandfather's house. I adjusted the bag's strap and rubbed my neck. I didn't understand Wilson's fascination with my messenger bag, but he had tried to take it twice. Maybe he had gotten Buck to take my suitcase. But why?

The counter was directly to my left, just as I remembered. A teenage daughter of one of the original McClungs rested elbows on the century-old glass case. She was helping a fresh-faced boy pick out the best to be had in snuff. Her attention stayed focused on the teen. Both seemed oblivious to the action that had occurred just outside the door, and now to me, inside the store. Perfect. I continued down an aisle, unnoticed.

The floor planks creaked and groaned with my steps. The grooved and pitted, uneven planks were original. They had been in place for over a hundred and twelve years. As a child, I'd always watched my feet coming down the main aisle. It amazed me to see my bare feet touch the same planks my barefoot grandfather had walked on as a child, and my father after him. There seemed to be something magical with walking in their past footsteps.

I moved toward the back. McClung's had one of the first indoor bathrooms in the area. And, I just remembered, that bathroom had a second door going out the back of the store. Supplies had originally come in through this back door before the area had been enclosed and made into a bathroom. The back wall was closest to the highway, the most convenient entry for the necessary plumbing when indoor bathrooms became the rage. I might be able to get out that back door, avoid Wilson and anyone left lingering from the diner, and trek over to Grandpa's house, unseen and unnoticed. I smiled at the thought.

The end of the aisle was capped with a rolling beer barrel display, locked into position, facing a short wall of refrigerated food and drinks. I made a left following to the end of the ell, where a metal minnow tank filled with water bubbled with the day's fresh offering in baits.

A sign taped to the store's once white cobblestone wall offered a dozen minnows for five dollars. I used to supply McClung's with their bait minnows. I could catch over sixty minnows out of Jimmy Creek, using a single slice of bread. Old Mr. McClung gave a dollar per dozen or candy of your choice. I always took the dollars.

The bathroom door was right where I remembered. I grabbed the doorknob, turned, opened, and marched into a dark, dank storage closet. I immediately gagged and covered my nose and mouth with my shirt. The dark closet smelled of mildew and an intense sour stench of rotted something.

It may have once been the bathroom, but that had been quite a few years ago. Now, it served as storage. I barely had room to move between boxes of canned beans and all types of sodas.

I turned to exit as a bell tinkled from the front. It froze me in place; someone was coming in the store. I held my breath, willing it not to be Wilson. A soft *whisk, whisk, whisk* stopped. A girl called out, "Can I help you all?"

Loud steps covered an answer. The sweeping started again. By the sounds, there were two people clunking loudly down the store's wooden planks toward my hiding place. They reached the coolers, stocked with sandwiches and sodas, before stopping. I opened the door a crack to peek out and to let in some air. The stench of oil wafted in, adding to the potent storage closet bouquet. I couldn't see anyone. I shifted and pressed my ear to the door opening.

One voice clearly stated, "We can't afford to stop now . . . just need a bit more time."

The other faced the minnow tank, its aerator hum making it hard to hear all that was said. ". . . get . . . jun outta . . . way . . . plenty . . ."

In reply came, "Might be time to do sumpthin' about that Injun . . ." I cringed hearing the slur: *Injun*. But I opened the door wider. I wanted to hear more.

". . . oil . . . results . . . do it . . ."

The two shuffled about. The movement covered the rest of the conversation. One set of heavy boots left the store. The other stopped for a six- or twelve-pack from the refrigerated end cap.

I peered out. I really wanted to see who this was. All I saw was his back. He was a hefty guy in dirty jeans, a baseball cap, and mud-caked work boots. He shuffled to the front counter, paid, and left.

The two sounded and smelled like they were part of fracking, and it didn't sound like it was the right part. I needed to get to Grandpa's house. Those two were probably Wilson's "them oil boys" and the cause of Grandpa's bad feeling. They sure gave me the creeps.

I turned into the storage closet and pulled my phone out to use as a flashlight. Perhaps the back door was still accessible.

My light passed over boxes piled atop and surrounding the still existing toilet. The back door was out of sight behind even more stacks of boxes. No way I was getting out the back door. I couldn't even get to it.

I turned to leave.

Another tinkle of the bell sounded, followed by a cheery "How can I help you?" A low grumble answered. The grumble stopped me. Grumbling was a Wilson trait. I turned the phone light off and quietly returned the phone to my pocket. I stayed still, tucked my nose into my shirt, and focused on listening.

Pressing my ear to the crack in the closed door, I heard another tinkle, more steps, and a "How are you all?" More steps and bell tinkles. I couldn't tell who was in or out. Then I heard a slow, steady thud coming down the aisle. It didn't hesitate at any of the shelves of colorful offerings. The steps continued, uninterrupted toward the back. Toward me.

I held my breath.

The steady, slow step halted just outside the storage door. The knob slowly turned.

I gasped and stepped back, my eyes riveted on the doorknob. The knob stopped abruptly. The man grumbled and shook the knob back and forth, each time blocked from turning it completely. I must have automatically engaged the lock when I closed the door.

There was a slow intake of breath, a foot sliding back, and then a big exhale.

I strained to hear more, made out the jingle of change and another heavy, slow breath. He was just outside the door. Waiting.

No. A grating, scraping sound started, stopped and started again, getting closer; then the door shuddered but remained closed. Slow deliberate footsteps receded. I tracked the steps to the bell's tinkle and the slap-slam of the screen door. If it was Wilson, now he was gone. Probably.

I tried to wait. I knew I needed to wait, make sure Wilson didn't lurk just outside, but I couldn't. Walls were closing in on me. I needed out of the storage closet. I turned the doorknob and pushed, only to bang my long Kiowa nose firmly into the door. I stepped back, rubbed at my eyes and nose. I wiped pain-induced tears away, again turned the knob, and this time pushed hard. The door moved a bit but bumped firmly into a barrier of some kind.

I put my eye to the small opening. Wilson had pushed the beer display in front of the door, blocking my exit. He had trapped me inside the storage closet. What was with this guy? First he wanted me with him, then he left me trapped. Twice now. I really needed to see Grandpa and get some answers. I huffed out stale air and pushed at the door once more. The end cap display did not move.

Another shove scraped it forward barely an inch.

I could shout for help and get out if I didn't mind the whole town knowing of my escapade. This was something that would be known all over the area before supper. No doubt, my parents would hear about it.

I wanted to get out without anyone knowing I'd been here. Maybe there was something I could use for leverage to push the end cap barrier. Before I could start a search, another tinkle of the door's bell rang out, followed by a hearty "Hey, Dot, how ya doing?"

I didn't hear Dot's answer. The bell was getting a workout as more feet came in and out. The store might be old, but it did good business.

Small, rapid footsteps danced at the front of the store, probably surrounding the candy selection, but yes, there was someone coming down the aisle. Again, the steps were slow and deliberate. Was Wilson coming back?

Footsteps stopped just beyond the storage door. I looked around the dim area for something to use as a weapon. A bottle caught my eye. I pulled a glass soda bottle out of its six-pack holster. My hand wrapped around its neck, and I held it high, like a club at the ready.

Through the door a low voice muttered, "What's this—" The rest was covered by a screeching, dragging sound. I was so intent on listening, I was surprised when the doorknob was wrenched from my other hand. I stumbled forward bearing my soda bottle club.

"You gonna hit me with that soda?" a voice from above chuckled. "Me, I'd much rather drink 'em."

A tall, clean-faced Kiowa man smiled down at me. "Whatcha doin' in the closet, Mud?"

Yes, my name is Mud.

Chapter Six

I got my Kiowa name when I was eleven.

My grandfather announced, “It is time.”

At first, no one responded. I had just returned from my first four-day vision quest with Grandpa. Lois, my oldest sister, wrinkled her nose. “It’s time for someone to take a shower.”

Her joke fell flat. While my father did not follow our Kiowa traditions, he honored them and his father, my grandfather.

Grandpa turned to my father. “Her name is calling. It is time for her naming ceremony.”

First, I froze, then forced myself forward. I was scared, but I needed to speak. “Grandpa, I failed. No vision came to me.”

Lois snickered. Our father gave her a silencing look.

I had stayed the four days—praying, yearning, chanting, and cleansing myself—but no defining vision came to me. Only cold, hunger, and fear. Fear of failure.

Grandpa turned, examined me. His eyes smiled at me, warmed me, reassured me. “No, Granddaughter, this one came to me.”

Grandpa turned back to my father. “We must plan her naming ceremony.”

My father smiled and answered, "*Haw.* Yes."

My Kiowa father, who like most in his generation shunned all things Indian in his attempt to blend in with the ruling white society that controlled his world, surprised me by rising before the sun to start the fire for my naming day ceremony. My sisters and brothers grumbled about the early rising. None had been named before. Neither of my two older sisters nor my younger twin brothers had expressed interest in being Kiowa. For them, it was a choice.

I had lain awake through the night, torn between fear and happiness. I was to have a Kiowa name. Yet I feared I did not deserve it.

At the foot of my bed lay a new pair of white deerskin moccasins. My mother, though not Kiowa, had made them for this day. The day I walked with purpose. My grandfather's sisters, my grandmothers, in the Kiowa Way, worked together to bead an intricate weaving of blue, yellow, and red designs. Blue for the sky, yellow for the sun, and red for the spirit, marking the progression their prayers traveled.

My father laid a rough, round cobblestone in the center of the firepit. Grandpa explained that the cobblestone came from within Mother Earth. It was part of her heart stone and lay in the center of the firepit as our hearts should at the center of our souls. Grandpa claimed that we would see the stone pulse with life as it was heated in the fire through the day and into the night. He was right.

Dad surrounded the heart stone with special wood, selected only at the full moon: wood intended for special ceremonies glowed blue to the trained eye. Grandpa tossed cedar into the fire. The sweet smoke from cedar ensured that no bad spirits or negative thoughts would come to the ceremony. Dad had the flames roaring in the predawn darkness.

I was afraid to look away from the fire. I needed to form a mask to hide my fear. No vision had come to me during my quest. I did not deserve a name. I breathed deep of the cedar smoke. I needed help to wash my doubts away.

I had seen several naming ceremonies, two done soon after a birth. To come into life with a Kiowa name was a rare blessing. Names are extremely important to Kiowas. The Kiowa naming ceremony honors the consciousness of an individual, a Kiowa finding their way, their identity. *Koy taw gee geah daw*—living the Kiowa Way.

I had wanted a Kiowa name for as long as I could remember. To be named meant I was Kiowa, that I belonged. And I so wanted to be part of my grandfather's tribe, to be Kiowa. I hoped for a family name, one handed down through the generations. A name I would carry as a reminder of our proud past, one that anchored me to the Tribe. Proved I was Kiowa despite my curly mop.

Flames reached upward as the sun rose to the music of Grandpa's welcoming-the-day chant. The fire burned all day and night of the ceremony. Its smoke would travel with the wind, spreading my naming to the world here and above.

My name would define me, let the Kiowas know I belonged. Yet I couldn't shake the feeling that I didn't belong or, worse, wasn't wanted. I choked on the cedar smoke.

I had been my grandfather's shadow for as long as I could remember. I trailed him everywhere. I still remember him gathered with his friends, all with gray-streaked braids down their backs, squatting in a circle, in the way it had been for generations. There, in the circle, they would talk of growing up with the Old Ones, their parents and grandparents. The ones who shared memories of hunting buffalo, racing ponies, and living free and happy in Kiowa country. I crawled closer and closer, through the story sharings, until I settled in a squat just behind my grandfather, absorbing the stories.

Family, friends, and many tribal leaders came to my naming ceremony. They came to honor my grandfather, a recognized Tribal Elder and the Tribe's sacred story keeper. Grandpa was one of the last readers of our three pictograph deerskin calendars. I had been trained to be the next.

Our tribe was one of four on the Great Plains that complemented its oral history with a written chronical painted on deerskins. The Dohason calendar, named for its creator, *Dohason*, or Little Bluff, the greatest principal chief in Kiowa history, chronicled Kiowa life from 1830 to 1865. Simple pictograph drawings noted a significant tribal event sketched above winter and summer markings through the years.

In formal storytelling ceremonies, Grandpa would start the telling. He recited the documented happening for the tribe in a given year and season; this prompted others to share what occurred in their band or family that year. Remembered stories, history, and legends would unfold through the night, bringing us all closer as a People with a shared history. Grandpa was the keeper of our sacred stories; he kept our past alive.

I had hoped a vision would come. Confirm that I was chosen to carry our stories forward. Yet for four days, nothing had come to me. No calling was confirmed.

I stared into the fire. I worried its smoke would have no true name to carry forth.

Before I was ready, Grandpa called me to stand at the front with him and the drummer.

I tried to look at Grandpa, let him know we needed to stop. But it was too late. Grandpa stepped forward, I lowered my head. I could not meet his eyes.

His voice rumbled, "This is a sacred ceremony for the Kiowa. As Kiowa, we all seek to honor our Creator, *Daw'Kee*. We first must know our self, be true to our self, to walk our true path in life, find our passion, live our potential. To live true to yourself is the way to honor *Daw'Kee*. This is the Kiowa Way, *Koy taw gee geah daw*."

"Haws" rang out, and heads nodded in agreement.

Grandpa looked beyond me, at the many faces of the tribe. "It is important to receive a Kiowa name, a true name. Names come at different times in life and in different ways, but a Kiowa name, a true name, when it comes, it must be given."

As if on cue, the gathered nodded and declared, *"Haw,"* Kiowa for *yes*.

My jaws clenched.

Grandpa continued, "My granddaughter's name was first whispered to me in a dream the stormy night she entered this world. It was sealed through actions of her childhood and first quest."

My bowed head jerked up. My eyes sought Grandpa's. He knew I had failed at my vision quest. Nothing had come to show me my way. Grandpa knew this. He knew I felt that I didn't fit: at home as the middle child, in the tribe as a curly-headed half-breed, and as a girl being trained as our next story keeper.

Grandpa looked into the distance; his eyes were too far for me to catch. He went on, "Many receive an ancestor name.

This is a strong thing, as it links our generations together and we remember. Family names are good things . . ."

Now Grandpa turned his eyes to me. They sparkled. He warmed me and chilled me.

His work-worn hands clutched his eagle-feather fan. Grandpa raised his deep brown eyes to *Daw'Kee*, the Creator, before he continued, "New names are good too. Today a new name has come to the Kiowa People."

The drummer began. As a faint heartbeat started, my eyes looked upward, my jaw clenched. I was excited and . . . scared. There was such responsibility with a Kiowa name.

The drumbeat grew louder, stronger.

Grandpa raised his fan and faced me. He looked deep into me. "This one must find her balance in two worlds. She must find the point where air and fire meet, that balancing point between earth and water. She will find the path, not lost in or between her worlds, but at the balancing point where the worlds come together. That is her way."

Grandpa chanted as he fanned me.

The tribe's heartbeat pounded in my blood.

Grandpa announced, "Her Kiowa name is *Ahn Tsah Hye-gyah-daw*, She Knows the Way."

I shook. It was a strong name.

EEEEEEYYYYYYEEEEEEEEEE whoops sounded in celebration of a new spirit in the tribe, a Kiowa named.

Smoke streamed upward and spread on the wind.

My heart soared. I had a Kiowa name. A new name. I repeated in my mind, *Ahn Tsah Hye-gyah-daw, She Knows the Way.*

I found Grandpa's eyes. They glowed with warmth.

I stood in the center of the universe, in balance.

A smile started.

All was good and right . . . for a hot minute.

In the distance, I heard my cousin Denny repeating, ". . . water and earth comes together . . ." Then his young, high voice rang out above all others: "Her name is Mud!"

My moment was shattered by silence, followed by laughter.

And with that, I was so named. Everyone in the area—the family, those at school—everyone called me Mud, until I went to California. Once there, I declared myself Mae and never muttered a word about "Mud."

Now little Denny towered over me. I rushed into his arms and gave him a ferocious hug, which startled him. Our family was not demonstrative; hugs and "I love you" came sparingly. But it had been years.

"I am so glad to see you!" I gushed.

Denny held me at arm's length, looked me over. "Well, you look the same—a sweaty mess as usual." He grinned and surprised me with a returned short hug.

Denny was two years older than me. Always the cool one, he was the first to get a motorcycle and the first to quit school. Denny had the TV-Indian chiseled good looks—dark chocolate-brown eyes that twinkled with trouble, and silky black hair that looked like it hadn't been cut since he was fifteen. He had grown to nearly six feet, unusual for Kiowas.

He stepped back. "It was quite a surprise to hear a buzz when I came in the diner about someone threatening Wilson out front." Denny gave me a grin. "I only caught sight of your back. But I know that walk anywhere." His smile broadened. "Are you home?"

I moved away from the stench of the storage closet to the slightly improved fish smell of the minnow tank, taking Denny with me. "Is Wilson still out front?"

Denny wrinkled his forehead. "Naw, he left, spitting gravel, quite a while ago. I left the diner and stayed outside a bit, waiting for you to come back out. I wanted to check if it really was you. Finally decided to come on in." Denny sniffed, wrinkled his long nose. "Why were you hanging out in the old bathroom?" Before I could answer he grabbed my arm and pulled at me. "And why are we at the bait tank? It doesn't smell much better here."

I let Denny pull me away from the tank. "I was hiding from Wilson, then he trapped me in that storage closet." I peered around Denny, made sure no one was around.

Denny laughed. "And why would Wilson trap you in there?"

I wasn't quite sure how to explain. My morning had been a whirlwind of strange happenings. I finally dived in with my biggest concern. "Denny, something is going on. Grandpa summoned me but never arrived at the airport. Instead, Wilson was there." Thinking aloud, I added, "And a couple others from the Legislature. Everyone acted strange . . . out of balance . . ."

Denny just smiled. "You always were making up stories for us kids. If you don't want to tell me what's going on with you and Wilson, just say that. I can mind my business." His smile faded. "Not like I've seen you in years . . ."

Making up stories. How could Denny think I was making things up?

"Denny, it's not like that. Something is going on with Grandpa." I stopped in the aisle. "Wilson claimed Grandpa sent him to pick me up at the airport, but I think Wilson deliberately trapped me in his truck . . . and that storage closet."

Denny shook his head. "Mud, Grandpa would never send Wilson to pick up anything, especially you. He doesn't trust him, called him a lying snake the whole time Wilson was a tribe legislator. You know that." He pushed his long hair back.

I tagged behind as Denny headed to the front of the store. "I did—I *do*, but Wilson was there, Grandpa wasn't, and Wilson said he told Grandpa he was picking me up."

Denny waved at the girl behind the counter. They exchanged quick smiles while she tended the register.

He had me thinking back to the airport. Had Wilson ever said that Grandpa sent him . . . or had he just implied it? Darn it! Wilson first claimed he was looking for James; later he changed his story and said he was there to pick me up.

Denny shook his head. "Don't matter—I can drop you off at Grandpa's house." He opened the store's screen door, watched a black wall of vertical thunderheads form. "If you come now."

I followed Denny out. The heat was stifling, the air thick. I was slow. "It had to be Wilson that blocked me in the storeroom. He's the only one who knew where I was."

Denny slowed, turned to look at me. "Him and everyone in the diner. Didn't take me no time to figure out where you were."

That stopped me. Denny was right, it could have been "them oil boys" that blocked the storeroom's door. They said they needed more time. Was Wilson working with them? Could the muttered *"Do sumpthin' . . . Injun"* mean do something with the Indian? With Wilson's help? Or was Grandpa "the Injun" they planned to do something about?

Why hadn't Grandpa left more information in his message? I stomped after Denny. He watched the black sky and hurried across the gravel parking area.

A thought occurred and I rushed to catch up. "Denny, have you heard anything about fracking around the old Jimmy Creek Spring?" That was the family's spring out by the Slick Hills, a low range of bald limestone hills.

He stopped to shake his head. "I thought you got educated in California. That's crazy talk." Denny used his chin to point toward a truck and moved to its driver's door. "Grandpa would not allow fracking anywhere near the spring or its source, '*deep within Mother Earth.*'" He mimicked Grandpa's rhythmic Kiowa accent.

Denny got into a nineties-era Ram pickup. "You comin'? I've gotta get the cows in before the storm starts."

On cue, thunder shook the air.

Chapter Seven

The thunderclap announced the coming onslaught. It started as large drops that beat at the truck until uniting in a downpour. Rain sheeted down Denny's windshield, unmoved by the frantic flapping wipers. His headlights exposed an ongoing wall of rain. Lightning flashes illuminated the road ahead.

Booming thunderclaps shook the truck. The storm's intensity startled and delighted me. It had been years since I had experienced a real thunderstorm.

Denny craned forward. "I figure something was going on out at the Complex. Grandpa went to Carnegie a couple times last week." He stole a quick glance at me. "And you know they usually come to him."

The Kiowa Tribal Complex in Carnegie housed all things Kiowa: the government, environment, land, and social programs, as well as language lessons and the senior and cultural centers, including the Kiowa Museum. Grandpa, as the tribe historian, often worked with the museum on Kiowa artifacts. He also made a point of donating the best of his own artwork to the museum—ensuring Kiowa representation of our visual history.

I leaned forward and peered through the sheet of rain, searching for the Canyon Creek bridge. The road shrank to a single lane crossing the old bridge. I willed the truck to stay on the road. "What started Grandpa's visits to the Complex?" The truck bumped onto the bridge. Water rushed past, licking at its edges. I released a sigh of relief.

Eyes locked on the road, Denny wrinkled his forehead before answering. "It was after a couple tourists stopped by Grandpa's house. I think they had one of his old pieces and wanted to buy another painting."

Grandpa painted Kiowa art in the traditional Great Plains flat style that immediately followed the ledger art era. The flat style, like ledger art, was painted without shadings or dimension. His art, done in rich primary colors, consisted of snapshots of daily Kiowa life shown with authentic regalia, weapons, tools, and settings of the time. Grandpa took authenticity to the extreme. He ground his paint colors and used only what had been available to the tribe pre-reservation. He had always sold his art from home. Grandpa had grown frustrated early on with the system that honored and enriched the seller more than the Indian artist.

Rapid thunderclaps were followed by lightning flashes. With every flash, I strained for a glimpse of the simple rectangle house surrounded by open pasture, with a dark grove trailing toward a creek in the back. The sign came into sight first. A wooden tipi swung wildly in the storm. Lightning flashes revealed faded printing: "J. B. Sawpole Kiowa Indian Artist." For as long as I could remember, that tipi sign had marked my grandparents' home. My heart flew just seeing it.

In the next instant, my jaw clenched. Grandpa and answers were minutes away. It was time to get this mess sorted so I could get back to work.

Denny drove past the swinging tipi sign and turned onto the muddy drive leading to the house. He broke the silence. "You know, there was something with Jimmy Creek Spring going low . . . maybe not tasting right . . . I don't quite recall." Keeping his eyes on the road, Denny shook his head. "I've been busy with calving. Haven't had much free time to get over here." He tilted his head toward Grandpa's house.

I stared at the house, a dark mass against a charcoal sky, coming into focus through freeze frames caught between lightning streaks. My jaw relaxed. This home had always held love and acceptance. And answers.

Denny stopped at the carport and looked out at the sky. "I gotta get to the cows. Really sorry to drop you and run."

The truck's headlight shone into the carport, illuminating a lone buffalo skull mounted to the center beam. Its blank eyes stared at me. Every Kiowa home I knew had a buffalo skull. It signified thanks to *Daw'Kee*, the Creator, for a home with plenty. Grandpa had made sure I had one at my house in Boulder Creek, California. We both chuckled at having a buffalo in the Redwoods.

Denny shifted into reverse before I had the door open.

"No problem. The cows need you." I stepped down from the truck and slammed its door closed. I intended to run under the carport, then into the kitchen through a side door.

Once outside, I was hit by the pungent zing scent of lightning. Refreshing and startling. I stopped to take a deep breath. The hot rain pelted me. In that moment, I caught a fleeting movement from the corner of my eye. I focused on the spot. The truck's retreating headlight caught a second movement. A figure at the back corner of the house going toward the black woods and creek below. The figure had obviously come from Grandpa's house.

It ran. Instinctually, I chased.

Bad instincts.

I'd forgotten the muddy mess created by the continuing downpour. Once off the gravel driveway, I slipped in the mud, sliding onto my knees. On my way down, I watched a hunched figure moving across the pasture into the dark woods. In the next flash of lightning, the figure was gone.

Despite the rain and mud, I stayed on the ground and stared into the blackness, hoping for just one more glance. One more chance to identify the running person. None came.

A vibration started in my front pocket.

A deep sigh escaped as I righted myself and retreated to the cover of the carport before pulling the phone from my pocket. My eyes lingered on where I had last seen the dark figure. I hoped to see another movement. Another look at the shape and I might be able to tell if it was one of the oil boys from McClung's.

The buzz became insistent. I answered the phone. "Yes."

A shrill voice rang out over the pounding rain. "Thomas called Richard!" Marcus sucked in a breath and released it before continuing at a high pitch. "Now, Richard wants the company's logo *animated.* Full 3-D animation in less than three days—no, two days, since there must be testing. This is *not* possible."

A thunder blast caused me to jump. "Marcus, calm down."

"What the hell is that?"

"A thunderstorm. I can't talk. I'm outside, dripping wet and muddy. You can handle this. Take a deep breath." I could hear a shrill yet faint *"Wait!"* as I disconnected and fumbled with the phone before shoving it into my pocket.

Rain-drenched, I ran to the kitchen door and let myself into the dark house. Instead of the usual warmth of the kitchen, there was cold emptiness. My eyes went to the kitchen sink. I could close my eyes and easily summon an image of my late grandma standing before the sink, wiping her hands on her apron as she turned with sparkling eyes to pull me in for a hug that filled the soul. I held the image close before letting it go.

I called into the grayness, "Grandpa!"

Where was he?

Thunder roared.

My phone rang.

No answer from Grandpa.

I fumbled with the light switches.

No power, no lights. *Great.*

An elongated lightning flash confirmed the furnishings in the small house had not changed locations since my last visit. Directly to my right was the dining room table. I touched the rigid seamed top of a vinyl dining chair. A shuffle to the left took me to the blanket-covered arm of a recliner in the furniture-crowded living room. I dropped onto the chair's arm.

No sign of Grandpa. I called out again. Nothing.

Thunder roared but couldn't drown out the insistent ring of my phone. I had to answer. Marcus was probably calling back.

I answered without looking at the screen. "This is Mae."

Instead of Marcus, an anxious-sounding Bernie said, "Mae, what's going on? Marcus said you hung up on him?"

I blew. I knew I shouldn't, but it was out before I could rein it back. "Bernie, I've been out of the office less than twenty-four hours. You both know what to do—just do it."

Grandpa should be here.

Silence on the line.

I leaned forward on the recliner's arm, strained to make out shapes in the gray light. "Bernie, I just got to my grandfather's house. We've got a storm going on." Supporting my words, thunder rocked the house.

Sweet Bernie. Despite my sharpness, she asked, "Are you all right?"

Lightning flashes confirmed Grandpa was not in the small living room. Where was he? Could Grandpa have been the figure outside? No, he had enough sense to stay out of a lightning storm. Grandpa had to be in one of the back rooms. Rain pounded the roof.

I had no time to explain to Bernie. "I need to see if my grandfather's here. I just have to go." I ended the call, slid the side button back to put it into silent mode, and shoved the phone into my pocket. Immediately, I regretted being short with Bernie. At work we spent most days together. I was closest to Bernie and often took her for granted.

Thunderheads collided with a deafening clap, followed by another flash of lightning. I pushed off the chair and peered down the dark hallway. The flashes of light didn't reach into the black corridor.

Arms outstretched, I moved down the hallway. He had to be in the back. Thunder rattled the windows. My already tender knee banged into a metal wall. It brought me down, swearing. I had forgotten the washer and dryer were in the hallway.

I gave my knee one last rub before getting up and moving toward the first door. The renowned no-no room of my youth, Grandpa's workroom, never to be entered by any of his twenty-eight grandchildren without permission.

As a child, I would sneak in. Taking what felt like hours to slide in undetected to sit, unmoving and believing myself unseen, amid his horde of necessary broken treasures, sometimes simply watching his colorful brushstrokes until a picture and story emerged, other times listening to him with the Old Ones speaking the rhythmic clipped sounds of Kiowa, and occasionally finding him snoring on a sagging couch on its last legs.

I knocked on the door, waited, then banged louder, to be heard over the pounding rain. Grandpa ignored everything while working.

Another deafening thunderclap, followed by rapid flashes that faintly reached into the hallway. The storm was going to be directly overhead soon.

I turned the knob, poked my head in, and once again called out, "Grandpa!"

Nothing.

From the doorway, I peered into the room, making out irregular shapes. He had what must be boxes stacked and lined in rows by the closet. I knew his makeshift easel desk, handmade from scraps scavenged from the households of his ten children, would be by the room's only window. Grandpa needed light to paint by.

My nose curled. The room had a strange acrid stench. Copper . . . probably another of Grandpa's color concoctions. I raised my shirt collar to my nose. A makeshift filter.

Lightning flashed again, revealing a glimpse of someone sitting at the desk, sleeping. I smiled. Only Grandpa could sleep through this storm.

Just as quickly, my morning frustrations boiled up. *How could he be sleeping?*

I stumbled as I stepped into the room. My foot rocked on and across a hard object. I reached down to pick it up. Once in my hand, the worn bone handle settled perfectly in my grasp. I didn't need the next lightning flash to recognize my grandfather's buffalo jawbone club—a tool he had handcrafted as a boy under the guidance of his grandfather, Wolfcub.

Grandpa had used this jawbone to bring down his first kill, a buffalo calf desperately needed by his hungry and cold family. All his grandkids had teethed on the jawbone club and, later, played mock battles with it.

Still holding the buffalo jawbone club, I moved into the room.

With the next lightning flash, I made out a slumped figure, braids skewed and draped across the desktop. Something looked wrong.

Terribly wrong.

He wasn't sleeping.

I couldn't breathe.

I finally squeezed out, "Grandpa!"

I forced in a breath. My nostrils filled with the copper scent. I gagged.

In the following rapid-fire roaring of clashes and flashes, I could see the exposed side of a bashed-in head, the skull splintered.

No one, no soul lived in that shell any longer.

Chapter Eight

My legs refused to move. I leaned forward, strained to look and not see. The storm's pounding rain and roaring thunder faded to white noise. I couldn't believe my eyes. My face crumpled and my heart began to break. I finally choked out a second "Grandpa!"—more a sob than a word.

I bent at the waist, holding myself tight. I couldn't get a deep enough breath. He had called me for help. A chill shook me. I had failed him.

I choked back sobs. Finally, a breath broke through my struggles and gave me enough fuel to slowly straighten. My eyes brimmed with unshed tears. I looked toward the gray shape.

He had a bad feeling. He knew.

I should have been here.

I set my jaw, forced myself to cross the paint-splattered floor. I didn't want to make this death a reality. But I had to see him. I needed to see him.

I owed him so much.

I knew I had disappointed him, and now I had failed him again.

"Oh, Grandpa, I am so sorry." I struggled for another breath. Choked on the smell of death.

I tried but couldn't summon an image of my grandfather. I didn't want this to be what I held forever more, but I owed him the respect. I needed to complete the long walk to his side. Finally, I stood beside Grandpa's easel desk. I forced myself to look down as a single stroke of lightning brought daylight to the room.

I stumbled back. I couldn't believe what the flash had revealed. The breath I didn't know I was holding broke free. Tears fell. I shook.

It wasn't Grandpa.

Thunder clapped. I took a breath in. Looked deeper into the grayness. From behind he did look like Grandpa. Up close the differences stood out. This man was narrow across the back, not broad and thick like Grandpa. The dead man's braids were longer. Grandpa's braids only reached his shoulders. He had cut his long braids after my grandmother's death.

Calmer, I looked back at the body. One of the dead man's hands seemed to reach up the front of the desk while the other had tried to protect his face from striking the wood desk, immediately following the fatal blow from behind. The destroyed head rested on one side, the face in shadows.

I forced myself forward to see the exposed face, strained through the grayness to confirm a growing suspicion. A lightning flash assisted again, this time to confirm the dead man's identity. Even in death, hard lines creased Wilson's face.

I felt weak; relief flooded through me, then guilt.

It was such a huge relief that it wasn't Grandpa, but this was a life gone. A real person. One who had been talking to me less than an hour ago. My body trembled. Despite the humidity and heat of the day, my body was bathed in a cold sweat.

What remained of Wilson sat in the desk's chair. He was sprawled across the top of the slightly slanted desk. In the dim light of the room, I could make out the deep puncture that had led to the destruction of his head, now misshaped. A sharp depression exposed bone splinters and tissues. A small, glistening pool of blood collected under the turned head.

Only then did I realize I was still holding what must be the murder weapon—Grandpa's buffalo jawbone club. I threw it from me. It landed with a thump by the desk.

My hands shook.

Lightning flashed, drawing my gaze to the window's rain-streaked pane. Without thought, I walked to the single-pane window, reached with still trembling hands to pull the lower sash upward, letting in the acrid sharp aroma of ozone while allowing the spirit of the dead man to escape. Rain splattered the window sill. I didn't care.

Unseeing, I looked out the window, took a deep breath, mentally recited the Wind Walker prayer.

The spirit finds its way Home
To the Other World
It soars on the wind
Rides above the grandeur and beauty of Mother Earth
To Daw'Kee, *our Creator*
Only the Sun and Earth remain forever

* * *

I prayed that Wilson's spirit would ride the winds back to the Creator, not be lost in the swirling storm of his death. I ended the prayer with the Kiowa's traditional "All My Relations," extending my blessing—positive energy—specifically to Wilson's family and on to embrace all our relations on Mother Earth, from those that slithered, crawled, or flew to the two-legged.

My phone vibrated. I hit the "Off" button and stuffed it in my back pocket.

My gaze shifted to the distant granite pillar of Medicine Bluff, the vertical remains of a once towering round hill, cleft apart, leaving half the dome intact, with no sign of the other half—a natural phenomenon of nature and the Creator. Plains Tribe people came from miles around to climb through the hundreds of feet of wilderness to reach the flat top of Medicine Bluff for spiritual renewal, guidance, and prayers. I pictured Wilson's spirit riding a cloudy steed to the top and beyond.

I hoped Wilson was at peace.

A slight rustle behind me pulled me from my thoughts. I didn't move. Really, I couldn't move. Fear froze me. Was the killer here? I wanted to run, screaming, for safety. But there was nowhere to go and no one to hear. My eyes flashed around the room.

I forced myself to continue standing at the window while I focused on listening. Another sound, but this was from outside. Through the rain, a flash; I thought I saw movement, a—

Another rustle.

Not outside; inside, with me. I shook.

I dropped my head, looked down and slightly behind me. I tried to appear as if in prayer while I scanned the room. It felt like someone was in the room with me. Air stirred. The trembles returned. I had to grasp the damp window sill to steady myself.

The killer was in the room with me.

I strained to hear over my pounding heart. More movement. I was sure it now came from near the closet. I couldn't remember if the closet door had been open before, but it was now.

In the past, that closet had been stuffed with a jumble of frames, painting canvases, and garage sale paintings to be painted over that Grandpa had collected through the years. Everything, especially canvases, found a second, third, or fourth use in my grandfather's home. To my grandmother's endless frustration, Grandpa never said no to a good piece of reusable junk.

Soft light streaked through the glass as the storm moved off to its next downpour. The noise was just to my right from the closet area. Stacks of boxes stood between me and the closet and the noise.

My mind buzzed while I remained staring out the window. I really didn't know what to do. Whoever was in the room seemed to be purposely quiet, in stealth mode. Did he plan on sneaking up on me from behind too, like Wilson?

I bent my knees, prepared to move, wherever I needed. My eyes moved from side to side, searching for a weapon. Where was the buffalo club?

No, no. *No.* I didn't want to touch the club ever again. I shifted my eyes around the room trying to find anything to use as a weapon. All I saw were well-used paintbrushes.

A grunt came from behind a stack of boxes. The nearest pillar of boxes shifted, wavered, then toppled down toward me. One box bounced off my shoulder, waking me to action. I leapt toward a fleeing figure. My first step landed in a partially torn and spilled box of empty frames. With my second, a frame wrapped around my ankle, bringing me down on my bruised knees.

The fleeing figure rammed into the hallway washer. I heard a solid thud as someone hit the floor. I ignored my complaining knees and race-crawled to the doorway. I had hopes of catching the killer. The thrill of the chase had taken over my brain and body.

The fleeing figure was faster than me—a darting blur in the dark hallway. Footsteps slapped on the linoleum, first loud, then fading, even as I moved forward into the hallway in time to hear the slam of the kitchen door.

Whoever it was . . . was gone.

Chapter Nine

An insistent banging started across the room at the front door. The banging intensified, demanding to be acknowledged—now. The door shook with the unaccustomed thuds.

Instinctually, I closed the no-no room door behind me. This consistent banging on the door was not typical. My heart jumped. Irrationally, I thought, *Police*, which was followed by an impulse to run. I stopped myself. Got control.

The banging came to an abrupt halt.

I reached the end of the hallway as the front door opened. "James . . . we have to talk. Where are you?" rang through the house as a dripping Anna burst directly into the living room. No one in the country locked their doors; that would seem unneighborly. But it appeared that everyone took Grandpa's unlocked doors as an open invitation to come on in.

Anna stopped short when she spotted me. Her head swiveled around the room. "I'm sorry for busting in like this." She faced me. "I really need to talk with James." Her face was full of worry.

I couldn't help thinking, *Me too*, but I answered, "I just got here." I continued, "Grandpa doesn't seem to be home."

I moved closer. Anna looked shaken. Her face was pale and pinched.

I'm not sure why, especially since I was concealing a body in the next room, but I felt compelled to soothe Anna. I found myself moving her further into the living room. "James, my grandpa, wanted me here to help." A calm came over me as we locked eyes. "How can I help him and you, Grandmother?" I asked, using the Kiowa term of respect for an older woman with wisdom.

"I'm . . . I'm scared for him. There is a storm over us." Anna set her earrings swinging as she looked back toward the front door and to me again. She seemed on edge.

Her words scared me. Where was Grandpa and what was going on?

I reached for Anna and brought her to the threadbare couch covered in Indian blankets. She plopped down and released a splattering of raindrops and a heavy sigh.

I squatted by her, stayed silent, waiting for her to continue. The story would come when she was ready. That was the Kiowa Way.

An internal battle waged across Anna's face. Finally, she turned to me. "It started last week. First it was the water. Then James insisted someone was selling museum pieces. One of his old paintings showed up where it shouldn't—"

Before Anna could finish, the front door opened, banging into the wall. Nita marched in, then stopped to face us. "Is he here?" Like a pecking pigeon her head bounced between us, waiting for a response.

Anna struggled up out of the sagging couch. "Nita, *Hawnay koy taw gee geah daw*—this is not the Kiowa Way. It is not right that you come like this with evil in your heart."

In the gray light, Nita's lined face seemed to twist in anger, then reformed before she spoke in a patronizing tone. "Anna, we have a responsibility. Personal feelings cannot play into what is best here." Nita's face stretched into a mask of a smile. "I'm dressed in my best for the Council meeting tonight at eight PM. I plan on showing the security footage. If James won't answer us, everyone needs to see what he has done."

I stood. "What are you talking about? What has my grandfather done?" I looked over at Anna. She flicked her eyes away.

Nita swung her fake smile at me. "Is he in the back?" She rocked forward in shiny new granny Mary Jane shoes.

I moved between Nita and the hallway. "My grandfather is not here." I forced my anger down, but my voice stayed tight. "I want to know what security footage you have. And what you are talking about."

Dancing a bit, Nita turned to Anna. "You didn't tell her?" Nita looked back at me. "Mud, isn't it? I remember you following James around everywhere. Getting special treatment." Her hair bounced.

Anna glared at Nita. "We were just sitting down when you came barging in. I truly don't see why you're in this. I'm taking care of things."

"Oh, I know how you *Ondes* are." Nita used the Kiowa word for "upper class."

"You really do think you're special, just 'cause you are a descendent of Chief So-and-So. I get tired of you all." Nita pushed forward toward Anna. "And here it is, evidence that one of you stole from the museum. I'm not letting this get silenced."

Anna stepped back. "Nita, how have you become so bitter? I don't remember you this way when we were in school together."

"I'm surprised you noticed me at all." Nita straightened an obviously new blouse. "You are not changing my mind; this is coming out. In fact, I may have the TV news at tonight's meeting." Nita looked at her watch. "Plenty of time to get the news station out to the Complex." She nodded her graying head in agreement with herself.

Nita turned to me with a smile that did not reach her eyes. "Where is James? Let's hear what he has to say about this."

I raised my voice. "Tell me what is going on here."

Anna reached for my hand. "I wanted to tell you. I don't believe it . . . then the footage . . ." Anna's voice died away. Her eyes refused to meet mine.

I dropped her hand, stepped back.

Anger broke. I lowered my voice and snarled at Nita, "Show me your security footage or get out of this house."

"Oh, you don't need to threaten me. I'll happily show you." Nita dug in her large, beaded bag and pulled out an iPad. She pressed a few buttons, tapped, then turned the screen to face me.

Anna dropped to the couch, retreating from the conversation. I had no time for her now. I looked back at Nita; her face glowed. "This is security footage of my desk right outside the museum." She moved closer to me, brought the iPad up between us, and pointed with a crooked finger. "See? There's James looking all around."

Nita leaned forward into my space. "Now watch, he goes to my desk. My desk with private matters, even if I'm left in that hallway . . . see there? He took it right off my desk." Her crooked finger with red nail polish tracked Grandpa across the screen.

I couldn't make out what Grandpa took from the desk.

I turned back to the screen.

Nita sang out, "Packaging and everything. And there he goes right out the door."

My stomach clenched.

I saw it, but it wasn't true. I stayed silent from fear of erupting. This did not show the whole story. I knew it.

Anna finally spoke. "James had a reason. He is not a thief." The words hung in the air.

Nita spun to face Anna. "Just like you to defend him, even with the evidence right here in front of your eyes." Nita's red painted nail thumped the iPad screen. "James Sawpole took the Jefferson peace medal. He knew what he was taking—you see him drop that medal right into the package and go out the door."

Involuntarily, I sucked in a breath. The Jefferson peace medal . . . *gone.*

Anna shifted on the couch. "I still don't understand why the peace medal was on your desk."

Nita quickly retorted, "That medal was all tarnished. I take care of things in the museum all the time. You know that." She shook her head. "No one ever notices all I do."

"At your desk?" Anna looked up from the couch.

Nita stepped closer to Anna. "No one ever took anything before. I didn't want those cameras, but I'm sure happy they're there now." Nita slid her iPad into her bag and looked back at me. "Bet your grandpa didn't know about the cameras when he made off with the medal."

I could hold it no longer. I snarled at Nita, "My grandfather is not a thief." This was an absolute truth. I knew it. "If he took the peace medal, he did it for the Tribe."

Nita moved across the room to where I stood. "Sure, let's ask him." She looked around the room. "Where is he? In his workroom?"

Nita moved forward and past me before I realized she was headed to the no-no room. I was slow to react. Nita was already several steps ahead of me. I could hear Anna getting up from the couch to follow.

I ran down the hall toward Nita. I needed to beat her to the door, stop her from opening that door and finding the body. In a flash I realized that I had last been seen with Wilson. Everyone at the diner had seen us argue, and my prints were on the club. If Nita and Anna didn't assume I did it, Nita would seize on this to make Grandpa appear guilty of both crimes. And he wasn't—couldn't be. I knew this in my heart. But an accusation like this, it would not just stain Grandpa's reputation; that it could be believed of him would rock my grandfather to his core.

Nita was at the door, reaching for the knob. Nothing else to do. Tensed to spring, I wasn't going to make it in time—

The no-no room door opened.

Nita's mouth dropped open in surprise as the doorknob was wrenched from her hand. A woman's gray shape filled the no-no room's doorway.

"Why, Nita, it's so nice to see you. I was just putting my baby down for a nap."

It had been ten years since I'd last seen her, but I knew her just by her shape. She closed the door behind her, came out of the room, and subtly moved the open-mouthed Nita down the hallway. "Now don't go in there and wake my baby."

Stunned into silence, I followed both women into the living room. Before reaching Anna standing at the couch, Nita spun around. "How did she get here?"

My thought exactly.

Before I could come up with an explanation why Georgie, Buck Crow's wife and my first love, was in my grandfather's workroom, Georgie spoke up. "Why, Nita, that's kinda rude. I'm sure no one asks you how guests arrive at your house."

Georgie turned to Anna at the couch, reaching out her hand. "Hi, Miz Anna, I'm Georgie Crow. I've seen you around, but we've never really met."

Nita jumped in. "Yeah, Anna. She's married to Wilson's grandson." She turned to look at Georgie. "They sure had high hopes for him."

Anna nodded her head at Georgie. "Nice to meet you, Georgie." She looked over to me. "Mud, when—"

Nita interrupted, "You got that nice new Soobuuroo now for the baby." For some reason she made a point of stretching out the brand name. "I could swear I heard Buck was selling all his dance regalia." Nita leaned toward Georgie.

Glaring while smiling, Georgie stepped back. "And just where would you hear something like that?"

Enjoying herself, Nita straightened up. "Oh, I hear things at the Complex. People always coming 'round." As if it just occurred to her: "Why, didn't Buck start working for that Gerald in town?"

My ears perked up at that. Gerald? The art gallery Gerald? Gerald with the two Jefferson peace medals, waiting for the third before sending the set to a private collector?

Nita continued, "Seems like someone was saying that Buck could get good prices for beadwork and regalia." Nita looked closely at Georgie, waiting for a response.

"Buck is always trying to help where he can." Georgie turned away from Nita, obviously finished with the conversation. I steadfastly avoided looking at Georgie.

Anna broke the uncomfortable silence, "Tell James I'll be at Red Buffalo Hall early. We need to talk." She shook her head and turned to leave. "Nita, you leaving with me? We need to let Mud find James. He's probably out by the spring." Anna urged Nita toward the front door. "And we've gotta set up for the meeting." Under her breath, I heard a muttered " . . . news stations."

I didn't give Nita a chance to respond. I herded both out the front door, closed it, locked it, turned my back to the door, and, for the first time looked directly at Georgie.

Chapter Ten

She was still homecoming queen beautiful.

Georgie had an effortless beauty. Her golden hair, though tousled, was just right. Her damp clothes fit perfectly, hugging her curves just enough. And her gold-flecked eyes were . . . locked on me. I took my eyes away. I had to force them elsewhere.

Softly I heard, "Mud. Mud, I didn't expect you . . . never would have—" She reached toward me.

Sudden anger welled up in me and spilled out. "Would have what? Never leave your baby in the room with a body? No, that's not it. Because that seems to be what you have done."

Georgie straightened, tossed her hair to the back. "No. What I have done is save your ass. What do you think those two would have done finding you hiding your grandpa's body in there?" Her voice rose on "in there."

Anger left as quickly as it had surged. Georgie didn't know who was dead. She must not have gotten close to the body. I hadn't thought it—would never think it of her—but did this prove Georgie was not the one to end Wilson's life? Or was she playing me?

I shook my head. She was up to something; she had been in the no-no room. Was she protecting Buck? Is that why she was here?

I kept my voice cool. "What were you doing in there?" I looked around the dim gray living room and couldn't resist adding, "What are you doing here?"

Georgie turned toward me, making her too close. "Oh, Mud. I am so sorry about James. I know how much you loved him. He . . ."

I didn't want to hear this, especially about Grandpa and not from her. I wanted information before she discovered it was Wilson in that room. I needed answers, not comforting. I pulled back. "Georgie, what are you doing here? Were you hiding in there? Why?"

"I was looking for Buck . . ." She trailed off.

This I could not believe. "In my grandpa's house—oh, yeah." A snort escaped.

Georgie's eyes bore into mine. She retorted with a sharp, "Yeah."

My voice rose in disbelief. "And just why did you think Buck Crow would be in my grandpa's house?"

Georgie stepped closer to me. She lowered her voice. "Mud, you don't have to be like this."

I smelled her perfume, Poison. She had started wearing it our junior year in high school. Our best year. I was overwhelmed with warm memories and feelings. I resisted, pushed the memories away.

I stayed planted. In as cold a voice as I could muster, I asked, "Like what?"

Georgie shook her head, continued looking at me. "Like this—hard."

With each shake of her head, I was engulfed in Poison and memories.

I stepped back, took a cleansing breath of fresh air, cleared my head and nostrils. I let my breath out slowly. "Georgie, I just want answers, and I know you well enough to know you are avoiding giving them."

She moved forward, looked earnestly at me. "Mud, that's not fair. I really didn't mean for things to change, to happen like it did with Buck."

Her gold-flecked eyes connected with mine—energy buzzed between us. I gasped, hoped she didn't notice my involuntary intake of breath. "Stop. That's ancient history. I care about now, today."

Images from my morning, Grandpa's call for help, and Wilson's body flooded back. My resolve to get information hardened. "Georgie, what were you doing here—in that room?"

Her eyes slid from mine. "Well, you heard them. James stole the peace medal."

I stepped forward. I couldn't hold it back. "You know my grandfather would never do something like that."

Georgie moved back, nudged a low-slung coffee table. "We both heard Nita . . . you saw it. There's proof—"

My head jerked up. Georgie stopped mid-sentence. I locked eyes with her. "You didn't know that before Nita arrived." The room's light was too gray to read Georgie's face. I went on: "Last time, before I call the police, what were you doing in that room?"

I knew I wouldn't, couldn't call the police, but Georgie didn't.

Georgie changed tactics, spoke in a soft voice. "Yes, I got here just before you. I knocked and knocked, but no one answered and that storm was coming."

Georgie's eyes pleaded for me to understand. "I called out when I came in the living room, thought I heard someone back in your grandpa's no-no room." Georgie stopped and smiled at me, remembering the old name.

I refused to return the smile. "Go on—what happened next?"

"Did I tell you it was dark?" Georgie looked around the room. "Darker than this. The storm was right over the house, and there were no lights on. No one answered me, but I heard a big thump. It was before the thunder and rain really let loose. I thought James might be hurt, so I went toward where the sound came from."

I stopped Georgie. "There was no one else here?"

"I didn't think so, but that's the thing: I was going really slow toward the hallway." Georgie looked around the small, over-furnished living room. "This living room is a mess to negotiate in the dark. It's been years since I've been here . . ." Georgie again trailed off, looking at me.

"Go on," I urged.

She stood there trying to look confident, but shifted on her feet. "I know you won't believe me, but I think James's spirit came out of the no-no room."

"Oh, come on, Georgie. Just tell me what happened."

Georgie huffed and turned away. I grabbed her shoulder, pulled her back toward me. "Tell me what made you think a spirit came out."

I kept my hand on her shoulder. Her sun-kissed hair tickled the top of my hand. A soft current thrummed between us.

Georgie's stance softened. "I don't know what it was, but something, like, flew by. I didn't see anything but a black shape, and then the front door slammed."

My fingers kneaded her shoulder. "Goofus, a spirit doesn't use a door." I felt tension release from Georgie's shoulders. My fingers moved across her upper back.

Georgie exhaled a slow, thoughtful, "Yeah. Okay, not a spirit. But something went past me in the dark." She looked up at me. She was a couple of inches shorter than my five-foot seven-inch frame. "You're right, I didn't think it was a spirit then." Georgie's face scrunched in thought. "I called for James again, but the storm hit and I just couldn't hear much of anything. I was down the hall when I thought I heard the kitchen door open." She leaned into my hands, looked guilty. "I just stood there trying to listen. Then I did hear someone stomping around. I got scared."

I squeezed and released her shoulders. The thrumming stopped.

"Stomping around. Are you saying I stomped around?" We smiled at each other; then I remembered and dropped my smile. "Go on."

Georgie sent another tentative smile my way. "Then I heard a phone ring, and you. I just froze at the no-no room door. I didn't know what to do."

My eyes sank into her gold-flecked puddles.

As if in a race to the finish, Georgie rushed on. "I slipped into your grandpa's no-no room. It was dark. I thought I could get out before you saw me. But no . . . you just kept coming down the hallway and right on into the room too. I just had time to crawl into the open closet." She stopped, looked up. "I saw you find James. Oh, Mud. I'm so sorry." Georgie reached to touch me.

For a fraction of a moment, I leaned in toward her. It seemed right to be enveloped in her arms, breathe in her Poison. Then I remembered and abruptly turned away. "Don't."

Georgie recoiled.

I continued, adding a hard edge to my voice, "You haven't explained why you're here. What is going on?"

Georgie stepped back. She gave me an appraising once-over, landing back on my face. I refused eye contact. "Okay . . . okay. I was looking for Buck. He said your grandpa had the peace medal. He really . . . wants it," she ended lamely.

I couldn't help my childish response. "What were you going to do to get the medal? Bash in a head?"

I felt Georgie's cringe. She backed away, bumped the low-slung coffee table hard enough to bring down a line of Chinet paper plates, each painted with a Kiowa camp setting through the seasons. She watched the cascading scenes before turning back to me.

"Mud." She stopped, seemed to choke, then started again. "Oh, Mud . . . you know me better than that. I couldn't hurt anyone." She looked at my crushed expression. "I couldn't hurt anyone, not like—like that. His head . . ."

I wanted to reach for her, comfort her. I wanted her to hurt. I wanted her gone.

Georgie still read me well. She must have watched each emotion rage through me until I seized control and my face settled back into a mask of indifference. I hoped that's what it looked like anyway. It's what I was trying for.

Georgie broke the brief silence. "Hey, I saw it . . . well, the body, when you did. It scared me to death. That's why I ran."

My fingers threaded through my tangled mop, tearing at the snags, leaving the curls in disarray. "You knew I was alone in the house . . . and yet you ran." I shook my head. "I don't get it. You're not making sense."

"Mud, I had to get out. I was scared." Her eyes reached for mine. "How was I going to explain being in your grandpa's room with . . . that."

I resisted melting into her gold-flecked eyes. "You still haven't explained. Try now."

Georgie looked deep into me, but I stayed blind to her attempt. I mentally congratulated myself on keeping my wall up, secure around my heart. She saw the change in my eyes, my stance, and moved to offense. "That peace medal doesn't belong to your grandpa. Buck said it belonged to the Tribe. Gerald offered a big reward to Buck." She looked up after this to gauge my reaction. "Buck wanted it for the Tribe, and the reward would give him a chance to go back to school. Mud, it would change things for us. All he wanted was to just find out if it was here—"

I stepped in close to her to hiss, "Reward! Is this what you've become? Sneak into another's home, think the worst of my grandfather, a man you know?" Now I did look into her eyes. "A good man." I stepped closer, looked down at her, shook my head. "This isn't—wasn't you."

She glared at me. "I—we don't have a fancy job like you. And now with the baby . . ."

I had forgotten about the baby. "Oh, please, tell me there is not a baby in that room." I shifted and pointed toward the no-no room.

Georgie stayed angry. “No! He’s with my mother. I said that to Nita to help you.” She shook her head. “I did not want that old biddy spreading the word about James before you could tell your family.”

This brought me up. I’d forgotten. Georgie still believed that it was Grandpa who had died in the no-no room.

Georgie misread my extended silence. “Mud, I’m really so sorry about James.”

She reached for me, pulled me in. I resisted. Poison surrounded me.

I melted.

I fit perfectly.

The shroud of dim gray lifted in a blinding flash when what seemed like every light in the house came on. The still unlocked kitchen door banged open—once again. Denny stood in the doorway with a triumphant smile. “I saw you all were still without power so I flipped the circuit switch—” His look went from me to Georgie and back to me. A knowing grin filled his face. “Well, isn’t this like old times?”

Chapter Eleven

I pushed Georgie away. "No. No, it's nothing like old times."

Denny smirked at me. Like most in my family, Denny knew that Georgie and I had been a couple in high school—until Buck.

Georgie flashed an angry glare at me. "Mud, all I've done is try to comfort you." She turned toward the front door in the living room. "I've had enough."

I moved to block her exit. "Oh no you don't, not yet. You have not explained what Buck was going to do if the peace medal was here."

Denny watched, his eyes bouncing between the two of us. "What are you all talking about?" He turned to me. "What peace medal?"

Georgie caught my eyes. "That doesn't seem to matter anymore." She tilted her head toward the no-no room. "There's more important things than that now." Her voice was thick with meaning.

Denny moved to join Georgie and me in the living room. His work boots dropped small clods of red mud onto the well-worn linoleum floor. "All right, enough of this high drama. What's going on?" He glanced between us, then settled on me.

I faced Denny, took a breath and paused a moment. I still did not want Georgie to know it was Wilson who was dead, and I didn't want Denny to think Grandpa was dead, and I wanted to get more info out of Georgie. This was not going to be easy.

I let out a breath and looked up at Denny. "I told you something was going on with Grandpa."

Denny looked around. "So, where is he?"

My stomach tightened. I ignored his question and continued, "Denny, you know that Grandpa calling me is pretty strange, but not being at the airport to meet me—" I slowly shook my head. "That was way out of character for him. Then, three people showed up looking for Grandpa at the airport."

I had Denny's full attention. He nodded and remained silent, then signaled for me to continue. Georgie stood by the door, listening. That made me uncomfortable.

"Well . . ." I hesitated, not quite sure what to reveal. Finally, I said, "There is security footage showing Grandpa taking the Jefferson peace medal from the Kiowa Museum."

Denny stood there looking at me, waiting for more. I finished with, "The Tribal Council is accusing Grandpa of stealing the medal."

Denny laughed at that. It just erupted from him. He sputtered, "That's a good one. Grandpa a thief." He let out another hoot.

Georgie turned to face Denny. "This is real. I heard Nita from the Kiowa Complex . . . they have footage." When Denny continued to smile, she stomped her foot for emphasis. "There's going to be a special meeting at Red Buffalo Hall tonight."

Georgie shifted from the still skeptical Denny to me. "You all have to give that medal back." Her golden hair bounced with each word.

I locked eyes with Georgie and spoke slowly. "Our grandfather did not steal anything. There is a reason he removed the peace medal from the museum." I took a step closer to Georgie. "Grandpa would not deprive the tribe of such an important historical piece. That is not his way." I ended with a forceful "I will find out what is going on."

Georgie stared back at me. "I don't know how you think you're going to find that out . . . now." Her eyes shifted toward the no-no room. "Seems pretty obvious what happened to the peace medal." Georgie moved away from the door. "I just hope it's still around here someplace." Her eyes traveled around the room.

Denny squared off with Georgie. "Are you calling my grandfather, James Sawpole, the Tribe's sacred story keeper, a recognized Tribal Elder with the highest standings—a thief?" His voice went up and his shoulders quivered. "You, of all people, have the gall to speak."

Georgie first cowered under the ferocity of Denny's words, then, she stepped close to him with clenched fists. "And just what does that mean, Denny Sawpole?"

Denny glared down at Georgie. "Your all-innocent act doesn't work on me." He glanced over at me then went on, "You know *exactly* what I mean."

Denny and Georgie locked eyes. "You're not blind to Buck's maneuvers," he accused. "Or do you want to pretend it's just a coincidence that Kiowas are selling their family artifacts for pennies after a Buck visit—"

Georgie jumped in. "Buck has been helping your people. He took this job with Gerald to help the Kiowas who had to sell their stuff."

Denny pushed back. "It's *stuff* when we sell it. Then in Gerald's gallery our *stuff* magically becomes priceless artifacts with prices hundreds of times the measly amount paid to the needy families."

Now Denny drew himself up to his full six feet, to tower over Georgie. "Yeah, and they *had* to sell their *stuff* to cover an unexpected expense. Funny how many times that happened after a Buck visit," Denny finished with a taunting tone.

They both seemed to have forgotten I was in the room. I stayed in place, watching the scene unfold, taking it all in—hating Buck a bit more, minute by minute.

Georgie leaned into Denny's towering form. "Denny, I don't appreciate what you're implying." She tapped her toe in a new white Nike. "Buck is making a living. We're just trying to get by."

Denny stepped back to take in Georgie, top to bottom. "You seem to be getting by pretty good." His voice had a hard edge. "You even left the price tag on your latest buy." He wrinkled his long nose at her. Georgie pushed a scrap of white paper down into her back pocket and shot a hateful look at him.

Ignoring the look, Denny eyed her unnaturally distressed jeans and designer top. "Those nice new pretend-old jeans cost quite a bit. You can't even get them in Lawton. That there is a trip to the City in your new Subarooo." Denny made the name sound like a wolf howl. Seemed like everyone here felt compelled to play with the manufacturer's name.

Georgie's face reddened; her voice became tight. "Buck is working hard to make good. He's going back to school with

Gerald's help, and he will finish this time. He wants to make his son proud." She said the last bit with conviction.

Denny shook his head, his eyes full of disgust. "You can't make your child proud when you're selling his heritage, his culture." His voice softened. "Georgie, you may not be Kiowa, but you've been around the tribes. You should care. Your son is Kiowa."

Georgie backed away, tossed her hair. "You know Buck had nothing to do with any of that. He only wants to help. That's why they come to him. Asking if he can speak to Gerald for them. Many are getting good money for their old beadwork and junk."

I could tell the moment Georgie said *junk* she wanted the word back. Once released, the word physically struck Denny. His head jerked back and his eyes went hard, followed by his tone. "Junk! They're treasures. Museums have been after these items for generations, and you call them *junk*?" He seemed to struggle for a moment before he was able to control his voice and continue. "You know Corky RedOak? He found out his son sold the family's beaded baby cradle to Gerald. Corky's great-grandmother beaded that cradle. She used dyed porcupine quills. Generations slept and stayed safe in that cradle. Now it's gone." Denny trailed off at the end.

Georgie pushed back at Denny. "You're blaming Buck for that?"

Denny snorted. "That and many others. Where do you think your money is coming from?"

Georgie shook her finger in Denny's face. "You know Corky's son Jason owned that cradle. It was passed on to him. Jason sold it to Gerald. No one forced him to do it."

Denny pushed Georgie's finger away. "Yeah, Jason sold it. He didn't have much choice. They needed money to get their car's flat tires fixed to get Corky into town for his radiation treatments."

Denny stepped back and dropped onto the old couch as if drained of energy. He slowly continued. "Georgie, Jason did not get even one percent of what that cradle sold for at the gallery; he got just enough to pay the bill for the new tires. A car that was doing fine before Buck saw the family cradle." In a taunting voice he added, "And it just happened that the cradle sold and was gone the same day Gerald got his hands on it." Denny looked down, shaking his head. "Like that wasn't planned."

I looked at Denny sitting on the couch. "Why didn't you tell me all this was going on earlier?"

Denny looked up. "You already don't like Buck." His eyes slid over to Georgie and back to me.

I felt my face heat up. "Buck's helping them strip our People of our culture. He's no better than a Fort Indian." Fort Indians of the past sold information or acted as scouts for the invading cavalries. They did the bidding of the soldiers, their actions often leading to the death of their own people for a bottle or a step up in the white society.

From behind me Georgie snapped, "I've heard enough."

I turned toward Georgie and demanded, "Would Buck kill for the peace medal?"

That brought her up short. She glared at me. "You may not like Buck, but he is not a killer." She carefully enunciated "he is not a killer," making sure I heard each word.

Denny stayed on the couch, sent me a confused look.

Georgie marched to the front door, then turned back toward me. "Mud, I am sorry about James." She faced the front door, fumbled with the doorknob, finally unlocked it, and continued her march out of the house, slamming the door behind her.

I caught a whiff of Poison as she left.

As I stared at the closed door, I realized that I had given Georgie my heart at fifteen and she had never given it back—until today.

Chapter Twelve

"Are you going to stare at that closed door all day?" Denny's face clearly expressed his exasperation. "Just what is going on here?"

Sweeping my right hand across my upraised left palm, I signaled in the old Plains Indian Tribes' sign language for Denny to hold—be silent.

The Kiowa elders—my grandfather, my great aunts, and great uncles—all signed unconsciously while speaking in Kiowa or English. In either language their hands flew in accompaniment to their words, adding a hypnotic show to the already rhythmic sounds. We older grandchildren picked up the sign language quickly, using it for our own, in play and, occasionally in school tests.

I smiled at Denny, softening the command, as I tiptoed to the living room front door and abruptly pulled it open, revealing an empty porch. Georgie was gone. I pulled the door shut, carefully locked it—enough with these nonstop visitors—and returned to the confused-looking Denny.

He pushed himself up from the couch. "All this . . ." he swept his hands encompassing the living room and kitchen area, but meaning my strange behavior. "This was fine as kids, but enough already." He moved toward the kitchen door.

Following, I spoke to his back. "I'm not making up a story, Denny."

It hit me. Grandpa was missing; there was a body in the no-no room. Grandpa was accused of stealing the Kiowa's Jefferson peace medal, the tribe's emblem of first contact. There might be illegal fracking at Grandpa's spring, and Grandpa was missing. Denny needed to know everything. I took him by the arm and moved him down the hall to the no-no room's door.

He looked down at me, started a half grin. "Don't tell me Grandpa napped through the storm and all that shouting."

Before he could turn to open the door, I pulled him back. "Denny, there's more." I hesitated, not sure how to tell him what was beyond the no-no room's door. I did not want him to open the door and think it was Grandpa at first glance, like I had.

Denny stopped to face me. "All right, Mud, enough storytelling . . . spill." His toe tapped out a steady impatient beat.

I nodded my head, set my jaw. He was right, time to get it out.

"Wils—" I stopped before speaking the dead man's name aloud, suddenly remembering the taboo. Speaking the name called the spirit back and anchored the spirit to this plane, slowing its ride with the wind to the Land Beyond.

I started again. "Buck Crow's grandfather is dead. His body is inside." I inclined my head toward the no-no room door.

Denny smirked. "Sure, you bashed in his head with the candlestick in the no-no room." He turned to go. "Enough, already."

My gasp at his words pulled him back toward me. I answered his unspoken question by opening the door. I walked into the room, looked back, and told him softly, "Denny, I'm telling the truth."

He started to speak, but his voice dropped away as his eyes slid from me to the body across the room.

I rushed to assure him. "It's not Grandpa. It's . . . it's Buck's grandfather."

Denny started for the body. I stopped him with a touch. "He's gone. There is no hope."

I watched Denny's eyes take in the scene and the situation through a series of glances. His eyes went to the bashed head, noted the deathly stillness, and slid over to the open window. Unconsciously he nodded his head once, muttered, "*Geah taw geah.* It is good." It was then that he saw Grandpa's buffalo jawbone club laying on the floor. I could see he knew instantly how the dead man had died. Denny's eyes returned to me. "Where is Grandpa?"

I choked out, "I don't know. I've not had a chance to do anything but keep people out of here." My eyes suddenly brimmed with tears.

"Why? We need the police on this now." Denny moved to the hallway and signaled for me to follow.

The unshed tears dried instantly. I rushed to stop him. Denny could not report this until Grandpa was here to explain.

"No, Denny, think how this looks." I needed Denny to agree with me, keep this quiet for now. I wanted to avoid Grandpa being attached to this or, worse, arrested. The stigma would never disappear.

I recounted to Denny the case against Grandpa. "They have footage of Grandpa taking the Jefferson peace medal, Buck's grandfather was looking for the medal. Now he's dead."

Making sure Denny was listening, I emphasized, "Dead in Grandpa's workroom. Killed by Grandpa's buffalo jawbone club." Now I had his attention.

"People will think he did this before Grandpa ever has a chance to say a word." I held Denny's eyes. "And you know Grandpa—he will get all prideful stubborn and won't say a word. He'll do the stoic, silent Indian act." I waited a beat before adding, "While something breaks inside him forever."

This last was true. If the Kiowa People doubted Grandpa's honesty, if they doubted him as an honorable person—he would never be the same.

Denny lowered his eyes. Shook his head. "This doesn't look good, but waiting . . ."

"Denny, that footage of Grandpa taking the peace medal, and now this." I tilted my head toward the room. "The police will take him into custody."

Denny shook his head. "No . . ."

I reached out and grasped his arm. He needed to understand. Grandpa could not be trapped in a jail, even for a short time. "Denny, he's an Indian. The police won't look any further than that. Indian kills Indian. Case closed."

We both remained silent for a beat, then Denny asked again, "Where's Grandpa?"

"Denny, I don't know." I nearly cried. "I haven't had time to look for him. The other room doors are open." I was afraid to continue but did. "If he was in there, he would have heard all the commotion. Unless he couldn't." I stopped talking. I tried to hold my face together. If it crumbled, I would collapse.

I hadn't thought of searching the other rooms for more bodies—I hadn't thought of searching for Grandpa's body. My face crumbled; my knees suddenly gave.

Denny caught me. "It's all right. Grandpa is alive." He squeezed my shoulders.

"Oh, Denny . . ." Words failed me.

Denny cocked his head as if a thought just occurred to him. "I bet he wasn't even here when . . . that happened." He used his chin to point to the no-no room. "No one but Grandpa sits at that desk. Not if he's home."

I took a deep breath in and righted myself. "That's true. But where is he?"

Denny looked down the hallway. "First, I'll check the other two rooms." He stopped, looked at me. "You okay?"

I nodded and watched him go into a bedroom.

Denny was in big-brother mode, protecting his little sister. In the Kiowa culture, there is no word for *cousin*. In fact, there's no such thing as a cousin. All children of your brothers and sisters were viewed as your own. They were children of your blood and flesh. We all had grown up as a huge brood of brothers and sisters.

But I wasn't a little sister to protect. Grandpa called me for help. I needed to step up.

I moved back to the no-no room's doorway. I didn't go in, but started a slow scan around the cluttered workroom, searching for anything that might indicate where Grandpa or the peace medal might be. With the lights on, I could see the fallen boxes from my unsuccessful chase after Georgie. I thought of her hiding in the room with the body. A shudder shook me. A small guttural sound must have escaped from me.

Denny glanced over as he moved on to the small back room. "Everything all right?"

"Oh yeah." I gave him a weak smile.

He moved out of sight.

I needed to woman up.

I stepped into the room. Other than the tumbled boxes, everything else was in order, undisturbed. It was obvious that no fight had taken place before the death blow was delivered. The blow had to have been sudden and unexpected.

Unconsciously, I moved closer to the desk. Examining the room, trying not to look at the body, while looking for the peace medal. I scanned the area. My eyes rested on the top of the desk. Something was different.

Grandpa left all correspondence clipped to the top of that desk. It was his communications center. Grandpa being Grandpa, he usually left his notes drawn out in pictographs for us to decipher. I bit my lower lip to stop a smile, thinking of Grandpa's "Gone fishing" note from years ago. It had been a simple line drawing of Grandpa, on the back of "Abe," his multifunction 1970s Lincoln sedan, with pole in hand, complete with a leaping hooked fish. The smile dropped as I moved closer to the body.

There, just above the dead man's outreached hand, was a torn note sheet. There was something scrawled on the white paper.

It wasn't drawn; it was handwritten. The bottom of the ink was smeared, as if the dead man's fingers, wet with recent rain, had touched the words at the end.

I couldn't read the note from here, yet my feet refused to move any closer. I leaned forward, squinted to improve my eye's reception. No luck. I still couldn't read the note from this distance. I needed to get closer to the body.

There were sounds from the hallway. Doors closing.

I told myself again, time to woman up.

Without wanting to, I moved forward to the desk. I stayed back away from the sitting body, yet close enough to read the hasty writing just above the dead man's outreached hand: *I am whe*

The door opened, and Denny said, "No sign of Grandpa or anything missing." He stopped short, sensed a change in me. "What's up?"

"Grandpa left a note." A small rumble, remnants of the thunderstorm, emphasized my words. "It says, 'I am whe . . .'" I pronounced *wheh* and then spelled out *"w-h-e."*

"Wheh? What's wheh?" Denny's voice rose in frustration. "You sure it's from Grandpa?"

I nodded. "Yeah, I know his writing." I was sure. "Denny, part of the note is missing."

Denny marched over to the desk. "What are you talking about?" His eyes went to the top of Grandpa's desk, taking in the outreached fingers holding down half of a note. The other half, ripped from the dead man's fingers.

Denny shook himself. In unspoken agreement, we moved away from the desk, back toward the doorway.

I took a moment to think back to when I first came into the room and discovered the body. The flash that had lit the room to reveal the dead man with outstretched hands. That image was seared in my mind. I turned to Denny. "The whole note was there when I first discovered him." I side-eyed the body. "I would remember seeing it if a note had been torn"—I gulped, then continued—"from his fingers."

"But you didn't read it?" Denny asked.

"No, I didn't have a chance. That's when Georgie ran from the room . . . but that was before I knew it was Georgie and after Anna, then Nita showed up . . ." I trailed off.

Denny had a strange look on his face. "All these people have been here, this morning?" His voice went up in disbelief.

I looked deep into his brown eyes. "It has been nonstop."

He shook his head. The no-no room door blew fully open behind Denny. He asked, "What's 'I am whe' supposed to mean?"

I turned toward him. "I think Grandpa was telling us where to find him and the medal." Another hollow bang in the background. I sure hoped the storm wasn't coming back, or being followed by something worse. We did not need a twister to come through.

Denny shook his head. "How do you figure that?" Before I could answer, he went on, "This is looking worse and worse for Grandpa." He repeated a litany of points against Grandpa. "He takes the peace medal. His handmade buffalo club is used to kill Wils—No, don't stop me, Mud. He disappears leaving a cryptic note." Denny's voice rose again. "He must have . . . I don't know . . ." Denny did stop as we both heard a loud bang, obviously not thunder, outside the opened no-no room door.

Someone was in the house and coming down the hallway toward us and the dead man.

Chapter Thirteen

Denny was closest to the open door; he spun and moved into the hallway. I was two steps behind. Before reaching the door, I stooped and grabbed a wood frame hanging out of a box. The empty frame wobbled in my hand. Denny looked back at me, taking in my set jaw and flimsy weapon. Denny flashed a smile that brightened his face as he whispered, "I feel safe with you at my back."

I had to laugh at myself. I dropped the frame before it fell apart, followed Denny out, and closed the no-no room's door. Denny stood at the end of the hall blocking my view into the kitchen. Somehow his lean frame seemed to expand, filling the hallway. Denny was facing someone, blocking their access. Neither spoke.

I slid from behind Denny.

A middle-aged man in a short-sleeved dress shirt and tie stood with his hand stretched toward Denny. The man began in a false-sounding cowboy accent. "Howdy there, I'm Gerald Mayfield." His tie danced with little yellow Stetsons that perfectly matched the yellow pointy toes of his spotless snakeskin boots. Fortunately, there was no matching yellow ten-gallon cowboy hat.

Denny ignored the outstretched arm. “I know what you are,” he growled out. “What are you doing here?” Denny’s eyes bored into the man.

The man’s eyes slid from Denny to me. A slow smile lifted his lips but did nothing for his cold blue eyes. He dropped his arm, reaching his hand into his pocket to jingle some change. “Well there, as I said, I’m Gerald. I own TribalVision Gallery in town.” My ears perked up.

Gerald went on, “My assistant told me this here case must be yours.” He rolled a suitcase toward me. Its wheels rumbled across the floor. Gerald presented the handle to me with a small flourish of his hand. His nails appeared polished.

Questions ran through my mind. Was the rolling case the rumble I’d heard earlier? Just how long had Gerald been in the house? What had he heard? Did he know about the body? Did he know anything about Grandpa!

I carefully kept my face blank as I slowly appraised him. Then I realized he was still bent, presenting my case to me. Flustered, I stuttered out, “Thank you,” and took the case.

Denny shifted closer to my side—warrior on guard, eyes alert. I really didn’t know how Gerald resisted the searing heat of Denny’s glare. I had melted under much less in our childhood.

I asked “Where did you find my case?”

Gerald did a good ole boy “aw shucks” downward shake of his head. “Ahh, I saw it there in the alley and thought my assistant had left my case out again.” Gerald made sure to make eye contact before shaking his head with exaggerated exasperation. “I just rolled ’er in and tucked it in my closet. I plum forgot about it until my assistant told me about your visit to my little ol’ place.” He rocked back and jingled his change.

Gerald could resist no longer; his eyes moved from me to the art that covered all available space on the walls, tables, and floor. Anything in my grandparents' house that did not move had been painted, including sleeping grandchildren on more than one occasion.

Gerald almost drooled taking in a large white canvas with a flat-style Kiowa fancy dancer halted mid-step from an unseen eagle whistle. His eyes traveled on to a watercolor of a Kiowa medicine man in the midst of a vision, talking to an owl. Gerald's eyes rose upward toward the ceiling to find the room ringed in determined war chiefs and warriors, all on mounts ready to descend on the enemy. Finally, his calculating eyes rolled back to me. "This is amazing." Probably the only truth he had spoken all day.

Denny stepped forward, forced Gerald back toward the kitchen. "Enough. You were not invited here. I want you to leave now."

Gerald feigned surprise. "Have we met before?" He eyeballed Denny. "I'm sure I would have remembered you."

The warrior within Denny emerged. "We've never met and I don't want to know you. I know what you are doing to my People."

In the years I had been gone, Denny had grown to be quite an advocate for our People. I had always thought of him as simple—simple needs, simple desires, a simple, happy guy. First to go fishing, first to attend a Gathering, first at the Powwow Dances, and first to offer a hand. I had been the simple one to not realize the depth of his feelings for the land, life, People, and the Kiowa Way. I had to smile; Grandpa had influenced more than just one of his grandkids.

I tuned back in to hear Denny finish with, ". . . you do not think or care for any but yourself. How many Indians have you stolen from?"

Gerald stayed calm under the barrage. He never looked directly at Denny, instead his eyes bounced around the rooms, appraising the art and family artifacts lying about. I imagined his eyes spinning wildly with internal calculations.

Sparing a glance at Denny, he replied, "I'm sorry you feel that way. I believe I help the people that come to me. I give them the best price in town." His thin lips slid upward as if on cue with *"best price in town."* His voice left me feeling oily.

Denny cut in, "You control the pricing. And I notice, nothing stays local. It all disappears." He leaned into Gerald.

Denny's pressing bulk finally got Gerald's attention. "I am in business to make a living. If I wasn't here, people would have nothing." He straightened, leaned toward Denny with a dead smile. "Without me, they get no help."

His smile only seemed to irritate Denny more. I knew that look well; Denny was going to blow. That couldn't happen yet. I had a few questions for Gerald before Denny kicked him out of the house. And Denny looked ready to physically remove the fake cowboy at any moment.

I moved forward between the two and herded Gerald into the kitchen, where the door to the carport outside stood slightly ajar. Gerald watched me look from the door to him. He answered my unspoken question. "I knocked several times at the front door, then remembered these old Indian houses have the side door that most use." He amped up the smile.

From behind me, Denny interjected, “Family use the kitchen door. What gave you the right to just come in our home?” His breath was hot on my neck.

Gerald addressed me, “I knew you would want your case.” He gestured to it where it sat abandoned in the hall. “And I had some business out this way.” Gerald tried to look sincere. “I knocked and hollered at you all from the front door. You all musta been pre-occ-u-pied.” His twang was back.

Denny pushed me aside, and Gerald moved further toward the kitchen door. He bumped the small laminate wood dining table with the plastic floral chairs that Grandma had always scrubbed clean daily, with pride. This was her first—and only—store-bought dining set. Her good china bowl with Grandpa’s buffalo horn spoon sat in a puddle of stiff oatmeal at the head of the table. A triangle slice of toast lay propped on the side of the bowl.

Denny continued toward Gerald, trapping him against the table. “How did you know Mud would be here?”

Gerald tried to step forward away from the table. “This is a small town. Everyone knows everyone. I heard that James Sawpole had a visiting granddaughter.” He nodded his head toward me, exposing a pink scalp under his yellow hair. “She left a card with ‘Sawpole’ on it, so I came by with her suitcase.” Gerald looked at Denny. “I gotta say this is not the greeting I expected.” They locked eyes until Gerald broke contact and turned to look at the table he remained jammed against. His gaze settled on the buffalo horn spoon. It and other items made and used in daily life in my grandfather’s childhood were often still in use around the house today. What some considered an artifact, we used as a needed spoon.

A larger buffalo horn dipper had stood in a white-enamel bucket on the kitchen counter, ready to serve cool well water to all thirsty grandkids passing through Grandma's kitchen every day of my childhood. I glanced over to the sink and saw the bucket and buffalo horn dipper on the counter—in place just as they should be.

I forced Gerald to look over to me. "Gerald, why didn't you call? I left a card—not an address."

He looked from me to Denny and back again before answering with a sneer. "I did call. There was no answer." I noticed there was no cowboy twang in his voice now.

Both Denny and Gerald watched as I dug my phone out of my back pocket. It was off. I pressed and held until the phone began its start-up process. I bit my bottom lip while looking down at it. I had turned it off and put it away when I found the body. An hour ago, according to my phone and all the waiting missed calls. It felt more like a lifetime ago.

I looked up. "Gerald, I'm sorry. Thank you so much for returning my suitcase." I looked closer at the returned case. The TSA locks were missing from all three zippers. They had been in place when I'd last seen the case in the alley. I turned back to Gerald. "It looks like someone went through my case. Was that you?"

Gerald looked surprised at my directness. It took a moment for him to reply. "I knew once I looked at that case closer, it weren't mine. Nope, ma'am, I didn't open your case. That there's how I found it." The cowboy act was back.

I ignored the annoying "ma'am" and pressed on, abruptly switching to another topic, hoping to make him fumble out an unknown truth. "Gerald, I noticed that you had two Jefferson peace medals in a setting for three in your shop. Who was providing the third . . . the Kiowa peace medal?"

I wanted to hear Gerald say Buck was selling the Jefferson peace medal to him. Of course, I expected him to claim that he didn't know it was stolen. I thought Gerald would give Buck up to save himself. The right words from Gerald could prove Grandpa was protecting the peace medal from a planned theft. He could prove Grandpa was not a thief.

Gerald merely smiled and turned his full attention to me. "Why, no one was giving me the third Jefferson peace medal. That there Jefferson peace medal is Kiowa property." The twang thickened.

He assumed a lecturing tone. "You should know that it is not an object that is for sale. If your granddaddy has it . . ." He stopped and looked intently at both Denny and me. "You all just gotta get it back to the Tribe. No questions asked." He ended with another oily slick smile.

Denny let out a hot breath behind me. Gerald's act wasn't fooling him. I pushed back at Gerald. "And what makes you think our grandfather would have the medal?"

Again with the slick smile. "Several Kiowas work for me. You know how word travels once that drum starts beating for you all." Gerald's eyes continued roaming the art on the walls.

I ignored his offensive tone. "Gerald, that doesn't explain your display case waiting for the third medal to complete the set of Jefferson peace medals being shipped out. And your assistant told me the set was already sold."

Gerald looked down at me. "Was that a question?" He didn't wait for an answer, simply waved his manicured fingers at me. "You must have misunderstood my assistant. Those were not the real Jefferson peace medals. Obviously." He exaggerated the roll as he shook his head. "No, no . . . no . . . no. No. Those were exquisite copies." Gerald gifted us with another disposable smile. "The last Jefferson peace medal *copy* was due today, but the thunderstorm delayed its delivery." Here the smile was replaced by a sad face.

I didn't believe this act, and I could tell Denny didn't either, but there was no way I could prove Gerald had the original peace medals with intent to get the third. Yet.

Gerald looked from me to Denny and back. "Ahh, I see the confusion now and yes siree, I can understand the hostility." He looked over to Denny slightly behind me. "So, it is true. Someone stole the real McCoy. I sure hate hearing that." Gerald returned to his brain-swirling head roll routine. "I sure do hope that medal is returned." Smiling brightly, he looked up. "And, well, this will just prove my case tonight."

He lured me in; I had to ask him, "What's happening tonight?"

Gerald was all slick confidence now. "I'll tell you now, 'cause you all will just hear it tonight at the Red Buffalo Hall meeting." He paused to confirm he had our attention before continuing. "You all have a right nice little museum, but it's been going downhill for quite a while. Yep, we been talkin' for a bit and now, it just plain made sense." Gerald's smile reached his cold blue eyes for the first time as he finished, "Your Kiowa Committee is voting me in as museum curator to get things all fixed up."

Denny immediately shouted, "Never!"

Gerald couldn't resist poking the warrior. "Oh yes. I'll start immediately. Your granddaddy's theft was the last straw.

The Committee wants an accounting and controls. Just what I bring to the table. And it doesn't hurt that I'm posting a little ol' reward for the missing peace medal." He turned to me. "Yes, I'm going to offer a very nice reward for the medal's return. No questions, just bring it to me."

Denny pushed forward. "You're the *last* person who will ever touch the Kiowa's Jefferson peace medal. Enough of your pollution. Get out."

Gerald stood still, eyes on Denny. Then slowly his gaze slid back to me. I felt him appraise me, up, down, and inside, and with a final calculating look he asked me, "Do you know what a treasure trove you have here?"

Denny froze.

I locked eyes with Gerald. "Yes. Our family has been very fortunate—rich with love in this home."

Gerald snickered. An ugly sound. "No, I mean real money. If someone wants to sell some of this art . . ." He looked at me again. "I could pay well for this. It's gotta be expensive running a business in Cally-forn-ya."

That was too much for Denny. He rushed toward Gerald.

I got between them. I didn't really want to stop Denny, but there had been enough blood shed in the house. I pointed to the kitchen door. "Let me be clear. There is no Sawpole interested in your money. You can't buy our culture."

Gerald walked to the side door. As he went out, he tossed over his shoulder, "I got a gallery full of artifacts that says everybody's got a price."

Chapter Fourteen

Denny growled behind me.

Once Gerald was out, I closed the kitchen door. Denny moved me to the side, reached out and twisted the never-before-used dead bolt.

We moved to the living room. I made sure the front door was still locked before turning to Denny. "Wow. You impressed me. I had no idea—"

Instead of being pleased, Denny snapped, "Of course you had no idea. You just left. Not just to go off to college, but never heard from again—gone."

I was speechless—quite literally. I had no idea how to respond. Denny misread my stunned silence. "You too good for us? You may have been the first to go off to college, but there's five now. All with degrees. Four came home: Sandy teaches in Elgin, Lila and Chuck in Cache, and Rick at Oklahoma University. They all found work around here. But you, you never came home—worse, you never *come* home." He ended as if worn down, his voice trailing off.

I stood and shook my head. Denny's outburst surprised me. I didn't think my absence was missed. There were a lot of us.

"Denny, I don't teach. What I do—working with start-up companies, telling their stories with computer graphics—can only be done where I live, in Silicon Valley."

I was surprised to see a slight sheen across Denny's eyes. He looked down and away before answering. "I keep hearing that the internet will let you work anywhere. Why not here?"

I reached to touch his arm. "Denny, I have to be where the customers are. My work is not all computers. I need to meet and work with the owners of companies before I can craft their stories."

I squeezed his arm. "I haven't had time to visit. I started my business right after graduation." I stepped back. "It's hard to leave when the business depends on me to keep it all going." I let my voice fade away at the end. I was making excuses. I knew it.

I looked intently at Denny, trying to catch his eye. He had been my hero, growing up. All things seemed to come easily to him. I was so proud when he included me in whatever adventure was being planned. Even if most ended in pain or punishment . . . or the usual combination of both. My older sisters were boring, but with Denny there was always excitement happening around him.

"I do miss you. Everyone. All this." I opened my arms to include the house and life in Oklahoma. And I did. There were days I yearned to be home.

"I've thought about returning, but, Denny, I really enjoy my work. I get to create stories for companies that are defining new markets and industries, and everything is immediate and critical." I couldn't help but smile.

I moved closer to Denny. I had his attention. "And I'm good at it. I'm good at finding the inner story of the company and the founders, and putting pictures to their words. I help get these companies started right." I felt proud.

As Denny looked down at me, a smile flirted with his face. "Sounds like you're following family tradition—you're just like Grandpa, a storyteller. Only you're just tellin' company stories."

This brought me up. "Yeah, I can see what you're saying." I ran my hands through my hair. "I've created a niche position for myself as a corporate storyteller."

I sent a smile to Denny, trying to coax more from him. "You're probably right—storytelling is in my blood."

Denny returned to a serious tone. "It's definitely in Grandpa's blood. He is a master storyteller."

I wasn't quite sure where Denny was headed with the conversation, but there was no denying the truth of his words. "Denny, Grandpa is amazing. I know that."

Denny fired back, "I thought you knew that. But you seemed to forget it once you got to California." Denny glared at me. "You didn't just leave us. You left him too." His words struck home, hard. He went on, unable to hold back. "Oh, we know he loves all his grandkids, but it was different with you two. You two had a soul connection." Denny stepped back. "We all knew you were the next story keeper. You knew it too. But you left."

I looked up at him, caught his eyes. I wanted him to hear the truth in my words, see the pain in my eyes. For as long as I could remember I had wanted to be the story keeper. It seemed like I had always known the stories of the Kiowa People etched onto the Dohason and Anko calendar hides.

Most of our Kiowa grandparents had been raised by those who had their stories scratched onto the last years of the calendars. My grandfather's mother and grandparents had been born free in Kiowa country, then died as U.S. POWs. They had survived the unspeakable destruction of a twelve-year war in their homeland and the subsequent roundup and march to Reservation life. Listening to Grandpa tell of Sun-Boy, his great-grandfather and our band's chief, the battles and struggles made the images on the calendars much more than stories to me. This had happened to family.

I had wanted to work with the tribe to preserve our stories. Make sure the Kiowas remembered and were remembered. But they didn't want me. The memory still burned. I'd always been teased about looking different, but it was when I was leading at a storytelling that I heard for the first time that I wasn't Kiowa enough.

"Denny, the tribe did not want me. It doesn't matter what I know." I shook my head, curls bouncing. "I don't look Kiowa enough for them."

His eyes stayed locked on mine. "Mud, you were fifteen. I saw you leading, telling the story. You had the young mesmerized until you let a few of the busybodies get to you. You were good."

I had been good. I knew I'd had the audience. I could feel the focus, see they were wrapped up in the story. I smiled; several kids had even cringed as I mimed four thuds on a cottonwood trunk during the telling. It was at the end that a woman, talking to no one and everyone, announced, "Look at that hair! Is she even an Indian?"

I lowered my eyes. "She voiced the whispers I had heard for years."

Denny looked at me and said, "I don't understand why you always put your looks down. My mom loves your hair."

I snorted. "Denny, we have the same mix, but you, your looks came out all Kiowa. Mine are whitewashed."

I tugged a handful of Denny's thick mane. "We have the same dark, thick hair. Mine curls; yours is all Indian straight."

I smiled and pulled on my earlobes as I told him, "We have the same long nose and earlobes that will end up brushing our shoulders when we are old and gray, but your brown eyes are expected, while my green ones throw my mixture of features into confusion."

I stepped back from Denny. "Here, where people are exposed to our tribes, I am an obvious Kiowa half-breed and treated as such from both sides."

Denny snorted. "Doesn't matter how much Indian you are, we get worse treatment in town. You still don't see Indians with anything but fast-food jobs." He shook his head and muttered, "Hate it, but gaming is the only way our People get good jobs or money to go to school for better jobs."

"Yeah, I'm not a fan. I think the Kiowa's prospect of gaming money is part to blame for the tribe's increased attitude of 'not enough Indian to be Indian.' They're afraid they will have to share."

Denny backed away. I could tell he was thinking. He slowly said, *"Hawnay,"* the Kiowa word for *no*. "There are a few—they are extremely vocal—but they are not the majority of the tribe."

I was surprised that he was protecting the Kiowas who ridiculed us for not being enough Indian when we were kids. I snorted. "Come on, Denny. You know how some of the Kiowa families are. It reminded me of Harry Potter and the intolerant pure bloods." I moved toward Denny. "Anything less than full blood is not Indian enough."

I looked Denny over. "Even with your good looks."

Denny struck a pose.

I reminded him, "Denny, as kids you heard them at the gatherings whispering about Grandpa's "band of mixed breeds."

This made Denny smile. "Maybe it stung you more. You did stand out, but I liked being part of Grandpa's band. We are all a mix of everything . . . and completely covered in Kiowa."

This made me break into a real smile. It felt good.

Denny added, "Grandpa and his brothers and sisters made sure we all knew we are Kiowa, no matter the shade of our skin."

My smile got bigger as I remembered our great-aunts and -uncles. "The old ones didn't care what we looked like. We had Kiowa blood, we were Kiowa. They just wanted the tribe to survive."

Denny walked to an old console television. Its top was covered with framed photos. Most were of bygone days and people. "Mud, I get asked about you all the time. People want to know when you're going to return or at least come back for gatherings. The older ones even, they ask about where's that spot of Mud that James couldn't get rid of."

I was surprised how pleased I was to hear this. I had told myself it didn't matter. I didn't need to be the story keeper.

Denny went on. "The Old Ones remind me that you know the stories as well as Grandpa." He grinned at me. "I tell them, I think you tell 'em better." This made me laugh. He shifted. "You kept all of us kids entranced with the stories you told of Grandpa's paintings, of the Kiowas."

Denny looked serious; I knew not to interrupt. He stepped to a painting showing a woman, wrapped in the remains of a shredded blanket, climbing, with bare feet, up a rocky hillside toward a distant campfire's glow. With just a few strokes, the plight of the Kiowa woman, of a culture, was exposed while also portraying an iron-will determination to survive—all captured in a single expression. This painting had never been for sale.

Denny faced the painting. "I had heard of how *Zoneetay* snuck out of Fort Sill to bring food and news to Chief SunBoy and the last of the free Kiowas, to support the resistance." He turned back to me with a glow on his face. "You made me see her as more than one of Grandpa's chronicle stories." He turned back to the painting. In awe he said, "This is Grandpa's grandmother." He shook his head. "Unbelievable, what she went through. The soldiers kept her in a covered icehouse pit for months in payment for her bravery." He turned back to me. "Yet she survived. And because of her, we are here. And because of you, I felt her story."

I moved to his side as he looked around the walls lined with art. "Mud, you brought the Kiowas alive for me."

I stuttered a protest, "I just repeated Grandpa's—" I stopped. Denny was right. I did try to make it more than a chronicle accounting from our history. These were our People, our stories. It had all happened so recently.

Oklahoma had been the dumping ground for all tribes pushed from their lands, but this had been our country. We had already been in Oklahoma. Because of that, the Kiowas were one of the last tribes put on a reservation and one of the few tribes left on their homeland.

This land had been home to the Kiowas for generations. We still lived amid Kiowa country. We walked our sacred lands and viewed our battlefields daily. We carried the names of our Kiowa survivors in the last names of our friends and our family. When I told the stories of our People, I wanted my audience to feel the recent past.

Denny ignored my interruption. "For us, you added something to his stories. Maybe it was your understanding, I don't know. But the history, the symbolism, that doesn't interest me like it does you and Grandpa."

I stayed quiet. Denny needed to be heard.

He stood tall. "But I am Kiowa, and I care about preserving who we are. Most of that comes from Grandpa, but a big chunk was from you."

His words stunned me.

Denny appeared shy suddenly. He looked around the furniture-crowded living room. "When we all camped out here in the wilds of the living room, you chose a painting to tell us about. You made me feel proud to be Kiowa, *Shawn Tdaun*, little sister."

Unexpected tears welled in my eyes. I struggled to hold them back.

I thought he was finished, but Denny turned to face me again. He took a moment before adding, "The tribe didn't reject you; you rejected us and ran away because a girl broke your heart."

Tears vanished. I clenched my jaw, struggled to hold back welling anger. There was truth to what Denny said, but he knew there was more to it. Hadn't he heard me?

Denny finished. "You may be a success in California, but you have forgotten who you are. Knowing that is truly what matters in life."

His final words rang true . . . and hurt.

A silence settled on us.

After a bit, Denny shook himself like a wet dog. He smiled. "All right, that went too deep."

I was quick to agree. "Yep. Way too deep for me right now." I squeezed his arm, wanting him to know I'd heard him.

I took a couple steps into the living room, and then it hit me. For a few minutes, I had forgotten. We had forgotten . . . There was a body in the next room.

I stumbled.

And Grandpa was missing.

Denny seemed to remember as I did. His face went pale. I stepped toward him. "Denny, are you all right?"

"All right?" A wild laugh escaped from him. "How did I forget for even a minute?" Without waiting for an answer, he continued in a rush, "There's a body in the no-no room. Let's see, Grandpa's missing, which looks like he ran away 'cause he's suspected of murder and stealing the Jefferson peace medal."

I let him get it out. Then he looked over at me. "Oh yeah, and didn't you say something was happening at Jimmy Creek? There might be wildcat fracking going on. And whoever the frackers are, they want Grandpa out of the way."

Denny dropped onto the low-slung couch, sinking deep into the old cushion. "We've got to find Grandpa before anything else happens. But how? He could be kidnapped." Denny looked up at me. "Did you think of that? What if those oil boys got hold of him? You thought they might be threatening him." He looked down. "I just don't know what to do."

I squatted in front of him. "Denny, we just have to get out of here before anyone else shows up." I forced his head up. "I have an idea—"

Just then, a loud rap sounded from the living room door.

Chapter Fifteen

At least no one barged in.

Denny knocked me aside as another hard rap got him out of the cushion's depth and to the door. He stood with it partially opened. I couldn't see who was there.

A faintly familiar gruff voice said, "Hello, I'm Roy Medford. Is James Sawpole here?"

My mind processed slowly. *Roy.* Roy, the water quality guy I'd met in town. The one that had talked with Anna and might know about fracking in the backcountry.

Denny said, "James is not here." He moved to close the door while the words were still hanging in the air. By then, I was beside him and able to halt the door's progress.

I leaned out. "Roy, is that you?" I elbowed Denny out of my way.

Roy looked from Denny over to me. A smile erupted. "Hey, I didn't get your name back at the shop." He shifted from the door.

I hesitated a moment before telling Roy, "My name is Mud."

I didn't think his smile could get bigger, but it did. "I love it." He reached his hand out to me. "Nice to meet you, again . . . Mud."

I stepped onto the porch, leaving Denny looking puzzled in the doorway.

The moment I took Roy's extended hand, I knew he had experience with Indians. He grasped mine, held, and released. No pumping action or, as many Kiowas believed, the shaking off of promises.

I smiled at him. "What are you doing here?"

Denny stomped his feet behind me.

Roy leaned back against the porch railing. "I have business with James Sawpole." He smiled. "How 'bout you?"

"James is my grandfather. I'm visiting." As I moved to the other side of the porch, I could see Denny signal me.

Roy looked disappointed. "Sorry to hear you're just visiting." His ready smile returned.

In the background, Denny muttered, "Mud, we need to get . . ."

I kept my attention on Roy, then sent a quick sign to Denny: "Just wait, listen."

I leaned toward Roy. "Hey, Grandpa's not here. Is there anything I can help with?"

Roy held up a large envelope. "I was bringing a report out for him."

Good thing my ears were covered by curls because they perked right up on hearing *report.* I forced my eyes off the report to a bed of bright yellow black-eyed Susan flowers. Still damp, the petals wore beads of diamonds that sparkled in the afternoon sun.

Denny decided to join us on the porch. He stepped out and closed the door firmly behind him. Neither of us wanted anyone inside that house.

"Roy, this is my cousin Denny." I turned to Denny, caught his eye, and sent him an "I'll lead" hand signal while saying aloud, "Denny this is Roy. He does water quality testing." I shifted to include Roy in my explanation to Denny. "We met in town."

Ignoring my signal, Denny demanded, "What's Grandpa testing?"

Roy's smile went down with the hand holding the report.

I looked over at Denny and sent him a glare. I turned back to Roy to explain, "Denny and I have been worried that fracking is going on somewhere on Grandpa's land."

Roy looked at his feet. A welcomed breeze carrying rain-washed air passed between us. He looked back up at me to ask, "Will James be back soon?"

I leaned against the porch rail. "Not sure when he'll return." I kept my eyes on Roy as I tilted my head toward Denny. "I was just telling my cousin that Grandpa called me for help. That's why I'm here." I leaned toward Roy and took a guess. "How did the tests on Jimmy Creek's water come out?" Denny stayed quiet. Birds sang in the distance.

Roy relaxed back onto the porch rail. "So, James talked to you about his troubles?" He slapped the envelope on the side of his jean-clad leg.

I locked eyes with him. "My grandpa said he had a bad feeling." I waited a beat before adding. "He wanted my help." I wasn't lying. Grandpa had called me for help. I just wished he had said more. That report could provide answers.

Roy shifted the envelope from hand to hand.

Denny's eyes followed. His body seemed poised to intercept.

I kept eye contact with Roy and reached for the envelope. He held it for a beat, then released it to me.

Denny snorted.

I refused to look at Denny, keeping my eyes and smile on Roy. I knew I wasn't going to understand this report without his help. And yeah, I was flirting again to get what I needed.

Denny became impatient. "Are you going to look at it?"

"Yep, Denny. Doing it now." I opened the envelope and pulled out several sheets. Most of the information was numbers, graphs, and tables. As expected, none of it made sense to me.

Denny demanded, "So what does it show? Is someone messing with the creek?"

Roy watched as I handed the report over to Denny. I turned back to Roy. "What does it mean? Is there fracking going on?" Another breeze blew carrying the smell of earth—fresh, clean, and ripe.

Roy's brow wrinkled. "There is a summary at the end . . ." Denny began to interrupt, but Roy spoke over him. "But the upshot is that there are signs of contaminants that are typically seen within the petroleum industry."

I watched Roy. "From fracking?"

Roy answered, "Well, I can tell you results indicate that somewhere upstream, at Jimmy Creek Spring or"—he rubbed his lightly whiskered chin—"possibly worse, in the aquifers. Yes, contaminants related to oil production are polluting the creek water."

I shifted on the rail. "If the water is contaminated, why didn't Grandpa see it?"

Roy's easy smile returned. It was obvious he liked his job. "I don't know what's happening here, but if it is fracking, they prefer to pull water down deep, from the aquifer level."

His gaze shifted between Denny and me, confirming we were interested and following his explanation. "Fracking can use hundreds of gallons of water a day. It's faster to get that by tapping directly into an underground river."

Denny asked, "If they're just taking water from the spring's underground source, why is the creek getting polluted?"

I thought I knew the answer to this, but it was good to hear Roy confirm it.

"Water gets used in the fracking process." He looked at Denny directly. "During that process, water is mixed with chemicals. Illegal fracking's excess water and chemicals are often pushed back into the aquifer source water." He finished with, "Contaminating all the groundwater."

Roy looked back at me. "To finally answer your question, it takes a while for the surface to react to what's happened down below, and even longer for contaminated drinking water to be detected."

Denny's face reddened. "Our spring water is contaminated. We gotta get this stopped—now."

Roy stood, "Hold up. You need to talk with James. He said he had it contained."

I placed my hand on Denny's arm, tried to keep him settled. "Contained? What does that mean?" I looked to Roy. He shrugged in answer.

My forehead wrinkled. "I just don't understand how wildcat—*illegal*—fracking could happen without someone seeing what's going on." I shook my head. "Even if it takes a while for the land to show there's contaminated water, isn't fracking noisy and messy?"

Roy leaned back against the rail. "A lot of the cattle land is pretty remote out here. Not as remote as what I've seen in Navaho land, but still remote, which is perfect for illegal fracking."

Denny agreed. "Yeah, these guys can be in the backcountry. Lots of land not visited for months at a time."

I nodded with Denny. We both had spent summers working fence lines to the farthest points of our family lands. There was no one and nothing around for miles.

Roy continued, "If they have a water source to tap, perfect. If not, they truck water in from nearby sources. Wildcatters can be in and out within a couple months, yet their damage can last for years."

Denny looked at Roy. "You know an awful lot." His tone caused me to glance over at him. His body seemed tense, on alert.

Roy straightened. "I've been in the business one way or 'nother for near twenty years. I know the business and the players. Frackers—those boys don't always play by the rules. They can be ruthless."

Chills shot up my neck. "How ruthless?" Roy had my full attention. Denny's too.

Roy sensed the change. "Hey, is James okay?" He looked from me to Denny, then back to me.

I didn't hesitate. "We think he's getting threats."

"Yeah," Roy nodded, "that's how it starts."

Denny moved forward. "Are you working for any fracking outfits around here?" There was an edge to his voice.

Roy's face tightened. "I'm independent." He glanced at me, "But I haven't heard of anyone around Jimmy Creek."

I touched Roy's shoulder. "Sorry, Roy, we're worried about our grandpa." I let things settle for a moment.

Denny stepped back.

Roy remained standing. "Well, obviously there is fracking around your grandfather's spring. Tests prove that." He looked past me to Denny. "But that's about all I know."

Denny gave a nod.

I shook my head. "Do you have any idea how we can find fracking in the area? This can't go on in secret, can it?"

Roy rubbed his whiskered chin. "To be honest, lots of land owners out here want fracking. It brings in much-needed cash. I see this tearing tribes—heck, *families*—apart." He finished with, "I don't have to tell you all, tribe people are the poorest in our nation."

Denny and I both nodded our agreement. I appreciated hearing the fact from a non-Indian. Few in the United States understood the poverty faced by most American Indians still today.

I could tell Roy was ready to leave, but I had a couple more questions.

"Do you know if the Kiowa Tribe is doing anything about wildcat fracking?" Before he answered, I added, "Grandpa can't fight this alone."

Denny said, "I've been to a couple of general meetings where fracking is brought up. Seems like the Tribal Council is split on it. Some see the dollars and the changes that it can do for the tribe; others see the destruction and what that will do *to* the tribe and surrounding communities."

Roy nodded in agreement. "Yep. Some tribe members are working with the illegal fracking groups. It's like the old days of hiding a moonshine still during Prohibition years." He moved toward the porch steps.

I caught Roy's eyes. "Do you know Anna ManyHorse? She's with the Kiowa Legislature." I added, "She was over this morning to talk with Grandpa. They're working together on this."

I knew I was misleading Roy a bit, but I wanted to learn what he knew about Anna before he left.

"I am working with the Kiowa Tribe, but I am not at liberty to discuss it." Roy added, "Sorry," and looked like he meant it.

I touched his arm. "No problem, I understand. I'm just worried." I felt his arm harden under my touch.

In a low voice he said, "Well, I'll say . . . I can't quite figure Anna out." He rubbed his whiskers. I held back from pushing and silently urged Denny to stay quiet. Finally, Roy added, "Let's just say the company she keeps confuses me."

I squeezed his arm in thanks.

Chapter Sixteen

I watched until Roy left. Then I turned and followed Denny into the house. Denny didn't wait for the door to close before announcing, "I'm more confused than ever."

I leaned against the door, still processing what Roy had shared, and muttered, "Yeah."

"Mud, we need to get the police here." He looked around the room, "Before someone else drops in."

That got my attention. "Denny, this doesn't change anything. We still need to find Grandpa first." I reached for his arm. "I know once we talk with Grandpa, we will know who killed Wils—" I stopped before finishing his name, remembering not to name the dead.

Denny moved past me. "We have no idea where Grandpa is. We don't even know what's going on here." He shook his head. "Mud, we need the police."

"Why? So, they can arrest Grandpa?" I followed on Denny's heels.

He turned to me. "Grandpa may be hurt." His voice broke. "Or worse."

The pain on Denny's face zapped all anger from me. "Oh, Denny." I moved toward him. "I think Grandpa is okay, wherever he is."

He pulled away. "Mud, wishful thinkin' isn't going to help—"

"Denny, Grandpa left a note." I paused a moment. I could see Denny processing. I went on, "Grandpa always left messages in that top corner of his desk. Today's note was left there before the thunderstorm. Grandpa was gone before Buck's grandfather died."

Denny shook his head. "Mud, you can't know that."

I moved to face him. "The ink ran where rain-wet fingers touched it." I waited for Denny to realize the note was in place before Wilson's death.

Denny registered understanding, but then his face darkened. "Why would Grandpa run off someplace?"

I held his eyes. "Denny, I do think Grandpa took the peace medal—"

His eyes broke with mine. "Bullshit—" Denny shook his head, his long hair flying from side to side.

In a rush I said, "Grandpa took the peace medal to *save* it. I think that's why Grandpa called me—to help him keep the medal from Buck."

At the word *Buck*, Denny's eyes slid back to me with a hard edge. "Enough already. You can't blame everything on Buck. And this, this . . ." Denny ran out of words.

His words stung, but I kept on. "I told you about seeing Buck earlier, but I didn't tell you that he was outside the back door of the TribalVision Art Gallery."

Denny looked disgusted. "Exactly where I would expect him to be. That's Gerald's gallery. Buck works there."

"Let me finish." I faced Denny. "I went inside the gallery while looking for my suitcase." That seemed like days rather than a couple of hours ago. "One of the first things I saw was a *Koitsenko* sash and lance. I think it was the Crow family's sash and lance."

That got Denny's attention. He didn't say anything, but his jaw clenched. I took it as a sign to go on. "I bet Buck sold his family's sash and lance to Gerald. Then his grandfather found out. That must be what those two were arguing about outside the gallery's back door."

Denny shook his head. "Buck's family would be mad if he sold the sash and lance. But Buck wouldn't kill his grandfather because of it."

I looked pointedly at Denny. "I also saw two of the large Jefferson peace medals in a display case intended for the set. It had an empty spot." He signaled for me to continue. "The assistant at the gallery told me Gerald was waiting for the third Jefferson peace medal before sending it off to a very rich and important collector."

I moved further in the room, and Denny followed. I had his full attention. "I think Buck planned on stealing the Kiowa's Jefferson peace medal and selling it to Gerald. That's the big 'reward' Georgie thinks she's helping Buck get." Denny shook his head when I mentioned Georgie. I ignored him and continued, "Grandpa saved the peace medal from Buck and is hiding." I finished with more conviction than I felt.

Denny looked thoughtful but said nothing.

I paced across the room. "Denny, what I don't understand is how this all happened." I continued talking, really thinking out loud as I paced. "And Buck . . . is Buck connected enough at the Complex to get Gerald a job there?"

Denny's eyes followed me as I moved toward the kitchen. I turned, looked at him. "So how did Gerald get on the inside enough to get this job offer?"

Denny finally spoke. "Mud, I'm not sure why that matters now."

I paced back toward him, but before I reached him, he cocked his head and added, "You know, though, I do remember hearing at one of the Complex meetings a resolution to go through boxes that have been stored in the back of the museum."

I moved closer, hoping he would remember more. Denny's eyes shifted up as if searching his memory for details. "I think Anna found the boxes. Everybody was pretty excited about 'em." He looked over at me.

I stopped pacing. "Anna was at the airport, then here looking for Grandpa—"

Denny sent an angry look at me. "Don't drag her into this. Anna is one of our best legislators. I've watched her fight for Kiowa rights at the state capitol. That woman makes a difference." He shook his head. "Anna cares about our artifacts. In fact, she oversees management of the museum."

Denny's quick defense of Anna surprised me. It was obvious I shouldn't say anything more about her, but I did have a thought to share. "Maybe Anna used Gerald's help to catalog the items in the storage boxes."

Denny snapped his fingers. "That's it! That's how Gerald knew about the Jefferson peace medal. I bet Gerald came across it in the stored boxes."

"Once he found it, Gerald probably arranged for the medal to be cleaned." I added, "Then he planned to get Buck to steal it."

Denny nodded. "Yeah, so the theft wouldn't point back to Gerald."

I liked it. It made sense out of this mess. I finished the story: "Grandpa discovered what was going on and took the peace medal to safety."

Denny wasn't nodding anymore. "Yeah, but why kill Buck's grandfather?"

I moved to a chair and rested on its arm. "I think Buck's grandfather was in on the theft. And the three had a falling out." I reminded Denny, "He and Buck were arguing outside Gerald's gallery. Buck expected his grandfather to give it to him this afternoon."

"The peace medal . . ."

I nodded. "Gerald was waiting for the third peace medal to ship out the completed set tonight."

Denny watched, waited for more.

I ran my hand through my hair, thinking. "Yeah . . . I think that's why Buck's grandfather picked me up at the airport. He was going to use me to get the peace medal from Grandpa."

I stood and returned to pacing. "Buck's grandfather must have come here in the hopes of getting the medal from Grandpa after I got away from him at McClung's."

Denny took my spot on the chair's arm and looked over at me. "Do you think he found the peace medal here?"

"Naw, I'm sure Grandpa has the medal with him. And Grandpa was gone long before Buck's grandfather and the killer arrived."

"By killer, you mean Gerald or Buck."

I set my jaw. "Or both."

Denny looked at his watch. "This is not looking good. If we don't get Grandpa and the peace medal to the meeting at eight tonight, Gerald will get everything he wants, and then he or Buck will get away with murder."

I found myself nodding in agreement but still thinking about Gerald. "Pretty slick story Gerald came up with to explain the peace medals I saw in his gallery. All he had to do is ship the ones I saw out, deny that he knew anything about the Kiowa peace medal, and all the evidence is gone. We can't prove he was expecting the real one or that Buck was getting the peace medal for him."

Denny slid onto the chair's cushion. "Mud, we really can't prove anything. And worse, we don't have any idea how to find Grandpa."

I moved to him. "We can prove things when we get Grandpa to the meeting. He will have the peace medal and an explanation. I know it."

He sank further into the cushion. "Mud, we don't have any idea where Grandpa is."

"Denny, I may not know where he is, but I'm sure Grandpa told us in his note."

Denny snorted. "That doesn't help much. Unless you understand what 'I am whe' means."

"I don't know where *whe* is or what follows the *w-h-e* in the note." I waited, to make sure I had Denny's attention. "But I do know who has the other half of the note."

Denny sat upright, waited for me to finish.

"We have to find Georgie."

Chapter Seventeen

Denny was out of the chair. "How do you know she has the note?"

"Georgie was in the no-no room alone twice. She's the only person who could have taken it." Then, struck by an image . . . "Remember the white tag she pushed into her back pocket?" I walked away from Denny, shaking my head.

"The price tag . . . Oh yeah." I could tell he was thinking. A shocked look crossed Denny's face. "She tore the note from under his fingers." Denny shook at the end, as if chilled by the thought.

I faced Denny. "Can't believe, I fell for her lies." I felt sick.

"I told you she was no good!"

I set my jaw. I didn't want to hear anymore. "Doesn't matter now. We need to find her and get the other half of the note. That's the only way we'll get to Grandpa." I ran my fingers through my tangled curls. I no longer knew where to locate Georgie. At one time, it had seemed like I could sense her presence from afar.

Denny smirked. "Finding Georgie is not a problem." He pulled his phone out. "Between the moccasin telegraph and that new blue Subaru"—Denny again nearly howled the car maker's name—"we can find her in no time." He looked pleased.

The moccasin telegraph was an almost magical means of communication across the old reservation land where tribe members stayed in tight communication with each other. I had forgotten the expression, and its effectiveness. Denny's fingers flew across the phone, texting. The moccasin telegraph had gone high tech. But he was right, someone would take notice and relay a location.

And just that quick, Denny's head pulled up from the screen. "Looks like she's still around here. Weezie passed her car out on Wolf Road."

I cocked my head. "Isn't that just up the hill from here?"

Denny slowly replied, "Yep," but he seemed distracted. He glanced toward the hallway.

I turned to leave, but he hung back. I stopped at the kitchen door. "Why aren't you moving? I thought you would be thrilled to go after Georgie."

"It's just . . ." Denny looked down the hall. "Should we leave him here . . . alone?"

A small shiver went down my back.

My first impulse was to urge Denny to just come along before we lost track of Georgie. I wanted that other half of the note. We needed to find Grandpa, make sure he was safe. But Denny had a point. It didn't feel right to just leave the house.

We couldn't stay or notify anyone—yet. But we could cleanse the house and protect any lingering spirit.

I walked down the hall past Denny and into the no-no room. Denny followed.

I went directly to the cluttered closet and reached for the top shelf. My hand nudged, then grasped a cloth-wrapped bulk. I pushed farther into the closet causing a small cascade of wooden frames to fall. I waited for the final clunk before reaching up with both arms to properly carry Grandpa's wrapped cedar prayer box out of the closet.

Denny came all the way into the room and took the prayer box from me. He unwrapped it and placed it on the floor. We squatted together, knee to knee, and together reached for and opened the cedar box. I removed a single eagle prayer feather, its shaft wrapped in once-white deer leather, now gold with age and years of use.

Denny took and lit a small cedar smudge stick. Its sweet perfume filled the room. The cedar cleansed and protected against evil spirits and all negative energy. The wafting smoke with our eagle-fanned prayers would ensure that the dead man's spirit—if still in the room—was protected and able to move forward in a positive way.

I stood and watched as Denny started at the east side and smudged all four directions in the room. He strode to the body, said a few words I could not hear, and smoked the body from feet to head. He circled the scalp's natural spiral where Kiowas believed the soul entered and left its chosen body. As Denny prayed, he walked with the smoke to the open window.

Smoke swirled around the body, lifted and wafted out the window, caught by a passing breeze. A murder of crows cawed in the distance. A single sunray broke through to shine into the room.

Denny left the smudge burning in the center of the room while I gathered everything and returned the cedar box to the closet.

I took a final look around the smoke-filled room. It felt right. Denny stood behind me and sighed. "That feels better, but I'm still not sure we should leave without reporting this."

I glanced at the dead man. From here, he looked peaceful.

"Denny, we can't do anything else for him except find his killer." My eyes stayed on the back of the dead man sprawled across Grandpa's easel desk. A jar filled with gray water and a single paintbrush sat on a shelf to the side. I wanted to go, but something held me at the open doorway.

Denny looked over my shoulder into the room. I felt him shudder. "He sure looks like Grandpa from here."

That was it.

I pulled the door closed and turned to face Denny. "What if . . ." I stopped.

Denny waited.

I started again. "What if someone wanted *Grandpa* dead?"

Denny took a sudden step back. "What are you saying?" He looked at the closed door. "That death isn't over the peace medal?"

I hurried on, "I really think it is. Gerald and Buck killed his grandfather over the peace medal—that all makes sense. But talking to Roy made me wonder . . . and what you just said."

Denny interrupted, "What did I say?"

I faced him. "That he looks like Grandpa." I stopped there for a beat, then said, "Denny, what if someone wanted Grandpa out of the way and they killed Buck's grandfather by mistake . . .?" My voice trailed off.

"Are you saying . . . those little frackers." Denny growled the end.

Denny opened the door of the no-no room, looked in, and repeated, "He sure does look like Grandpa sitting at that desk."

I moved Denny aside and pulled the door securely closed.

Was I forcing the pieces to fit, just to make Buck the guilty one? Could this death be about fracking and a mistaken identity?

Denny saw the doubt in my eyes. He voiced his concern. "But why would anyone want Grandpa dead?"

"Remember the oil boys at McClung's? What if it's them using Jimmy Creek Spring water for fracking?" I didn't expect an answer, and I kept talking. "They said they needed an Indian"—I couldn't bring myself to use the 'Injun' slur—"'out of the way.' You know Grandpa would never allow damage to the land." I looked at Denny to gauge his reaction.

"You had me believin' Buck and Gerald did that." Denny used his chin to point at the no-no room door.

I met his eyes. "Denny, I do think Buck's grandfather was the intended victim, and everything with Buck and Gerald fits, but we need to look at all possibilities." I hated to say it, but it was true. "We've got two strong motives for murder here. Just depends on who was the intended victim."

Denny snarled. "Those frackers would try to kill Grandpa?"

"I don't know, but people kill for less."

Denny shook his head.

I moved from the no-no room door, down the hall. "After we get the note, I think we need to go by Jimmy Creek. See what things look like there . . . see if we can find where the fracking is located." A thought struck. "Grandpa may even be at Jimmy Creek."

Denny hung back. "I may know where those frackers are." He saw the question in my eyes and answered. "I've seen the guys you described around. Not much out here—you know how newbies are noticed."

I nodded in agreement.

Denny set his jaw. "Those two have a trailer office setup on the old Cross place not too far from the backside of Jimmy Creek Spring in the Slick Hills. Yeah. We can check on them after"—an unpleasant smile crossed his face—"we talk to Georgie."

Denny walked out the kitchen door to his truck. I hurried to the passenger side, pulled myself in, and pushed my lime-green messenger bag to the floor. I had completely forgotten about it. Wilson tugging on the bag's strap came to mind. Why would he want Richard's IPO papers? That made no sense, like everything else. I shook my head. Just a couple of hours ago, I'd thought that bag contained everything I needed in life.

We bumped through rain-filled mudholes down Grandpa's driveway toward a rise on Wolf Road. No sign of Georgie. My hands clenched into fists. We needed her to find Grandpa. Where could she be?

Parked on the side of Wolf Road, Denny sent out more texts.

I looked out the windshield at the countryside while we waited for replies. My eyes followed the creek line to the timber in the back of Grandpa's house. Denny's fingers beat on the steering wheel, impatient for answers.

My back pocket vibrated. I really tried to ignore it, but Denny started looking around the truck for the source. I gave in, pulled the phone out, and let Denny know I needed to answer. He nodded and stayed focused on his cell's screen.

Before I could speak, Thomas chuckled. I knew that nasty sound—it was his tell. Anytime Thomas was sure of a winning hand, that chuckle slipped out. I had heard it in many business negotiations.

"How can I help you, Tommy?" I knew he hated the name he had used when we first met, but I couldn't resist tweaking him.

"It is Thomas." There was a deep breath before he added, "It's what I'm helping *you* with that matters."

The creak of his chair going back and the scuff of heels hitting the top of his desk followed before Thomas continued, "Richard, *our client*, was thrilled that I stepped in to correct your huge mistake."

I sucked in a breath. He heard it and chuckled again. "Thomas, what did you do?" This was our biggest deal. The agency could go national if everything went right. We had been on track. The story was defined, the presentations drafted, supporting graphics made, and rehearsals beginning. The client, Richard, had been happy.

Again, that chuckle. "I pointed out the obvious flaw in his big company launch. That new company logo needed to fly. It needed to announce itself."

I had to stay quiet, hear it all.

His feet came off the desk and landed on the floor; the chair gave a long squeal. He went on, "Richard was thrilled with my suggestion. When Marcus arrived at his office—you know, for the meeting you wouldn't let me attend—Richard told Marcus about his desire for the logo improvement and the need to get it in the final deliverables." I could hear the smile in his voice. "Yep, Richard appreciated my input by the end of our call."

It took a long moment before I could speak. "Tommy, you may have scored points for yourself." I stopped, held the anger in to finish. "But you sabotaged us, the agency. Richard's IPO is happening in less than three days."

"So?" came across the line.

I looked at the phone in disbelief before going on. "That's less than two days to create a 3-D logo animation." My voice got tense. "We don't have the resources to create a logo effect that does nothing for the real story of the company."

A squeak slipped out of Thomas as he realized the problems he'd created. "Uh . . . uh," he stuttered, "like you always say, your part is getting the story told." The line went dead.

Thanks, Thomas. I'd better check with Bernie and Marcus. This would send them into a panic. Before the phone was answered, I felt eyes on me and stopped the call.

"Who and what was that?" Denny asked.

I shoved the phone into my pocket. I'd get back to the agency in a bit. I turned my attention to Denny and spoke more sharply than I should have. "Hear anything on Georgie?"

"Whoa there." Denny put his palm up. "I'm not your whipping boy."

I looked out the windshield, tracking the creek again to Grandpa's house below us. I muttered, "Sorry. It's a bad time for me to be away. We're doing a big company launch." The old tipi sign swung in a breeze far below. "And I'm having problems with my business partner." I shook my head. "Enough—now is not the time."

Denny glanced over. "Sounds like a bad marriage. You all didn't get to know each other before jumpin' into bed." Advice from a thirty-year-old single guy.

I stared at him. "Thanks for putting that ugly image in my mind." I shook my head. "Any luck finding Georgie?" I was getting anxious about everything.

Denny's eyes went back to his phone. Mine wandered to the flower beds around Grandpa's front porch down below. The yellow black-eyed Susans really popped. They looked nice.

"Nothing," Denny said. "It's like she disappeared." He tossed the phone onto the center console.

I pointed through the windshield. "Follow the creek down into the timber over there."

He didn't bother looking. "Yeah, that's the creek behind Grandpa's house. You know those little creeks all run into Canyon Creek."

"Denny, look." He followed my pointing finger. "From this rise, Grandpa's house and land are on display for anyone wanting to watch happenings at the house."

Denny banged on the steering wheel. "Georgie's been watching us. She saw us coming and hightailed it."

I had to agree. From this vantage point, she would have been able to see we were headed her way and would have had plenty of time to hide down a seldom-traveled dirt road, anywhere.

He turned to me. "Guess this proves she killed Buck's grandpa."

I slowly shook my head. "No, no . . . she couldn't." I stopped. I would never have thought Georgie could take a life, but I'd also never dreamed she would marry Buck.

I didn't want to believe I could have loved a murderer.

Chapter Eighteen

"We've waited long enough. Georgie's hiding," Denny declared.

"I think you're right." We both knew that Georgie was familiar with these back roads. She could stay tucked away and unseen all the way back to Lawton.

I turned to Denny. "Let's go to Jimmy Creek." I forced a smile. "Grandpa may be there, waiting for us."

Denny followed gravel roads to Highway 115 toward Meers, a one-store town nestled in the Wichita Mountain foothills. The store was in the center of a "Y" intersection, with one arm going toward the Slick Hills and the other toward the Wichita Wildlife Refuge.

He took the right arm toward Jimmy Creek and the Slick Hills. The land was rocky, with soft, rolling hilltops. Most used it for ranching and scraping out an alfalfa cutting or two. The rocky area was water rich. In the old days it had been a favorite spring and summer camp for the Kiowa and Comanche tribes.

Grandpa had been left Jimmy Creek and its surrounding one hundred sixty acres from his grandpa Jimmy Wolfcub. We used the old homestead around Jimmy Creek for huge extended family gatherings every year.

Coming around a curve, it was easy to spot the Jimmy Creek–fed pastures. Green and gold grasses led to rare shade from cottonwood and willow trees along the creek bed.

"Everything looks good," I said.

Denny glanced over at me and back to the road. "Let's get a closer look. On over by the creek's swimming hole."

Denny turned off the road onto a dirt lane. He stopped and looked over at me. "Don't tell me you forgot who's responsible for opening pasture gates."

I laughed and jumped out of the truck. "I just figured gates would be on automatic openers by now." I walked in front of the truck over to the gate posts.

Denny hung out the open window. "You kidding? We still got people without power in their homes around here."

As I unhooked the gate and pulled it open, Denny muttered, "Gone too long." He was right. Since living in Silicon Valley, I had started taking life's basics for granted. How easily I had forgotten the families living without power or running water on reservations and what had been reservation lands. Native Americans, America's proud first Americans, are the poorest in our nation—an unseen and overlooked minority. I shook my head and made a mental promise to do better.

Denny drove through the opening. I pushed the gate closed and pulled a hoop of wire securely over the posts. It was only then that I noticed new gate post holes in progress, with tools and a tarped pile to the side of the dirt road.

I went over to the tarp and pulled it back. Materials for a new gate with slatted metal covering and placement for a very secure lock lay in place. Grandpa must have been working on this when something pulled him away. The peace medal . . . probably.

Denny continued to idle, waiting for me to get back in the truck. I moved up to his window. "Come check this out."

He threw the truck into park, came to the side of the dirt road, and looked down at the metal slats and gate material. "Wow! That's a lot of gate and a lot of money."

"It does show that Grandpa wanted to keep someone off the property. You sure don't need all this to keep cows in."

We both headed back to the truck. I had to ask Denny, "Did Grandpa tell you he was being threatened?"

He shook his head. "I heard nothing about this." Denny put the truck in gear. "Grandpa hates asking for help. He thinks he can still do it all." He kept his eyes on the muddy road that headed across the cow pasture to the creek. "It's calving season, and I've been cutting alfalfa." Denny maneuvered around a deep rut before going on. "Grandpa probably figured I was too busy to help." He slapped the steering wheel. "And that man is stubborn."

I caught his eye. "We'll find Grandpa. Get this all cleared up."

I didn't voice my worries: that Grandpa was in danger if the murder was over fracking—the oil boys could be after him—or that Buck and Gerald were after Grandpa and the peace medal, and they may have killed once already. And then there was Georgie. We needed to find Grandpa—first.

The truck pulled in under the shade of a cottonwood. Twinkling in the sun, the creek water skipped from one rock to another. It looked cool, crisp, and inviting. Without thought, I rushed over to the creek's edge, reached in, cupped the cold water in my hands, and splashed it onto my face. The cool felt wonderful, but the water wasn't crisp. It left a slick feeling on my face and arms.

My look stopped Denny from drinking the water cupped in his hands. "What's wrong?"

"I don't know . . . but don't drink it." I rubbed my face with the front of my shirt. "It feels slick."

"Get back," a voice boomed from above at the same time a shell was racked into a shotgun. Hair stood up on my neck. I froze.

My eyes lifted to Denny. His eyes were focused over my shoulder, where the shotgun must be. Denny pushed me aside. "Earl, what are you doing? Point that shotgun elsewhere."

Denny marched on up the bank to an unusually large mixed-Indian man in faded jean overalls and old muddy Converses. Denny pushed the shotgun barrel down.

"I didn't see it was you, Denny." Earl White raised his shotgun to point at me. "I just saw the back of her." I noticed his little toe poked through the side of one tennis shoe.

Denny pushed the shotgun down again. "That's my cousin Mud." He looked annoyed. "Earl, you know Mud."

Earl squinted at me. "Yeah, I remember . . . the curly-headed story keeper." He smiled at me, a smile that radiated to his hazel-colored eyes. He swung the shotgun barrel my way again. I moved.

He nodded. "She was a couple years behind you and me. I guess it's okay you two are here." Earl looked off into the distance. "I'm watchin' till James gits back."

My heart sank. Grandpa wasn't here. I shook off my disappointment, walked over to join Earl and Denny. "Why are you watching?"

He looked over at me and back to Denny. "Isn't it obvious? Just look at what they done." Earl pointed at the creek with his shotgun.

I stepped back toward the bank. He was right, it was obvious, now that I took a moment to look at the whole creek. Belly-up minnows clustered at the creek's edge, and a rainbow slick glistened where the sun touched the flowing water.

I turned back to Earl. "What happened?

"James said they're hurting Mother Earth deep inside. It's making her water dirty and slow." Earl nodded at us, moved the shotgun up and down in time with his head. "Things are worse at my pasture downstream."

Denny moved to Earl. "I didn't know this was happening. How?" Denny was unable to say more.

Earl lowered his head and shook it. "It started with them coming in here for truckloads of water." He swung the shotgun up. "Now they're getting it down deep."

Denny reached for the shotgun, pulled the stock downward.

I stepped forward, said one word. "Frackers."

Earl nodded. "They're taking Jimmy Creek Spring water from the underground, draining it at the source to keep those fracking drills humming."

"Earl, do you know who is doing this?" I asked.

Earl turned and spat. "Oh yeah, we know the two boys. We done chased them off the property enough times. But they're just hired guns. James said we need to find the money behind them."

Denny held the shotgun's stock to still it. "Is it a big guy usually traveling with a small rodeo-dude type?"

Earl nodded his head, listening to Denny. "Yeah, you see them around. They do the dirty work."

I stepped in. "Who do they work for? Is there a name on the office, the trucks?" I looked between Denny and Earl.

Earl wiped his mouth with his gun hand, swinging the racked and loaded shotgun wildly around. "Well, these guys aren't with any legit outfit. So, James and I are takin' care of things till help comes." He let a sly grin seep across his face.

Denny asked, "What do you mean?"

Earl leveled his shotgun and swung it around. "Right now, we're on guard. James messed with the pumps and stopped the fracking for a few days." When Denny pushed the shotgun stock down, Earl gave us a gap-toothed grin. "Those boys aren't happy with us."

I bit my lip. Grandpa may have messed with the wrong people. The body in the no-no room came to mind. We needed to find Grandpa.

Denny looked over at me, then back to Earl. "Earl, did they threaten my grandfather?"

Earl was delighted to tell his story. "Oh yeah. Those boys got real mad when James bought all the material for the new gate." He waved his shotgun toward the tarped materials. "They been coming in here and taking truckloads of water for that fracking goin' on over the hills a ways. Well, we stopped that." Earl waved his shotgun triumphantly in the air. "And the gate will fix it for good."

Denny and I exchanged worried glances.

Earl's forehead wrinkled. "But that's when they started takin' water from underground, and that really made things bad." Earl raised the shotgun, pointed it toward the creek. "The fish are dyin', the water's real low, and the surroundin' plants are goin' yella too soon. The water's poisonin' the deer, elk, and even the cows. Meat's no good. It poisons the vultures and other carcass eaters. Just a vicious circle of harm."

Denny looked sick.

I got a bad feeling. "Earl, what did James do to stop them taking the water from the spring's source?"

"Well, he told them to stop stabbing Mother Earth or he would stop it." Earl looked at me. "Those boys just laughed, said they were on private property with permission, and that fracking just kept going." Earl shook his head. "They went back in their trailer, laughin'."

Denny turned his attention to Earl. "What else happened?"

We knew our stubborn grandfather; this would not be the end of it.

Earl lifted his shotgun to his shoulder and smiled. "That James, he said we just needed to sweeten things up."

I shook my head, I was afraid to ask, but had to know. "What did he do?"

Earl let a laugh out. "James poured sugar in the drill engines. He thought that would slow them down while he went to the Kiowa Council to get it all shut down. 'Cause they may be on private land, but they don't have no rights to the spring water."

A faint hum vibrated the air. Earl lifted his head. "Well, that didn't take them long 'nuff. I hope James got help comin'." He looked back at Denny. "I was hopin' you was with James."

Denny leaned toward Earl. "Did my grandpa say he was coming for me?"

Earl took his battered Deere cap off; he rubbed his head with the same hand. "Well, he said he'd get help, startin' with an order to stop now." The hat went back over the sweat-flattened hair.

I looked over to Earl. “Who did he tell this to?”

“Them boys. They came over all mad. Accused James of messin’ with the engines.” Earl looked to Denny. “’Course we didn’t say nothin’ about the sugar.” Then he shifted back to me. “That ol’ James walked right up to the big ’un and told him to git off his property and git his pipe out of his water.” Earl started laughing. “James backed that big guy all the way back to the road and into their truck.” He turned serious. “That little ’un hung out the truck’s window. He tol’ James they’d be done and gone before we could do anything about it.”

Earl looked intently at Denny. “That really got James riled up. He told those two boys they would have to kill him before they’d get anymore of his water.”

My head jerked up. “What did the fracker say?” I liked the feel of the word. It was rough and cheap like I expected someone involved with illegal fracking to be.

Earl shook his head. “That big ’un just laughed.”

My jaw clenched. *Those frackers.*

Earl looked at us both. “That duded-up guy said, ‘That could be arranged.’”

I pictured the body with gray braids sprawled across Grandpa’s desk.

Denny locked eyes with me. I knew he saw it too.

Had those oil boys meant to kill Grandpa . . . and got the wrong Indian?

Chapter Nineteen

Denny's hands tightened on the steering wheel. "Where can Grandpa be?"

I looked out at Earl, standing by the creek. The yellow vegetation spread outward from its once life-giving water source. I hated to voice it, but I had to. "I don't know." Then I remembered the note. "But I do think Grandpa chose to go wherever he is." I needed to hold on to this belief. Grandpa was all right, we just needed to get the other half of the note. It would tell us where to find him.

Denny banged on the steering wheel. "Where is that Georgie?" He took out his phone and sent another flurry of texts.

We needed to do something until we found Georgie. Those oil boys came to mind. "Do you know where to find the fracking office?"

"Oh yeah." Denny nodded. "What are you thinkin'?"

"Let's go for a visit. I don't think they know where Grandpa is, but there's Buck's grandfather's death."

That's all Denny needed to hear. His truck tires spat red mud as we climbed back onto the highway's blacktop, leaving Earl on guard at Jimmy Creek.

Rain-fresh air, raw with the scent of earth, filled the truck's cab. The rolling highway cut between pasture after pasture of deep green alfalfa fields mixed with fenced grazing land for cattle. This was broken up by an occasional dirt lane or a more traveled, two-lane gravel road that cut across the highway every few miles.

We rode in heavy silence until Denny turned onto one of the gravel roads. He leaned forward, looked intently out the window, then turned onto a single-lane dirt road that soon devolved into muddy ruts. It was obvious from the parallel lines of deep ruts that trucks with heavy loads had been traveling on this dirt road a lot.

Lush green alfalfa fields gave way to brown and yellow rotted vegetation and chopped, exposed red dirt and mud—everywhere. Denny slowed to a near crawl, maneuvering through the muddy red ruts and puddles.

"Looks like Mother Earth has been cut opened and is oozing blood." I took my eyes from the ravaged ground. "Grandpa must have been sick when he saw this."

Denny added, "And angry."

I looked across to him. His jaw was locked in the clenched position, his eyes on the rutted road ahead. "Denny, we can't bust in and demand answers from them."

"Who says?"

"Come on, Denny—we need to stay focused. That means figuring out if these two had anything to do with Grandpa's disappearance or Buck's grandfather's death." I watched his face for a response. There was none. I continued, "Then we can deal with the water and fracking."

Through his clenched jaw Denny said, "They threatened our grandfather."

That made *my* jaw clench. I forced it to release. "We need to find out if their threats became murder—first. If these oil boys didn't do it. . . ." Here, I had to catch his eye. "If they didn't do it, and they don't know where Grandpa is, then we will deal with the fracking tomorrow."

Denny grunted in answer.

I went on, "We will have Grandpa and more information, so he'll be better able to get this shut down." I kept my eyes on Denny. "Tomorrow. Right?"

Denny answered, "If you say so."

I could get no more from him.

A low, constant, grinding hum droned through to the cab. I looked about, searching for the source. Off to the right, in the near distance, stood a line of derricks. Denny made a right toward the only working derrick. We bounced down what was more a choppy, muddy trail than a road. It ended in front of a single-wide office trailer sitting atop cement pillars that barely kept the trailer above the surrounding muddy field. Additional cement blocks created mud-splattered steps to the front door.

Denny turned the truck off and glanced over. "Took a bit to get here, but this setup is pretty close to Jimmy Creek Spring, as the crow flies." He pointed off in the horizon. "Grandpa's land ends just over that hill."

I looked where Denny indicated. "Yep. I can see how they can drill from here and tap into the source of the spring." I shifted in the truck's seat, took in the chopped raw land and machinery. "What I don't get is how this can be happening without everyone in the area knowing."

"You heard Roy: some know and want it, others may be afraid to talk, and there's always those who feel hopeless."

I shifted back to look at him. "What do you mean, 'hopeless'?"

Denny shook his head at me. "Mud, this is happening to Indians on backcountry, Indian-owned land. No one cares, and we don't have the money to fight them legally." He looked around the bare, churned field.

It was an old story.

I shook my head. I had escaped this life. How could I have forgotten it so easily, so quickly? Was I more *Hanpoko* than Kiowa?

I looked back to the office.

"There's a couple pickups over to the side." I motioned with my head. "No outbuildings—just that office." I looked back at Denny. "No place to hide Grandpa out here."

Denny nodded.

As I watched, the front window blinds parted and closed.

As if this was a signal, Denny slapped the steering wheel. He had his door opened and slammed before I could get out of the truck. I chased after him on the narrow cement block path. It was slow going. I had to watch my feet to keep from falling off the uneven walkway.

I hurried to catch Denny, now entering the trailer.

"Hey, no one said come in. What do you think you're doing here?" came from a man sitting at a desk positioned off to the side of the one-room office.

Denny marched straight ahead to a second desk with a hefty man behind it and placed both hands on the desk to stare directly at the seated man.

"I want to know which of you did it," Denny demanded.

Behind him, I shook my head. Guess we were going to go in and demand answers, after all.

Denny blocked most of my view of the man in front, but I was able to see the smaller guy coming from behind his desk toward Denny. He came with clenched fists and mean eyes. I tapped Denny's back and signaled. Denny turned his head and halted the small man with a single glare.

No one moved or said a word.

I shifted to enter fully.

The office seemed to be more storage than office. Pipes, their connections, and oversized nuts and bolts were scattered and stacked everywhere. Just to the right of the door, pipes of varying sizes were stacked in a waist-high pyramid. There was no place to hide Grandpa.

The smaller man shuffled his feet before asking, "Did what?"

I looked him over. He was "duded up" with rigid seam creases down the center of each jean leg and a silver belt buckle practically large enough to topple him if he leaned too far forward. Perfect brown hair curtained his face.

Denny declared, "Messed with James Sawpole." His eyes stayed locked on the small man, who was now sweating in his crisp, button-down shirt.

The hefty guy let out a nervous laugh. It was cut off abruptly as Denny rotated his head to settle his glare back on the big guy.

An angry Kiowa was a fierce sight, but I wasn't sure how long Denny's glares would hold these two off. I picked up a four-foot length of pipe from the top of the pyramid. It was a bit longer than a baseball bat and a lot heavier.

The smaller man quietly moving toward Denny stopped. He eyed the pipe in my hand, then announced, "We don't know who you're talking about." His beady eyes shifted to Denny. "Just leave."

I rested the pipe on my shoulder and eyed the small man.

Glancing between the small man and me, the hefty guy helped by saying, "We know James Sawpole. Gene, he's that Injun."

Denny straightened to focus his glare back at Gene. In return, Gene sent a laser look at the hefty-sized guy and told him, "Shaddup, Wayne."

I shifted to Wayne. "You." I used the pipe to point at him. "You were there." I said no more, let it hang between us while I kept my eyes on his. Wayne's eyes darted wildly about.

Denny's glare kept Gene in place.

Wayne pushed back from his desk. He looked over to Gene and whined, "I told ya she saw me."

My mind raced. Did these oil guys kill Buck's grandfather and think I saw it? I tapped my hand with the pipe. Waiting to see what else leaked from the hefty-sized Wayne.

Denny wasn't as patient. He turned to Wayne and pushed the desk into the large man's stomach. "Tell me what you did." Denny followed the desk, leaned in to Wayne, and added a low *"Now."*

From the side, I heard a drawer open. Gene was at his desk. The small man had moved while our attention was focused on Wayne. Without hesitation, I brought the pipe down on top of Wayne's desk. The resulting explosion was much louder than expected, but it had the desired effect of freezing everyone. I stepped over to Gene. "Bring your empty hands up slowly." I kept the pipe up, ready for swinging.

Gene left in the drawer whatever was in it. His thigh shoved the drawer closed as his empty hands came up to rest on the edge of his desk. Using the pipe, I indicated for Gene to stay.

I swung the pipe to my shoulder, moved a glaring Denny to the side, and shifted back to face Wayne. This gave me the first good look I'd had of him. He'd had muscles . . . once. His front matched the back I had seen at McClung's. I had no doubt these were the two oil boys I heard wanting an Indian out of the way.

I moved the pipe to my waist, still at the ready. I couldn't keep contempt out of my low voice. "You went too far with James Sawpole."

Wayne shifted his eyes to Gene. "I was doin' what they told me." He turned back to me.

Gene dropped into his chair and repeated, "Shaddup, Wayne."

I turned to face Gene. "Are you in charge?" I tapped my other hand with the end of the pipe. "You want to explain?"

I could feel Denny at my back. I knew he had it.

Gene crossed his arms. "Explain what?"

Denny stepped forward to Gene. "What you were doing at Sawpole's house."

Wayne started, "Well, that—

Gene interrupted, "We weren't there."

I dropped the end of the pipe on Wayne's desk, a soft tap. "That's not true." I shifted, stared at Wayne, then gave the desk a solid tap. "You were there when he was killed." I wanted Wayne to feel threatened.

Wayne's eyes opened wide, his upper lip quivered, and sweat collected on his brow. He squirmed as he revealed, "That Sawpole Injun was dead when we got there." I winced at the slur and his total disregard for a life lost, but noted he said *Sawpole.*

Gene came out of his chair. He moved toward Wayne. "I mean it. Just shaddup!"

Denny held his hand up, halted Gene.

I moved a bit closer, decided to gamble. "And I heard you in McClung's say you wanted James out of the way. Seems like motive, opportunity . . . and we know you have the means."

Gene shifted; his hands tightened into fists. He took a moment, then nodded, as if confirming a thought with himself. "Yeah, we wanted him out of the way." Gene faced me. "But not like that. Not like that." He shook his head. "There's much easier ways to get what we needed than that."

Denny pushed forward. "You went there to threaten my grandfather."

Gene protested, "Hey, back off. We didn't kill your grandpa."

Wayne pushed up from his seat, moved toward Denny. I hefted the pipe again, looked over at Wayne with intent in my eyes. My knees bent, I shifted my weight, readied.

Wayne watched. Sweat collected into beads across his upper lip. His eyes stayed on me, and he stopped.

Denny turned, took in the scene, and laughed. He spoke to the room. "She will use it. Mud went through college on a fastball scholarship." He laughed again. "Yep, our home-run all-star."

Gene reviewed the situation before giving Wayne a slight incline of his head. Wayne dropped back into his chair. I relaxed my stance but kept alert and the pipe ready at my side. I urged Gene, "Go on with your story."

Gene kept his eye on me and the pipe. "We just need a little more time. Then we're out of here before anyone else knows what hit them."

Denny stepped toward Gene. "That's a real bad choice of words, considering . . ." His voice purred with menace.

Gene lifted his hands. "Is that how it was done? Someone hit him?" His open palms faced Denny. "I just meant that we're packed and out of the area before anyone has time to legislate us out of here."

Wayne spoke up, "Couldn't really tell from the window how he died. I thought he was shot." Without thought Wayne added, "But I knew the boss would be happy the Injun was out of the way."

I hit Wayne's desk with the metal pipe. The bang startled everyone again. In a low voice, I demanded, "Can you—please—stop saying that."

Wayne answered with a blank look and muttered, "What? Sayin' what?"

I loomed over Wayne sitting at his desk, which now sported two cylinder-shaped dents. I let my anger be heard, "Your Indian slur is as bad for reservation Indians as the n-word. It's ugly." I clenched my jaw and spat out, "*Injun.* Stop using it!"

Gene laughed. "You're worried about a word?" He shook his head. "All right, out with it. What kinda cut you two *Indians* lookin' for?"

I turned back to Gene. Still mad. "We want it to stop. You're obviously pulling water from Jimmy Creek Spring to use for your fracking. James Sawpole has not granted you rights for use of his water."

An odd expression crossed Gene's face. "You got proof of that? 'Cause we got an agreement with old Sawpole . . . poor dead James Sawpole . . ." Gene let a twisted smile out. "Guess you can just take us to court to prove he didn't grant us rights to the water source."

Denny lurched toward Gene. I moved to block him. "Denny, he's not worth it." Using the pipe, I pushed Denny back toward the door. "We'll take care of it with the law and the tribe's help."

Gene taunted. "With Sawpole bein' dead and all, we got plenty of time to finish here, before the courts get anything done."

Wayne looked over to Gene. Responding to a signal, he lumbered up and pushed his desk away. The pyramid of pipes shook, a few rolled from the top, clanging to the floor.

Feeling more confident, Gene gave us a half smile. "You two just move along. We got nothin' more to say."

Denny stopped and faced them. "What did you intend to do to my grandfather?"

Gene's face slid into a full twisted smile. "Don't matter—you heard Wayne. Sawpole was already dead before we got there."

Wayne nodded in agreement. His enthusiasm rocked a pile of fist-sized bolts from the desk, sending them thudding across the floor.

Gene glared at Wayne and kicked aside a rolling bolt before adding, "You saw us outside. We were never inside."

Wayne moved to the front of his desk, stepped on a bolt, slipped, and recovered. He took a moment to steady himself before declaring to me, "I saw you at the window." Wayne looked over to Gene. "Scared me, huh?"

Gene gave a single nod to confirm.

I remembered the rustling noise I heard from the outside when I was standing at the no-no room window. It must have been the big guy. Wayne outside, sneaking around in the storm, and Georgie inside the no-no room, trying to sneak out. And a dead man at the desk.

Wayne shifted to lean against his desk. "We saw him just before you did." He settled a butt cheek on the edge. "And boy, did I want out of there."

"What was the plan?" I leaned toward Wayne, kept the pipe in sight.

Gene stepped forward and returned to his favorite line: "Shaddup, Wayne."

Not sure, Wayne glanced at me before he answered, "Well, we didn't get no farther than lookin' in windows." Wayne stopped, shook his head, and mumbled, "Then I saw him." His eyes widened.

"Did you see anyone else?" I watched both men. Without hesitation, Wayne shook his head. Gene just smiled.

Denny leaned into Wayne.

This brought Gene to Wayne's side. "Time for you all to leave. We got nothin' more to say."

I touched Denny and dropped the heavy pipe. "They're right." Denny stayed in place. Softly to Denny I added, "Enough for now. We need to find Georgie."

Denny was not happy.

I pushed him to the doorway, then turned and told the oil boys, "We'll be back with proof that James did not grant water rights." I aimed a sputtering Denny at the door. "And with our Kiowa legislator, to get this fracking stopped."

To our backs Gene called out, "You do that—bring your Kiowa legislator." He laughed. "She'll be lots of help." Wayne joined with loud guffaws.

I shoved Denny out the office door. He was fuming. "What are you doing? Those jerks admitted to using Grandpa's water. We gotta make them stop."

"We can and we will. But not now." I directed Denny back toward his truck and spoke to the back of his head, "Those two didn't kill Buck's grandfather, and they don't know where Grandpa is."

Denny muttered under his breath. I watched my step on the rocky cement blocks. I was not going to plop face-first in the mud now . . . not in front of those two frackers. I knew at least one of them would be peeking through the blinds. A glint where there should be none caught my eye. I bent, grabbed a mud-encrusted round object, and shoved it in my pocket. Never could leave a coin on the ground.

Denny got into the driver's seat and I moved to the passenger door. Once inside the truck's cab, I continued, "Grandpa's not dead. We get Grandpa, the Tribe rep, and maybe the Bureau of Indian Affairs down here and get this fracking stopped."

Denny looked out at the churned land. "Why didn't Grandpa get this stopped already?"

That was a good point. Another question for Grandpa. The list was growing.

I grabbed his forearm. "Denny, we will be back to stop the fracking tomorrow."

Denny started to smile at that. "It will be fun to bring Grandpa here, alive, get the water theft stopped and then the fracking halted." He smiled bigger. "Rub that wicked grin off Gene's face."

I nodded. "It would have been smarter for Gene to pretend they weren't using the water. Now they can't deny it. They made the water rights claim in front of both of us. We can get this stopped as soon as we get Grandpa." And answers.

Denny started the engine and the slow, bumpy ride away from fracking. Back on the highway, he turned to me. "What makes you so sure those oil boys didn't do the killing?"

A laugh slipped out. "Watching that klutz in the fracking office. He bumped into things, made a mess just standing up . . . made it obvious that no fight took place in the no-no room. Especially with that Wayne guy."

Denny wrinkled his forehead. "What do you mean?"

"Well, think about the no-no room. Sure, there's clutter, but nothing was broken, shoved out of place. Grandpa's desk is sitting exactly where it sat ten years ago."

Denny nodded. *"Haw"* slipped out.

I flashed a smile at him. "The water in that old jar Grandpa used for cleaning paintbrushes was still sitting on the shelf—with water in it. There wasn't a fight in that room."

I continued thinking out loud. "Buck's grandfather was killed up close—to use that buffalo jawbone club you have to be within arm's distance. That close to your victim . . ." I stopped, forced my mind to shape the crime scene, then continued. "You know who you're hitting. That was a single, well-placed blow."

Denny shook his head. "You're forgetting it was dark and from behind."

He had a point, but . . . "I don't think it was dark when the killer first arrived." I waited for Denny's reaction.

"What makes you say that?"

"Georgie said she heard the loud bump just after the lights went out." I thought back, tried to recall the details. "She heard something and went to the no-no room to check on Grandpa."

Denny made a scoffing sound, a full-throated snort. "You trust Georgie." He shook his head. "I cannot believe you." He turned to look at me. "She tore the note from a dead man's hand."

The image made me shiver in the cab's heat. I refused to believe Georgie was a murderer. She could not have changed that much. But tearing the note away, that rocked me.

Denny declared, "All right, I agree."

His words brought me back to the current conversation, but I was lost. "You agree to what?"

He glanced over. "You're right. Those little frackers didn't kill Buck's grandfather." Denny returned his attention to the road. "Gene has Wayne do everything, and Wayne is *Mawbane*." He spat the Kiowa word out.

I had to smile. *Mawbane* was either one of the worse insults slung from a Kiowa or could be a lighthearted jab. *Mawbane* literally translated to "one who does not think," a terrible insult from the Kiowa perspective. Depending on context, voice tone, and hand gesture, the word's meaning was either the ultimate slur or else just playful name calling. In this case, it was an insult.

"Glad you agree." I looked over to Denny. "We will mark *them* off as murder suspects."

Something Wayne said echoed in my mind: *"The boss would be happy the Injun was out of the way."*

The fracking boys were off my list, but I couldn't say the same for their boss.

Chapter Twenty

Denny interrupted my thoughts of murder.

"I gotta eat something."

How could he be hungry now? We needed to get a line on Georgie. But a glance convinced me that Denny did need food. His starved look reminded me that he became single-minded when hungry.

"Meers is coming up. I'm going to get a burger." He looked at me and added, "Should I get a Meers Burger?"

I glanced out the window as we approached the century-old clapboard Meer's diner. Grandpa had told us the single building was the whole town of Meers when he was young. It served as the only grocery store, trading post, gas station, restaurant, and post office for miles, in the days when a mile was hard to travel.

Meers had first been established as a mining town in 1901. The wood-plank building was now a tourist destination, as much for its relic form as its noted "Oklahoma's Best Burgers." The one-hundred percent Longhorn burger was nearly dinner-plate size and came with mustard, onions, tomatoes, and lettuce. Deemed the perfect burger, it was a must stop for all taking part in the annual Tour de Meers cycling event. As I looked around, seeing all the cars, it was clear it also had become a hot lunch spot.

Denny's question really was, "Did I want to split a plate-sized Meers Burger?"

I shook my head and followed with "Naw, not for me." My stomach was tied up in knots as I tried to figure out where Grandpa might be and why a man was killed. I wish I knew who had been the intended victim. I was sure that would point to the killer. Or at least the motive. Was the murder over water for fracking or about the peace medal? And Grandpa, where was he? I held on to the thought he was safe. I really had to.

Before I could ask, Denny stated, "Nothing on Georgie." He turned a hopeful face to me. "But who knows, someone might know somethin' at Meers."

If there was news, Denny would get it. He was connected to the moccasin telegraph and tied to the farmers' network. Those old boys saw lots from the fields and loved to gossip. Denny would work the locals for any sighting of Georgie. And I could use the time Denny was away to think. Things kept happening too fast. I needed a moment or two to myself. There was something, just on the edge of awareness. Something I was forgetting . . .

Denny left the truck idling and its AC on full blast while he went in to get his order. The truck's converted engine purred on its clean-running propane. I enjoyed the cool air stream. All vents on the right side were strategically pointed at me. I was finally feeling cool, relaxing into the seat, when I saw it, a flash of blue in the very back of the parking lot. A bright blue car. I leaned forward in my seat. Could it be a Subaru?

It was.

I nearly howled *Subarooo* in delight. I was sure it had to be Georgie. The car was tucked in beside a panel truck and a trash bin in the service area. Hidden. I had spotted it only because of my slouch and a chance reflection off the car's bright new paint.

I slid out of the truck and stayed low as I edged toward the blue car. There was a golden head in the driver's seat. Georgie was turned away, focused on the store's side porch and door. But I knew that head of hair. It was her.

I moved from a front fender toward Georgie in her car. Something in her manner stopped me. I squatted down behind a fender to watch. Georgie was intent on someone or something. I stayed low and started a scan of the parking lot. Last thing I wanted was Buck or Gerald to sneak up on me.

The slap-slam of the store's wooden screen door pulled my eyes up to a raised porch. Anna stood on the store's seldom-used side porch. She had the air of someone waiting . . . expecting.

The chime of an opening car door pulled my attention back to Georgie. She was getting out of the car, but her focus stayed on the side porch—on Anna. Georgie softly closed the car door, stopping the chime, yet made no motion forward. She stared up at the porch. Waiting.

Oblivious to Georgie, Anna stood in the porch doorway, watching the front. Anna's face was pinched in the same scowl she'd worn earlier, but now her tightly controlled braid was in disarray. Escaped strands stuck out everywhere. Her colorful Indian blanket blazer was gone. In its place was a wrinkled blouse and pants that looked as if they had been wet and left on to dry. She glanced at her watch and then back out at the parked cars in front. She was looking for someone.

I edged forward toward Georgie, using another truck for cover. I had both women in sight—Georgie was two truck fronts away, while a car and a blacktop strip separated me from Anna on the porch. I didn't want either to see me. They had acted like they didn't know each other at Grandpa's house. Now Anna was looking for someone and Georgie was here, waiting for someone.

Uncomfortable in my squat, I shifted. Something poked my thigh, so I shifted again. The poke receded.

Anna walked to the far side of the porch. As she moved, her head swiveled while she looked around. Her silver earring disk seemed to dance in the sunlight. As Anna reached the end of the porch, she turned around and lifted her wrist to look at her watch. She shook her head. No silver disk danced.

I edged to the front fender of the panel truck. This got me closer to Georgie while still keeping them both in view. Georgie rocked forward toward the side porch steps, then back again like she couldn't make up her mind whether to go or stay.

Anna stood in profile from this angle. She placed her hands on the porch railing, facing the front, intent on watching everyone who entered, not noticing Georgie and me to the side.

Just as Georgie decided to make a move, Denny came out the side door with a small burger in one hand and a bag in the other. He moved to a trash receptacle, seemed to finish the burger with a single gulp, and tossed its wrappings. Georgie stopped in place to watch. Anna turned from the rail. The movement caught Denny's eye. He broke into a smile and went to greet Anna. Her shoulders dropped, but she met Denny with a politician's smile. Denny didn't seem to notice.

Georgie watched for a few moments, then eased back to the driver's door of the Subaru.

I took another step and inadvertently scuffed the toe of my sneaker.

The sound alerted Georgie—Grandpa would have been ashamed that I had made such a rookie mistake and given my position away. She turned and saw me. Her eyes went wide, and she opened the Subaru door between us, trying to get into the car. I pushed on the door, forcing it closed, and Georgie against the side of her car. I moved closer, took a deep breath of her Poison perfume, and looked into her eyes. "You have some explaining to do."

Georgie's eyes went everywhere but to me. I leaned into her, pressed her back up against the car. My nose brushed past her cheek as I hissed into her ear, "Where is it?" Her Poison was strong here. I took a deep breath of it. That scent . . . the memories. I closed my eyes for a beat.

Almost involuntarily, my hand came around, cupped her firm buttocks, then moved up to rest at her back pocket. I felt her take a sharp breath in. She surprised me when she let her body relax into me. My hand slid into her rear pocket, and I exhaled slowly. Georgie's cheek rubbed softly on mine as she turned to whisper, "I don't have it." Her breath was hot on my neck.

I rested into her a moment too long before pulling away. When she started to stand upright, I shoved her back against the car. Georgie cocked her head at me. "We never played rough before." She smiled. "You've learned new things." Her smile was ugly.

I turned away, shoving my hands into my pockets. It took a moment before I could reply, "No. Pain has never been my thing." When I looked back, Georgie had her sweet smile on.

She leaned forward and in a low voice told me, "No, you were always gentle." There was a longing in her eyes. Or maybe that was a reflection of my own longing.

I shook my head to clear my thoughts. "I want it now." My hand stayed on her shoulder. Poison was in the air.

Georgie cocked her head, tried to read me. Getting nothing, she answered in a defensive tone, "I don't have the peace medal." She shrugged my restraining hand off her shoulder. "And before you ask, I don't know where Buck is." She stood upright, scanned Meer's side porch where Denny and Anna stood talking. They had not noticed us.

I shifted to block her view. "You know what I want. I can't believe you took it." I shivered as I added, "Like that."

Georgie's body went rigid. I had her full attention. "That—that was an accident. The paper was . . . was damp." She looked uncomfortable with the admission.

I shook my head. "You took it from a dead man."

She saw the disgust. It angered her. "James was gone." Georgie pushed me away. "I came back to get that peace medal. My family needs the reward." Her eyes slipped back to the porch.

I blocked Georgie from opening the car door. "Give me the note."

Georgie turned to me. "I don't have it."

I pushed her back against the car. "Tell me the truth." Then I leaned in close, "Now." This time I was all business.

Georgie stared back. "All right, Mud, just give me some space."

I took a step back. She watched me before finally speaking. "Everything I told you this morning—that was all true."

A snort escaped. Georgie gave me a look. I returned it and said, "Why should I believe anything you say? You stole a note from a dead man."

Georgie pushed at my shoulder. "Don't judge me. I did what I needed to do for my family."

She saw me looking through the finger-smeared back window of her car, at the elaborate child seat, with a giraffe holding court over numerous toys strewn around the car interior. Her voice softened. "A baby changes you instantly." She looked at me. "I want him to have so much."

I took in the new car, the child seat with a sheepskin cover, the toys everywhere. I could see that.

Georgie took my silence as understanding and began to tell me what she had left out earlier. "When I ran away from you in the dark, I only pretended to run out the kitchen door." Her shoulders relaxed as she continued. "I opened and slammed the door, then stood to the side. It was still dark and before you saw me, Anna came." She smiled. "And boy, that was a relief. I slid right back down the hall and into the no-no room. I didn't want to look at your grandfather—but I needed to find that peace medal."

She still thought that my grandpa was the dead man . . . or she was a good actor. I kept my face blank but nodded. Shifting a bit, I stole a side glance at the porch. Denny and Anna were still there. I returned my attention to Georgie.

She explained, "Babies are just so expensive. Mud, you would not believe everything you have to buy." She pointed through the back window. "That seat . . . that seat cost over four hundred dollars. And he's already too big for it."

I was tired of hearing about her troubles. "Georgie, stop stalling."

For a moment, it looked like she was going to protest. Then she took a deep breath and started again. "Remember, it was dark. I looked everywhere, except . . . The last place, the very last place was right there at the desk with it . . . him." Georgie shivered in the increasing heat.

I watched her face as she replayed what happened in the room.

"That darn Nita came marching down the hall. I heard you all out there but never thought you would let them in . . . with that"—her lip curled in distaste—"that body. But I heard Nita's pounding feet. She was getting close."

Georgie's face went white. "I'd just seen the note, and it was smeared. I got closer, just to read it, that's all I was goin' to do." Her eyes pleaded with me to believe her. I gave a small nod and she went on. "It was dark so I had to get close, but I didn't want to get too close to the body."

She stole a glance at me again.

"Go on." I reached to touch her shoulder in support. To the side, Denny was talking as he ate fries from the bag. Anna seemed to listen while watching the front. Neither noticed us.

Georgie said, "Well, I couldn't read it." She stomped her new-Nike-clad foot. "I had to get closer and I had just touched it—the note, not *it*." She stopped to whisper, "Not the body."

I squeezed her shoulder, urged her on with a look.

A scowl crossed her face. "That's when that darn busybody came running down the hall. It's really Nita's fault."

I struggled to keep an impatient tone out of my voice. "*What* is Nita's fault?"

"Everything!" Georgie snapped back.

I needed a deep breath; I tried to not breathe in the Poison.

Georgie glared. "Well, she scared me." Another stomp of her white Nike before she went on. "I turned to the door, and half that note came with me. See? It's Nita's doin' 'cause then I launched right into keeping her out of that room for you." Georgie looked expectant, like I owed her a thank-you.

My jaw was clenched, but I got the words out. "Give me the note."

"Mud, I gotta tell you. That note didn't make sense." She stole a side glance at the porch.

It would make sense to me. That note half would make everything clear. I knew it. I moved closer. "Georgie, just give me the note."

She started shaking her head. "That's just it. I don't have it anymore." She stole another glance up at Denny and Anna before moving to open her car door.

I pushed the door before Georgie could bend and get in, pinning her. "Then what did the note say, and where is it?" Chimes sounded.

Georgie shoved at the door. "Okay. Okay. The note wasn't about the peace medal at all. It was regarding seeking." Georgie watched for a reaction. The chimes continued their alarm.

My face remained blank, and so did my mind. "Regarding seeking?"

"Yep, that's what it said . . . regarding seeking." Georgie pushed the car door open. "The rest must have been left behind. But that note had nothing to do with the peace medal." She slid into the driver's seat. "I tossed it."

"Where, Georgie . . ." I struggled to control my voice. "Where did you throw away the note you took from a dead man?" I wanted honesty.

"Don't make it sound like that." Georgie tossed her golden hair back. "If James hadn't taken the peace medal—well, I'm sorry, Mud, but he brought it on himself."

I stepped back in stunned silence.

Georgie took advantage of my retreat. She closed the Subaru door and silenced the chimes. Then she lowered the window. "I won't deny I want to get that reward. I hung around a bit to watch you, see if you were going to get the peace medal, but then I decided to . . ." She stopped to think, then went on. "I decided to get something to eat here before I go on up to see if Buck's working on old man Crow's pastures."

This was news to me. "Buck's grandfather has property out here?"

Georgie stole a glance at the porch, making sure Denny and Anna were still up there before she answered. "Yep, a side of his family was part of your mountain band. He's got some property out back of the Slick Hills." She started the car, "Gotta head out, see if Buck's there."

My mind was on overload. As I stepped back, Georgie looked up at me. "You know, Mud, we really should team up to find the peace medal. Buck and I get the reward, you get to clear James's name of the theft. Good final act for him." She gave me her sweetest smile.

My head started shaking before my mouth could utter, "No."

She threw out, "Think about it." The window went up. Georgie couldn't keep her eyes from traveling back to the porch one more time before her car spit gravel on its way out.

I got back inside Denny's truck in a daze. It took a moment before I remembered to check on Denny and Anna. They were still on the porch. I couldn't hear what was happening, but I could tell from gestures and expressions that Denny was bringing Anna to the truck.

Denny pulled the passenger door open. He had a huge smile on his face. "Mud, you know Anna, our legislator?" He urged Anna forward to the door's opening. "I caught her as she was leaving." Out of Anna's sight, Denny signed, "Tell her."

I didn't know if he meant the murder, fracking, or both, but I wasn't sharing any of it with her. I wanted to talk with Grandpa first.

Anna moved forward as I signaled "no" to Denny.

"Ah, Mud, yes, I was trying to tell Denny that we talked earlier." Anna looked over at me. "Twice actually." She gave a shaky smile.

I looked up at Denny. "Remember, I mentioned Anna was looking for Grandpa this morning." Turning to include Anna, I continued, "She's with the group accusing Grandpa of stealing the Jefferson peace medal."

Denny's brown eyes widened, then narrowed at me. "Mud—"

Anna interrupted, "Now, Mud, that is not true. I had to call the meeting. I had no choice on that, but I would never believe James stole the peace medal." She looked toward the now-empty side porch.

I stared at Anna, ignored Denny's squirming. "You didn't sound so sure when Nita was accusing my grandfather of theft." I was making Denny uncomfortable; I could see it in his eyes and his gestures to me to stop.

Anna took my comment head on. "But there is footage of him doing just that." Her eyes never made contact with mine—they moved, watching for something, someone. Anna added, "I had no choice but to inform the Council and call for the meeting."

Denny repeated to me, "See? Anna had no choice—she had to do her job. Grandpa will clear it all up."

Anna whipped her head around to focus on Denny. "Have you talked to James?" A few more strands of hair broke free of her braid.

"We're looking for—" Before Denny could add more, I interrupted with a few coughs.

Anna waited until my coughing fit was over to add, "I do want to talk to James. We were going to meet this morning," she explained to Denny.

I announced, "He'll be at the meeting tonight."

Anna turned to look at me. A glint caught my eye. She had a handmade silver Kiowa sun disk with dangling sunrays on her ear. A simple but elegant earring.

"Where—where is he?" Anna reached for my arm.

I didn't answer Anna's question. I countered with my own. "What's going on with fracking around the Slick Hills?"

Anna was taken by surprise. "What? Fracking?" Her arm dropped back to her side. She got control of her face before she turned it to me. "Whatever made you think about that?"

Denny's eyes pivoted from Anna to me. I faced her from my seated position. "Fracking was brought up this morning."

We both watched Anna. Her worried look lightened. "You must have heard that from Wilson." She waved her hand in the air. "You should know, he lies a lot."

Denny asked: "How do you know that?"

For the first time, Anna smiled. It lit her face, erased all signs of the perpetual scowl. She said, "He clears his throat." She turned to look at both of us. "James told me that once and he was right. You watch: every time Wilson lies, he first clears his throat." She let out a laugh. "Can't believe the man doesn't know he has such an obvious tell."

Denny and I glanced at each other.

Anna went on, "You'll know Wilson's lying once he starts clearing ways for the lies."

I thought of all the throat-clearing Wilson had done throughout our morning together. I wasn't sure he'd ever spoken the truth to me.

A buzz started from my back pocket. I reached without looking and sent the call to voicemail.

I looked up at Anna. Her dangling earring swung with each move of her head.

I refused to drop the questions. "Why were you meeting with James?"

Denny gave me a look and a sign. I was being too direct, too pushy, but I wanted an answer. I turned to Anna. Waited.

She shifted, watched a couple go into Meers. Still I waited. I stopped Denny from speaking with a quick "silent" signal. Finally, Anna looked at both of us. "James called me. Said he wanted to meet." Her brown eyes glared.

I waited to hear if there was more.

She returned to watching Meer's front door and muttered, "He left me with more questions than answers."

"About fracking?" I shot at her again.

Anna shook her head, and more strands escaped from her braid. "I really do need to take care of things at the complex." She turned to Denny. "Been doing much more delegating, but there's never enough time to get everything done." Denny nodded in agreement.

Anna turned her attention to me. "Tell James. . . ." She stopped, hesitating before going on. "I'll see you at the meeting." She followed with "Before, if possible."

As Anna turned to leave, I noticed the other earring was missing. I hoped she'd find the mate. It would be a shame to break up such a unique set.

Denny was still standing at the passenger door. "We coulda told her what we know about the fracking problem." This was followed with a louder, "Shoulda told her about the body."

I shushed Denny. "No. I'm not sure we can trust her."

He threw his arms up. "What do you mean?" Before I answered, he continued, "Grandpa does. She's been over to his house. We've talked about me being part of the Council . . . eventually."

This brought me up. Unfortunately, a surprised "You?" squeaked out.

Denny eyed me. "Yes, me." He sounded angry. "Not everyone has to have a college education to find their place in the world."

"Denny, it's not that." I shifted to look at him and received a prick in my thigh. "There is no one I believe could do more for the Tribe." I shoved my hand in my pocket, brought out the coin I had found earlier. "Just didn't know you wanted to be involved . . . that way," I finished lamely.

I rubbed mud from the covered disk and discovered the point that had been prodding me.

Denny stuttered, "I didn't—not politics, really. But I care about our tribe and what's happening to us." He finished strong: "And this seemed to be the way."

Absentmindedly, I picked at the mud covering on the disk. Denny would be a good representative and spokesperson for our mountain band of Kiowas. I nodded my encouragement. "I'm glad you're doing it." I caught Denny's eyes. "We need stronger representation in the Tribe and the state."

He gave me a shy smile. "I'm not doing anything yet. Just talkin' about it." He turned serious. "We've talked about needing reps in office that are in it for the People and not the money opportunities."

I sat up in the truck's seat. "That is definitely you." Denny would have my vote.

He gave me a half smile.

I realized Denny needed to hear my support. "Seriously, Denny, I do think you would make a difference." I reached to squeeze his forearm. "You really care."

He surprised me by answering, "So does Anna."

I shook my head. Slowly, I answered, "I'm just not so sure about her."

Denny shot back, "I am. And Grandpa trusts her." He said the last like that settled everything.

I couldn't let it drop. There was something off with Anna. "Denny, I hear you, but Anna's hiding something. Maybe . . . with fracking."

Denny stepped back from the truck's door opening. "You don't know that."

I couldn't keep surprise out of my face or voice. "Denny, she avoided talking about fracking just now." He tightened his lips. I went on. "Something is up with her and fracking."

I wrapped the dirty disk in the bottom fold of my shirt and rubbed at it. The last chunk of mud coating crumbled.

I kept my eyes on Denny. He wasn't going to like what I was thinking. "Remember Gene asked us what kind of 'cut' we wanted?"

Before I finished, Denny had set his jaw and started shaking his head. "You're not changing my mind about Anna. She's a good legislator." His eyes watched my hands. "What are you doing?" An edge of irritation seeped into his tone.

I pulled the disk up, cleared of mud. It was a silver Kiowa sun disk with dangling silver sunshine rays. "I found this."

Denny reached for it. "Anna must have dropped her earring when she was talking to us."

I pulled the earring back. "No. She didn't lose it here."

The earring dangled from my fingers as something Roy, the water quality guy, had said about Anna came to mind: ". . . the company she keeps confuses me."

I looked at the silver disk sparkling in the sun light. "I found this earring on the steps at the fracking office."

Chapter Twenty-One

Denny stared at the earring, stepped back, and shook his head. He slammed the truck's passenger door. Without a word, he got in the driver's seat. I put the earring back into my pocket. It pricked me. I shifted in the seat.

"Denny, I know you don't want to hear this, but we do need to consider Anna as a suspect." I thought he was going to do the silent Indian routine, instead he surprised me with a response.

"I thought you said all this was Buck's doing." Denny rested his hands on the steering wheel.

I nodded. "I do think Buck killed his grandfather over the peace medal." The peace medal's theft seemed to be what set so many things in motion. It had to be the root cause, didn't it? "Why else would Grandpa call me for help?" I turned to Denny, "You're more help with fracking than I would be."

He nodded in agreement.

I spoke my fractured thoughts aloud. "No, Grandpa sent for me because of something with the Tribe and that means it had to be the peace medal theft."

We sat in the idling truck; its AC kept us cool.

Denny slapped the steering wheel. "Then why get me worked up about Anna?"

"Denny, Grandpa may have called me because of trouble with the peace medal, but that was before there was a murder." I let that sink in, then added, "We don't know who the intended victim was, so we can't be sure of the why." I stopped. I didn't want to upset Denny, but I was not going to hold back. "And there is something going on with Anna." I continued in a rush, "It looks like she's working with the frackers. You heard them laughing when we threatened to get our legislator. They knew our legislator was female—they said *she*. And I found her earring on the fracking office steps."

Denny stayed quiet, but I could tell he was thinking about what I had said.

I didn't want to, but I had to add, "Denny, Anna is the only one who has two possible motives for this killing." His jaw clenched, but I went on. "One, she's involved with the frackers, either as boss or getting a cut." Denny didn't like where I was going, but he was listening. "Anna may have wanted Grandpa out of the way and gotten Buck's grandfather by mistake."

Denny couldn't hold it in. "*Hawnay!* No! Absolutely not possible." His hands gripped the steering wheel driving nowhere; his knuckles went white. "You forget, Anna knew the dead man. She would not mistake him for Grandpa."

Denny had a point. This set my mind spinning. Maybe Anna intended to kill Wilson. According to Georgie, he had property in the Slick Hills. Wilson may have been involved with fracking or blocking Anna from fracking or . . . too much for now. Too much for Denny.

It took a moment before I announced what I thought was Anna's second possible motive: "If Anna and Gerald are working together, she may be after the peace medal." I stopped, bit my lip, then finally said, "And willing to kill for it."

Stuttering words came from Denny but made no sense. He was too angry to get a full sentence out. I was glad we were parked.

I spoke over his sputters. "Anna and Gerald could have discovered the peace medal in the museum's stored goods and arranged its theft and sale." Denny's objections subsided. He was listening. I lowered my voice. "Buck's grandfather got in their way of getting the peace medal and ended up dead in the no-no room." My eyes went to Denny.

A full minute of silence elapsed before Denny quietly admitted, "This may not look good for Anna." He turned to face me. "But I believe in her, and so does Grandpa." Denny set his jaw.

Anna had as many reasons to kill as Buck. One of the two had to be the killer. But I needed evidence, not a list of reasons. I looked around the parking area. Not much moved in the afternoon heat. Most customers stayed in the store to eat their burgers. My eyes wandered to the empty side porch, and then I remembered. "Denny, I found Georgie. She was here watching Anna, I think."

Denny rushed in with questions. "Where is she? Where is the note?" His body twisted in the truck seat to face me. "Where is Grandpa?" His look demanded answers.

I hesitated. "That I don't know." Denny's face reddened, and I quickly added, "Yet." Denny watched as I squirmed in the seat and reached into my pocket past the earring. Found it and pulled out a crumpled white paper. "I have the other half of Grandpa's note." I held it up and quickly explained, "I slipped it out of Georgie's back pocket without her knowing." Here I swallowed hard, thinking of Georgie against the car, my hand sliding into her rear pocket.

Denny grabbed for the note half. By reflex, I pulled it back. "I haven't had a chance to look at it yet, and Georgie said that it didn't make sense. She claims it says something like *'regarding seeking.*'"

I thought about Georgie lying, saying that she had thrown the note away. I had given her a final chance to be honest, to tell me the whole truth. Instead, Georgie had lied about not having it, and I'd stolen the note from her back pocket. Well, now she didn't have it.

Denny reached for the note again. This time, I let him have it. He seemed surprised but wasted no time opening the half note. He read it and tossed the crumpled paper toward me. "Enough! Georgie's right. It makes no sense."

I retrieved the wad. Ink had run on one side. Fear or the truck's AC gave me chills. This note had to make sense. It needed to lead us to Grandpa. My jaws clenched. Everything hinged on finding Grandpa.

I straightened the wrinkled paper. The ink was smeared, but the letters and words were clear: *re you seek.*

For an instant, it made no sense.

I felt eyes on me. Denny waited, expecting me to have an answer. I had none. Avoiding Denny, I gazed out the windshield. There were fewer cars around. The lunch crowd was fading.

I looked back down at the letters and words.

Of course.

I looked around the inside of the truck, glancing at Denny. "You see my—" I cut myself off when I spotted my messenger bag in the footwell.

Denny shook his head. "Mud, enough already."

Distracted, I told him, "Just give me a minute." I pulled the bag up and flipped through the stack of unopened mail until I found one that was rigid. In a rush, I pulled out a white cardboard express mail envelope, firm enough to write on, and grabbed a pen. The messenger bag dropped to the floorboard.

"Mud, is this leading somewhere?" Denny sounded exasperated.

I turned to him. "The first half of the note said, '*I am w-h-e*.'" I enunciated the phrase ending with the letters as I wrote each on the cardboard mailer. I looked back at Denny to make sure he was listening.

He said, "I get it! What does the note say?" He pushed his dark hair back.

I put my hand up. "Just wait . . ." I looked at the smeared half note and added *r e you seek* to the back of the mailer. I started nodding, excited. "Denny, it reads: *I am where you seek*." I said it again, loud and with a silly grin. "I am where you seek. Grandpa is telling us where he is." I couldn't keep the excitement out of my voice, "Grandpa is *where we seek*!" I waved the same-day mailer at him.

Denny looked at me like I had lost my mind. "Like that makes any more sense. We've been seeking Grandpa all over. We haven't found him, so he's not where I sought." Denny gripped the steering wheel. "Mud, stop waving that at me. We've got to go back and call the police."

I squeezed his arm. "Denny, Grandpa is where we have both gone for insights and introspection. It's where our family has gone to seek spiritual guidance for generations."

His rigid arm relaxed. Denny's eyes opened wide. "That's it!"

We both came out with the answer and laughed. "Grandpa is on the vision quest ledge." I waved the mailer in celebration.

His face brightened. "You're right. *I am where you seek.* It makes sense."

When Kiowa children come of age, they are taught introspection and personal growth through seeking in a vision quest. The last several generations of our family have gone to a specific ledge in the Ghost Mountains for their four-day vision quests. Not all of us experienced a vision, but we all became thoughtful adults—well, most of us.

Grandpa must have gone to the ledge to seek guidance and balance. I felt certain we would find him on the family ledge. Denny and I kept grinning at each other.

"Denny, all we have to do is go to the Ghost Mountains in the Wildlife Refuge and get Grandpa off the ledge." I giggled at the sound of "get Grandpa off the ledge." Without thinking, I tucked the mailer between the seat and console, out of the way.

Denny's grin increased, not from the joke, but from relief. This felt right.

He relaxed into the driver's seat. "We get Grandpa and the peace medal off the ledge." Denny gave me a smile, then continued, "Get both to the Complex for tonight's meeting at eight." He nodded his head. "Yep, Grandpa explains that he was keeping the peace medal safe from Buck and Gerald.

That will blow up the meeting at Red Buffalo Hall." A satisfied smile spread across Denny's face. "Grandpa can expose Buck and Gerald to everyone gathered."

I chimed in, "Grandpa proves his innocence without anyone ever thinking the worst of him."

Denny was excited now. "This won't bring back the family regalia and artifacts the People have lost already, but it will prove what Buck and Gerald have been up to."

I finished for Denny. "And show how their greed led to murder."

Reminded of the lost life, we both said a silent prayer for the newly released soul riding the wind on to the next world.

Denny put the truck in gear and started driving toward the nearby Ghost Mountains. I glanced back at Meer's side porch in time to catch a glimpse of Gerald leaning out over the rail with his eyes locked on us. My last image was his yellow tie waving over the porch like a warning flag.

I didn't say anything to Denny.

Chapter Twenty-Two

The Ghost Mountains lay inside the Wichita Wildlife Refuge. Rolling ranch lands led the way to the park's fifty-nine thousand acres of wilderness and wildlife. As kids, the Wildlife Refuge had been our backyard. With an easy horse ride or hike across family lands, we would spend free days transported into the world of our ancestors. We walked Kiowa country, explored old camp grounds, pretended to hunt buffalo from horseback, and played Indians and cowboys. In our world, the Indians always won.

I glanced at Denny. A black cloud had settled on us. After our initial joy at solving the note, we'd been quiet. Each working through private thoughts. I looked out the window and watched the Mountains get closer. "Denny, remember Grandpa's 'listen to the animals talk' game?"

I was relieved when he responded, imitating Grandpa's clipped, rhythmic English: *"'Even the annoying buzz of the small cicadas have something to tell us.'"*

"'If you are willing to listen,'" we both chorused.

Denny's laugh broke the gloom. "I don't think our parents knew he was leaving us for hours in the middle of the Wildlife Refuge when we were so young."

"You could go home anytime." I defended Grandpa's actions with a smile.

"If you could find your way home, alone," Denny finished, still grinning, "Otherwise, you had to stay put until he retrieved you."

"I did learn a lot from him. Yeah . . . if a cicada stops buzzing suddenly, I better stop and look around." I smiled back at Denny. "Grandpa made us comfortable, safe out here in the country." I looked around the countryside as it evolved to rough foothills.

An insistent buzz brought me back from the past. Denny looked over. I pulled the phone from my pocket. It was the office. I really did not want to deal with this now, but I had to. I swiped to answer with a brisk, "This is Mu—Mae." Denny snickered at my near mistake.

"Mae, where have you been?" The voice from the phone rose in volume as it continued. "Things aren't looking good. Mae, do you hear me?"

"Bernie, I'm here. Talk to me." I turned away from Denny to focus on Bernie.

She burst out with, "Things are blowing up, and you disappeared. Do you know how many messages I've left for you in the last hour?"

The car's tires rumbled across the planks of the Medicine Creek Bridge. We were approaching the Wildlife Refuge. I was surprised I still had cell reception. "Bernie, I don't have time. Just tell me what you need." I was too abrupt—I heard it in Bernie's quick intake of breath. But I knew Bernie and Marcus could handle my few days away. They should not need to be in constant contact with me.

Except . . . for Thomas. I cringed when I remembered the trouble Thomas started with the client's last-minute logo change. I should have called Bernie after my conversation with Thomas, taken time to work out a solution. I'd been too distracted.

Before I could speak, Bernie responded, "All righty then. Marcus wants to talk to you about the client's latest demands *and* Thomas's continued disruptions to the work flow. Thomas wants no calls from you, but Richard, the client, does want a call from you."

"Bernie, I'm sorry." I knew my apology startled her by the long silence on the other end of the line. I went on to explain: "I should have contacted you when I heard of the changes Thomas instigated."

Lamely, I added, "I'm not juggling well today." I waited a beat before going on, "I know you and Marcus are a strong team, and can handle the next few days. I really want you two to manage the client and the last of getting the show together. You're ready."

Bernie seemed more suspicious then supported. "What does that mean?"

I promptly replied, "That I think you are capable of managing clients directly. I'm glad you're stepping out from behind the curtain."

Denny kept his eyes on the curves in the road. Yet I knew he was listening.

Bernie took a moment before replying, "Well, you've stunned me into silence. Not sure how to respond to all that." Even her constant keyboard tapping had stopped in the background.

I laughed. "I'm sure you will figure out an appropriate response by our next call." The silence lingered a bit too long. I could tell there was something more bothering Bernie. Years of working long hours together to establish the agency had bonded us. I prompted, "Bernie, what else?"

She sucked in a breath, before saying, "Mae, he's talking to attorneys."

I was confused. "Who's talking to attorneys?" Denny glanced over at me with a questioning look. I shrugged and returned my attention to Bernie.

A long breath hissed into the phone as Bernie said, "Thomas, of course." Unable to contain her curiosity she continued, "What's happening? I heard him talking to someone about 'a dissolution' before he closed his office door." Bernie lowered her voice. "That's like a business divorce, right?"

My stomach clenched. It was my turn to suck in a breath. Things with Thomas and the partnership—this was happening way too fast. The partnership was failing, but not the agency—my agency—another gut twist. I pushed it aside. I had to, for now.

I looked up at the approaching Ghost Mountains, then focused my attention back on Bernie. "I'll talk to Thomas. First, transfer me to Marcus." I didn't feel it, but I had to be light for Bernie. "And Bernie, don't worry. I'll make sure I get you in any divorce."

"Mae, how can you say don't worry! The energy here is not cool." Bernie sounded anxious. More than I'd heard in her before.

Despite the situation, I kept a smile on. I wanted her to hear it in my voice. "I'll take care of things. Just go ahead and transfer me to Marcus." I hoped my warmth came across the cell lines.

I glanced over at Denny. He was no longer listening. The curves through the foothills absorbed his attention.

Marcus came on the line in a rush. "Mae, I really cannot deal with the client and Thomas. Both are being impossible, and I have no bandwidth left." He let out an exaggerated breath to punctuate his point.

I chuckled a bit. "Marcus, you only need to work with the client and make him happy. I will deal with Thomas. Remind your crew who their manager is. You got this."

Denny kept his eyes on the road, but he smiled.

Marcus didn't sound relieved. "You heard Thomas promised the world to Richard before I got to the client's office. Now Richard is not letting go of the idea of a 3-D logo opening for his launch." I could hear Marcus shaking his head as he continued, "Impossible in the time we have left."

Marcus was right. There was no way to add 3-D animation to a logo being showcased in time with everything else that needed to be done. But we might be able to simulate a 3-D look.

I reminded Marcus, "We were playing with textures on Richard's logo a few weeks back, before the crunch started for the IPO launch. Pull a couple of those files. It won't be 3-D, but we can give his logo a textured effect for the opening. I think that, with movement, will be enough to satisfy Richard."

My suggestion was met with silence. Finally, Marcus muttered, "Hmm, these aren't bad. This could work. . . ."

Bernie must have come up behind Marcus. I could hear an exchange but couldn't make out the words. They seemed in agreement when Marcus's voice returned. "I'll see what we can do. Are you calling Richard?"

I smiled at hearing a hint of excitement in Marcus's voice. "Marcus, you continue working with the client. Remember, Richard is extremely nervous and thinks he needs the extra pizzazz of 3-D. Remind him, the company is the pizzazz. No smoke and mirrors needed when he has the real thing. Pull Bernie in as needed for client support." I repeated with emphasis, "You have this."

A distracted, "Yeah, yeah, we can bring it on from here to—Gotta go. Here's Bernie."

Bernie was direct and to the point. "What about Thomas? He's not so easy to distract."

This was true, but I needed to offer reassurance. "You just stay focused on the show. I'll deal with Thomas."

The truck slowed as we rumbled over the tubed cattle guard marking entry into the Wichita Mountains Wildlife Refuge.

Bernie started, "But—"

I cut in, "No *buts*. Thomas is my problem. You keep the show on track until I get back."

Denny turned onto a dirt road. We bounced along the path until stopped by a wall of trees.

Bernie asked, "When is that?"

I looked over at Denny; we were parking. I answered Bernie, "Soon." And gave her all my attention. "Hey, I appreciate all you do for the agency . . . and me. You make my life better. I don't tell you that often enough." For the second time, I left Bernie speechless. I laughed into the silence. "Bernie, transfer me on over to Thomas."

This brought a fast response from her. "You sure?"

I forced myself to continue smiling, I wanted the positive energy for myself and to send over the airwaves to Bernie. "I'm sure." As the call was transferred, I heard the music of Bernie tapping away on her computer's keyboard.

Thomas picked up before the first ring ended. He launched right in. "I have been waiting for your call."

I knew it wasn't me he wanted to hear from. Before I was able to clarify, Thomas went on, "So you found a loophole?" I froze, waiting to see if he added anything more. Unfortunately, he didn't.

My mind spun with questions. What kind of loophole was Thomas looking for? Something with our business agreement? I couldn't confront him right now. I needed to wait until I was back in the office with our contract in front of me. Thomas had taken care of the agency's incorporations and filings while I had been absorbed with clients and building the business. Once I had been thrilled that Thomas managed the details of our corporation. Now I realized how foolish I had been. I had been *Mawbane.*

Thomas inquired, "Hello . . . you there?"

I shook off my worries. "Hey, Thomas. It's Mae. Just wanted to remind you one more time, that we both have our specialties in the business. Mine is with the clients and production. You are all back office." Thomas was silent. I went on, "I am the reason we have clients. Bernie, Marcus, and I are on Richard's IPO. We have it handled—"

Here Thomas couldn't help interrupting with a loud snort. "If you mean by *handled*, having a dissatisfied VIP, then yeah, you've got it handled." He was back to being overconfident.

I leaned into the phone. "Richard was a very satisfied client before you encouraged him to make unnecessary changes."

He had no reply. But I didn't need to be right; I needed Thomas to behave. A thought came to me, time to appeal to his greed. "Thomas, for this launch to be a huge success for the client and the agency"—I paused to make sure I had his attention—"Marcus and Bernie must handle all client communications and production. They know the client, product, and most important, Marcus and Bernie know what they are doing. Please, just let them do it." I said this with no heat, no malice. A simple request.

Denny shifted in his seat, glanced over at me.

Thomas started to comment. I wasn't ready for any. I went on, not loud but firm, "Richard does not need to feel uneasy at this stage." I reminded him, "I have worked with Richard and his executive staff for six months to craft the right story and segments for each executive to share during the company's public offering launch. Marcus has created the perfect look and feel for the new company, and Bernie is making sure the story embedded in the speeches and graphics come together for each presenter. We are why the agency has done so well."

I heard Thomas breathe heavily into the phone, but no words came out. He could not argue with the truth.

I decided to tackle the real problem. "We can work out the changes needed in the agency when I return." I bit the inside of my cheek. I should have dealt with our issues before things got to the breaking point. "It's time we talked about the agency and our future together."

I waited for a response from Thomas. When he said nothing, I repeated, "Thomas, for Richard to stay happy, it means we need to deliver a successful IPO. You remember, we get quite a bonus with this launch if all goes well."

A choked "Bonus?" came across the line.

"Yes, Thomas." If he had been in the office more, he would have known, "We get a stock bonus. Richard was quite generous. The more successful Richard's launch, the better for the agency."

This time I got a response.

The line went dead.

Chapter Twenty-Three

Denny looked at me with a strange expression. I gave him a questioning glance. He said, "You're kinda a badass."

My Mae persona obviously amused him. I had to tell him the truth: "You know it."

Denny laughed as he got out of the truck. He reached back in and leaned the seat all the way forward. He kept a grin on his face while he shuffled tools and fast food remains around in search of something behind his driver's seat.

I slid out of the truck, tangled my left foot with my right, and kicked my bag to the damp ground. One corner of the bag landed in a mud puddle. I pulled the messenger bag up and wiped the red-colored mud off the bag as best I could. It would stain. Oklahoma's iron-rich red dirt was infamous. My bag was marked forevermore. I kinda liked it.

Denny was off to the side, just out of sight. I pulled the seat's latch and pushed the bag into a small space behind the seat, then slammed the passenger seat back into place. Denny had a huge smile on his face when I looked up. It was obvious he had something to say. I asked, "What?"

He laughed. "I was impressed with you being big boss and all." Denny held my eyes. "Then you go and tangle your feet. Same ol' Mud."

I had no choice but to join him. The laughter felt good.

I moved to the front of the truck. Seemingly endless rows of twelve- to fifteen-foot-tall cedars, standing in straight, rigid lines, faced me. Each row was so close that the tree's canopies touched, creating a couple miles of dark forest before breaking free to a rolling mixed-grass prairie that led to the granite peaks of the Ghost Mountains.

In early Oklahoma, wood was scarce. The cedars were planted exactly six feet apart by the government in the 1900s, with the intent to harvest all for use as fence posts. By the time the cedar fence-post forest was ready to harvest, more efficient materials were available.

The forest remained growing together into a maze of matching trees that looked the same everywhere you turned, and at every turn, you were met with shifting shades of gray as the canopies above soaked up all sunlight except for an escaped shaft here and there. It was easy to be lost in the Parallel Forest for hours. As kids around a camp fire, we heard stories of souls lost forever in the clutches of the dark forest.

I stepped away from the wall of trees.

A cool breeze blew across my face. I closed my eyes and took in a deep breath of rain-fresh air. Birds of all kind were in full chorus. Chirps, whistles, and chortles accompanied a shrill cry as a soaring hawk called to another. I pulled back my shoulders, opened my arms, and settled my mind.

I took a moment to be present in Kiowa country.

The air smelled washed, like fresh earth. Wind blew the leaves overhead, rippling them together and emulating the sound of a gentle waterfall. My eyes opened to a clear, crisp blue sky, with no signs of the angry clouds that had ruled the sky and wind just a couple hours earlier.

I heard a high sharp *kieed*, and then, like magic, a scissor-tailed flycatcher, Oklahoma's state bird, danced in front of me. Its sleek black and white body fluted down to a sweeping eight-inch, split-tail feather that let the bird dart up, down, and all around after its quick-moving insect prey. Before disappearing, the bird stared at me. Its orange and turquoise mascara-style eyes marked it as male and beautiful.

From behind me, Denny announced, "Things aren't as they appear. Isn't that right, Mud?"

I turned to Denny. "That's what Grandpa and the Old Ones would say. When you see a scissortail, it's telling you to think again, review your assumptions."

Denny nodded in agreement. "Maybe it means you should rethink your thoughts about Anna."

I shook my head at Denny. "It means the storm brought out lots of flies for the birds to eat." I moved toward him. He held something in his hand. "What do you have?"

Denny looked serious. "Mud, we have to do this right. Can't just march up there, you know." He blew on a tightly bound sage bundle, encouraging embers to glow. "We need to be cleansed of all negative energy and thoughts." Denny started at my feet, washing me in the skunk-like smoke, cleansing me for our journey to the family's spiritual place. Our place of worship. As Denny washed me in the sage smoke, he chanted a prayer for success on our paths.

Once finished with me, he washed himself in the pungent smoke. At the end, Denny planted the bundle upright to continue safely burning to its natural end. The smoke streamed forward, wafting up and away into the sky. Almost unconsciously, I stepped into the ribbon of sage smoke, letting it engulf me. I took a deep breath in, held it, then slowly released it. I cupped the smoke forward onto my head, clearing it, cleansing it, hoping for guidance.

I stepped out, ready. Through the forest, beyond the prairie grass, rose the granite towers of the Ghost Mountains. We couldn't see the faces within the granite rocks from here—the rows of trees blocked all but the highest points of the mountain—but I was sure Grandpa was sitting up there, talking with the granite-faced wise ones.

"Let's go—" All other words were drowned out in the revving roar of a van slipping down the muddy road toward us.

I moved with Denny to the back of his truck. The white van wasn't intended for dirt roads, especially muddy ones. It bumped from one side of the slick road to the other and then slipped back before stopping directly behind Denny's truck.

The van continued to rock even as the driver door flew open. Buck burst out, slipped, slid, and regained his balance. Both van and Buck came to a final stop in front of Denny.

Buck pushed Denny aside to reach me. "Where is it?"

Denny shoved forward, placing himself between Buck and me. "What is it with you? You all were ten or twelve when she made you cry. Get over it already." Denny used his extra inches to loom over Buck.

Buck rammed his barrel chest into Denny. "Get out of the way. This has nothing to do with you." Buck's typical Kiowa build—short, broad, and strong—pushed into Denny's lean frame.

Denny chest-bumped back.

Tension was ramping up quickly—too quickly. The situation needed to be diffused. I stepped closer to Buck. I wanted to see his guilt when I told him, "Buck, your grandfather is—"

Before I finished, sour, angry lines crossed Buck's face. He turned to me. "I don't care about the old man. Gerald said you had the peace medal James took?" He looked around, opened his arms. "Where is it?"

Denny spat out, "*Aim bote gkoat.* You are greedy." This was a terrible insult to a Kiowa. We are taught early to take only what is needed and share abundance with family and others.

Buck's face reddened and his eyes bulged. "I have a child now. I gotta take care of him. This medal fixes everything." He seemed to come back to himself and looked directly at me. "Gerald saw you all. You have the medal. I want it now."

Denny and I exchanged looks, unsure why Gerald thought we had the peace medal. I reached toward Buck. "The medal doesn't do you any good now. You can't sell it. Thanks to the moccasin telegraph, everyone in the Tribe knows it's missing by now." I couldn't resist asking, "You planned on selling the peace medal to Gerald, right?"

Buck slapped my hand away. "Just tell me where it is, squaw." Spittle stuck to the ragged beard hair around his mouth.

I recoiled. *Squaw* was a demeaning word to call an Indian woman. My hands clenched into a fist. Buck's nose looked ripe.

Denny pushed forward. "You better listen up, 'cause things are not looking good for you." He took another step into Buck's personal space. "And don't touch my cousin again, ever."

Buck held his ground. The two glared and puffed at each other. *Hair trigger* came to mind. I needed to do something before punches flew. There was one sure-fire way.

I taunted, "Georgie doesn't seem very happy with you." As I hoped, Buck turned back to me. I continued, "Does she know you sold your family *Koitsenko* sash and lance?"

Hot hatred shot from Buck's eyes. "Georgie knows what she needs to know." He stepped toward me. "And she knows the reward on the peace medal is what our family needs to get right now." His scraggly beard seemed to vibrate with his rage.

Denny shifted forward, nudged in between Buck and me. "Is that the lie you all decided on . . . *reward*? Mud may be a fool for Georgie, but I'm not. Georgie enjoys all the new stuff you've been bringing home way too much." Denny's face twisted with disgust. "I've got no doubt she knows you're robbing our People. Like you, she doesn't care." Denny eyed Buck's new work boots and jeans. "You sold our People out."

Buck backed from Denny. "I did not. They made their own choices." He added, "I got them the best prices around."

Denny wasn't having it. "You sabotaged them." He pushed forward into Buck's face. "You made sure that those families—Kiowa families—needed money right then. They had no choice but to sell family treasures for the only price around." Denny's eyes bored into Buck.

Buck stepped back. He refused to look directly at Denny when he answered, "You can't prove nothin'."

Denny wasn't finished. "You went after every family in the Black Leggings Society. People you knew." Denny's face was full of disgust. "You knew what treasure each family had and who was easy pickings."

I stepped forward. "It's going to be pretty easy to prove all the connections, Buck. Denny has a list of all the families who sold artifacts to Gerald after talking to you." I looked over at Denny, hoping he could confirm this. He nodded yes.

Denny added, "They all mentioned you as the go-between, and they all had an emergency bill of some sort come up after they saw you and first said no to you and Gerald. That's all. Not just a few families, but everyone you talked to with artifacts."

I spoke slow and steady, directly to Buck. "I saw your family's *Koitsenko* sash and lance in Gerald's gallery—for sale. People know your grandfather would never sell such a treasure. But you would." I accused him: "My grandfather took the peace medal to keep it away from you."

Buck couldn't hide the surprise that crossed his bearded face.

Unconsciously, I clenched my fists again. "You suddenly have money. You're driving around in a new car, getting new things as more Kiowa treasures disappear. It all connects to you, right back to the theft of the peace medal and the dea—"

Buck cut me off. "I didn't know nothin' about the medal until your grandpa stole it. Getting it back was going to make everything right."

Denny couldn't hold back. He grabbed Buck by the shoulders. "What you did can never be made right. You've killed your—"

Buck threw his arms upward, pushing Denny's hands off him. "Get off me! I didn't want to do it." Buck gave Denny a pleading look. "He made me."

Denny stepped back, shocked.

I leaned forward, anxious to hear Buck's confession. This would clear Grandpa. I wanted to hear Buck say who had made him a killer.

Buck's gaze stayed on Denny. "My grandpa found out I sold the sash and lance." Buck shook his head, let a faint smile show. "Man, I got some good cash for that." Almost as an afterthought, he whispered, "But I needed more."

Buck focused on Denny as he tried to explain his actions. "I have a son. I needed more money. Gerald made it easy. All I had to do was find out who still had artifacts at home."

"Not bad enough that you sold your son's heritage." Denny didn't hide his disgust. "You started stealing it from others."

Buck squared himself to Denny, puffed his chest out. Denny stared back, settled into himself. "Buck, just give me one more reason." He dead-smiled into Buck's bearded face. "'Cause I won't stop when you start crying."

Buck first tried for a menacing glare back at Denny. It melted under Denny's malevolent smile. Buck shifted tactics to defense. "I didn't know anything about that medal. Just that it was missing and your grandfather took it." He stepped back, put distance between himself and Denny, then continued, "Gerald said he would give the old man the sash and lance back, and me a nice reward. All I had to do was get that medal."

I noticed Buck had not voiced the dead man's name.

Buck turned to me. "I could get enough to take care of everything. Stop hawking small things . . . I just needed this last big killing."

On *killing*, Denny and I locked eyes.

I urged Buck on. "Tell us about the killing."

Buck backed away, his eyes darting about rapidly. "It was supposed to be once and done. That's it. Then he made me do it again and again."

Chapter Twenty-Four

Was Buck talking about *killing*? Had he taken more than one life?

The thought stunned me into silence while Buck went on. "I knew it was wrong, but after the first one . . . he had me then." Buck appealed to Denny. "I just wanted to start over. But he wouldn't let me stop after that, kept saying he would tell"—Buck lowered his head—"that he would shame me with the Tribe."

Denny stated the name: "Gerald."

Buck turned to me, his face charged with emotion and dread. "If they knew, if the Tribe found out what I did . . . I would be shunned. Worse, my family would be shunned. My son would grow up ashamed of me."

Denny and I exchanged looks. Finally, I said softly, "Buck, why your grandfather?"

He turned on me, took a menacing step forward. I held my ground. Buck took two more steps, then turned and slammed his fist into a nearby cedar tree. I heard the crunch of bone and bark splintering. The canopy above shook, and a bird flew off, shrieking a warning.

Buck let his hand drop to his side. I noticed small beads of blood pool and drop to the ground. He continued to face the tree. I felt Denny at my side; he must have moved forward when Buck was coming toward me. We glanced at each other. Was Buck going to confess to killing his grandfather?

I stepped toward Buck, urged softly, "Buck, why?"

Buck shifted toward us. He focused on me for a moment before his gaze slid away. In a voice as distant as his gaze, Buck said, "Yeah, Gerald. He saw the family's *Koitsenko* sash and lance at a Powwow. You know how my grandpa loves to plant the sacred Wild Dogs' sash and lance in front of his camp area at each gathering. Gerald saw it and had to have it. He kept after me. All the time, always increasing the price he would pay for it." He shook his head. "Gerald knew I wanted to go back to college."

Buck turned pleading eyes on us. "I would finish school this time. Georgie would be happy. I could get a good job coaching. I just needed enough for one year."

Unconsciously, I shook my head. "So, you sold your great-grandfather's *Koitsenko* sash and lance. One of the last remaining in the tribe." I stopped and looked away, too mad to continue.

Denny moved forward. "Looks like you sold your family treasure and just spent the money on new stuff." He locked eyes with Buck. "So much for school."

Buck raised his bearded chin in defiance. "I had to take care of other things first. And it woulda all gone according to plan if I'd gotten the peace medal. That reward fixed everything."

Denny stepped toward Buck. "So, was it worth killing him?"

Buck's eyes narrowed as he studied Denny, then me. "Killing who? What are you trying to pin on me?"

I butted in before Buck became too defiant. "Buck, we found your grandfather"—I stopped, not really wanting to say it, but I did—"dead at my grandpa's house."

Buck's color rose. "What are you playing at?" His eyes darted from me to Denny.

Denny studied Buck, then softly added, "Buck, it's true. Someone killed your grandfather."

Buck's lips moved; a cry of agony escaped. He dropped to his knees. "I told Grandpa I was sorry." Buck sobbed. "He said I'd shamed him." Another gasp and sob escaped. "I was supposed to be great. I got the girl. I got a scholarship. But they didn't want an Indian to do good." Buck began to rock. "I know I could make him proud of me again. I just needed one more chance."

I stood to the side, uncomfortable, not sure what to do. Denny stepped forward and squatted next to the rocking Buck. He slid his arm across Buck's broad shoulder. "Your grandfather knew you were trying."

I could just make out Buck's muffled, "Who . . . who did it?"

Denny remained silent, squatting by Buck.

I spoke to the back of Buck's head. "I thought you did."

Buck whirled on me. "Me? You thought me . . . I shamed my grandfather . . . but kill? Never a killer." All signs of remorse were wiped away with Buck's rising rage. "You . . ." Buck puffed to his full height and eyed me. "Grandpa said you knew where the peace medal was, and he would get it from you." Buck moved forward, menace in his steps. I stayed.

He breathed down on me. "You were with him all morning." His breath smelled of onions and beer. "What did you do to my grandfather?" Specs of saliva spewed out with his final words.

Denny was on his feet, at my side. "Your grandfather left Mud at McClung's. As everyone at the diner will tell you. He was alive and driving toward the Sawpole house while we were inside McClung's store."

Buck clenched his fists, gasped, and released the injured one. He choked out, "So who killed my grandfather?" His eyes bore into me.

I finally spoke. "Georgie found the body." I hurried to add, "She thought it was James who was killed. Georgie said someone was in the house before she arrived. Someone pushed past her in the dark hallway. It must have been the killer. But Georgie said she didn't see who it was."

At this, Denny shook his head and muttered, "If you believe her."

I defended Georgie. "It was in the middle of the thunderstorm, and the house was dark." I trailed off, not knowing what else to add. Somehow, I did believe Georgie's accounting.

Buck said in a flat tone, "Georgie didn't do it." He said nothing more. I watched his face struggle for composure as his eyes filled.

Then who? I wanted to scream. I'd really thought Buck had done it, but his reaction to the death was one of pure shock. Buck couldn't fake that display of surprise and grief at hearing of his grandfather's murder.

Denny caught my eye and signaled me to step to the side, out of Buck's hearing. He whispered, "Mud, we've got to take Buck back."

This caught me off guard. "What do you mean *back*?" I didn't keep my voice low. I glanced over at Buck to see if he'd heard. He was where we had left him, his slack face staring into the dark forest.

Denny's answer got my attention. "We have to take Buck to his grandfather's body and let the authorities know what happened—now."

I didn't hesitate. "We need to find Grandpa and the peace medal first so Grandpa can explain everything tonight." I emphasized, "If we don't, Grandpa looks guilty. The theft. The murder. Everything." My hands rested on my hips.

Denny stayed silent as Buck swayed in the breeze. A sob broke from him.

I faced Denny. "I'm not going back."

"Mud, I have to take Buck to his grandfather." Denny looked to the front of the van. Buck was bent over in pain. A choked sob escaped.

"Just let Buck go on his own. Now that we know he didn't do it." I glanced over. Buck remained bent, cradling his injured hand. I knew Denny wouldn't leave Buck to deal with his grandfather's death alone. But I wanted Denny with me.

"Mud, you know I can't." Denny watched Buck. "I'll take him to Grandpa's house. Buck needs to be with the body."

I could hear Buck's continued sobs. I kept my eyes down. "That means I'll have to go alone to find Grandpa." I swallowed nervously. It had been over ten years since I had been up to the vision quest ledge. I knew where it was—anyway, I was pretty sure.

Denny noticed my nervousness. "Mud, you'll be up and back with Grandpa within a couple hours. Heck, the police will probably just be arriving. You know how it is out here. We don't get quick service, no matter the emergency."

I only heard Denny say, "back with Grandpa" before firing off, "Denny, I'm not going back to the house with Grandpa. I'm taking him to the meeting at Red Buffalo Hall at the Tribal Complex. I'm getting Grandpa's name cleared before the police or anyone thinks of charging him with this theft and murder."

Denny looked perplexed. "That was going to work when we thought Buck killed his grandfather." He shook his head. "Now, we don't know who did what, or even why."

"We know Grandpa is innocent."

Denny's eyes went past me to search out Buck.

My mind scrambled, reached to connect darting dots. "Just because it wasn't Buck doesn't mean it wasn't Gerald." I knew better than to mention Anna.

I started seeing possibilities pointing to Gerald as the killer. I reminded Denny, "You saw how Gerald helped himself into Grandpa's house like he had been there before."

Denny pulled his eyes back to me; he was considering my new scenario. I piled on more hastily thought-up evidence. "We know Gerald is the one after the peace medal. He had Buck and Wils—" I stopped in time from saying the dead man's name; I couldn't break the old Kiowa taboo of not using the recently dead's name in fear of anchoring the spirit to this plane. I continued, "and Buck's grandfather trying to get the peace medal."

Birds chirped in the treetops. The cicadas annoying buzz returned. Buck must be calming down.

I bit my lower lip in concentration. This scenario was making sense. "Gerald wanted the Jefferson peace medal bad enough to offer Buck money and the return of their *Koitsenko* sash and lance. Maybe it was just Gerald who had done the killing. Gerald got carried away in his zeal for the peace medal."

After I said *zeal* I knew I had lost Denny. I nearly lost myself. *Zeal* had just slipped out of my marketing brain.

Denny had a look of disgust. "You don't kill someone out of 'zeal.'" He lowered his head. "Geez, Mud."

Buck muttered and shuffled off to the side. Disturbed squirrels scolded him.

I focused on Denny. "Definitely wrong word choice. But, Denny, you know what I mean." I caught his eyes again. "Maybe it was just Gerald that did it. He wouldn't want to lose Buck and all the treasures Buck finds for him."

Denny nodded his head in agreement. "I can see that." He locked eyes with me, this time making sure he had my attention before continuing, "Or I can see Georgie doing it. I know you don't want to hear this, but we know she was in the house alone before you arrived. That's a fact. You've been basing everything else off what she told you, not facts."

I noticed Buck move from the front of the van. He seemed to aim himself toward Denny.

Denny looked intently at me. "We know Georgie lies. She lied to you through the last of your high school senior year about Buck. You even said Georgie lied about having the note." He insisted, "You don't want to see it, but it could have been her." He shivered. "She tore a note from a dead man's fingers."

Denny was right—I didn't want to believe that Georgie could . . . *would* kill for money. Then I remembered Georgie's expression as she looked at the Subaru's finger-smeared rear window. Her face had softened while her eyes had hardened. Georgie wanted her son to have everything.

As if reading my mind, Denny added, "Georgie is not the girl you were in love with. You don't know her anymore."

"Denny, I know you won't believe me, but I am over Georgie." I set my jaw. "This afternoon I saw her . . . differently. I'm done with her." I didn't wait to hear Denny's response. I didn't need his confirmation. I knew it, felt it. I was free of being in love with Georgie, finally.

I added, "Right now, all that matters is that Grandpa goes to the meeting at Red Buffalo Hall tonight."

Denny pushed his dark hair from his face. "We need to take different paths." He kept his eyes on me. "But I'll see you at the Complex tonight."

I looked up at him. "I really wish you were going with me to get Grandpa."

Before Denny could reply, our attention was pulled by the slam of a car door. We had forgotten about Buck. While we were arguing, he had gotten into his van.

In two strides, Denny was at the van and pulled the door open. "Buck, you can't drive right now. I'll take you to your grandfather."

Buck's forehead rested on top of the steering wheel. His voice came out muffled. "I heard you talking about Georgie. She didn't do nothin'. She nagged me to stop working for Gerald all the time."

Buck pulled his head up as Denny began pulling him from the driver's seat. He sneered at me around Denny's shoulder. "That is until I got her liking nice things." Finally, out of the van, Denny shuffled Buck toward the passenger side, even as

Buck continued talking at me about Georgie. "Yeah, she got new things, but only what I would buy her. She wouldn't do nothin' to my grandpa. She does what I tell her to do."

I couldn't help but notice Buck emphasized "what I buy her" and "what I tell her." If he had so much control over her, then he should be able to answer my question: "Why was she at my grandfather's house?"

Buck's bluster returned, all signs of remorse gone. "I sent her to get that damn peace medal from James." Denny stopped moving Buck to let him talk. "I needed to get the medal to Gerald so he could ship it off. He has a buyer waiting." He glared at me. "My money's waiting. I told Georgie to get over there and get the peace medal."

Denny urged Buck on toward the passenger side of the van before he asked Buck, "Would Georgie kill for the peace medal?"

My *"No!"* shot out before Buck had time to digest the question.

They both looked at me. Buck glared. Denny lowered his eyes. He looked disappointed in me. I was too.

Denny leaned Buck against the side of the van. He told me, "I need to take Buck to his grandfather's body." He continued to talk as he held Buck upright and opened the van's passenger door. "You need to find Grandpa." He pushed Buck toward the open door. Buck put up a halting resistance before he finally slipped into the passenger seat and buckled up. Denny closed the door and moved to the driver's side.

I reached for his arm. "Denny . . ."

He looked up, squinted in the late afternoon sun. "You better get a move on."

I hesitated, squeezed Denny's arm. Kiowas don't say *good-bye*. It's too final. When we part, we say, as I did now to Denny, "*Heg-gaw aim oye bone thaw.* I'll see you again."

Denny smiled. "Hey, you better get going."

He looked upward, tilted his head toward the Ghost Mountains. "Grandpa's up there, waiting for you." He waited a beat to add "*Ahn Tsah Hye-gyah-daw*," then got into the van and drove away.

I stood staring at the muddy tracks left in the wake of the departing van. It was the first time Denny had ever used my true name, *Ahn Tsah Hye-gyah-daw*—She Knows the Way.

Chapter Twenty-Five

Alone, I walked back to the wall of trees. Smoke was still wafting up from the sage bundle Denny had used earlier. Without hesitation, I stepped into the smoke to purify myself once again before starting my trek to the ledge on top of the closest pinnacle in the Ghost Mountains. My exchange with Buck had brought on too many negative emotions.

As I washed with the sage smoke, I tried to release my worries for the agency, Grandpa, and the Tribe. I physically opened, with my arms stretched to the sky above, and mentally released my spirit to the wind—opened myself to discovery. I stepped out of the pungent smoke and sent a silent prayer with the drifting smoke upward to *Daw'Kee*, the Creator, this time asking guidance in finding the truth.

I faced the Parallel Forest. Everything seemed fresh, washed by the earlier rain and wind. Before stepping into the dark woods, I took a moment to listen to the animals as my grandpa had trained us. Birds gossiped in the canopy above; squirrels leapt from branch to branch; insects chirped in competition with each other; the cicadas' constant high-pitch rattle annoyed. Everyone in the neighborhood was out, talking and playing, no danger in sight or sound.

Yet my neck tingled, right to the bottom of my skull. I continued facing the forest, sure I was being watched. I slowly faced the four directions, pretending to offer another prayer skyward. I used this motion to look about for anyone or any animal watching me. There were no slow movements, no sudden quieting or startled squawks.

The chilled feeling of being stalked passed. Animals of all kinds and sizes continued to chatter. I had felt like I was being watched, but the nearby animals said otherwise.

I shook my unease off and looked up into the blinding sun to note its location in the sky. It was going to be dark in the Parallel Forest with the trees' overgrown canopies blocking most sunlight, but there would be shafts of light breaking through occasionally. I could use these light shafts to determine direction if I strayed from my path.

I oriented myself while facing the Parallel Forest and the Ghost Mountains. Beyond was due south. I squinted upward; it was getting to be late afternoon. The sun was headed west, leaving light shafts that fell to the east. It took me a moment to reason it out, but I got there. I needed to keep the light shafts on my left side, my east side, to stay southbound.

I took two steps in, before I stopped and returned. I rushed back to Denny's truck, grabbed a water canteen and the truck keys. Denny, like the country boy he was, had left his keys in the ignition of the unlocked truck.

I returned to the forest and marched in. By the fifth step I was engulfed in a veil of charcoal murkiness that left everything colorless in shifting shadows, with occasional shafts of light slashing through. The darkness seemed to mute the birds' chatter while amplifying the clicks and chirps of various small, dark-loving mammals and insects. The shroud of dark did nothing to mute the annoying screech of nearby cicadas.

I walked in a well-trodden six-foot path between the rows of cedars. This should be a straight march to the other side of the Forest.

A sharp squawk from above pulled my eyes upward while I continued moving forward. I scanned for signs of movement in the dark canopied sky and promptly bounced into a cedar. I landed on my bruised knees. The red dirt provided a soft landing in between the trees. The canopies overhead had kept the rain out, so it wasn't muddy. But it still left a dusty red mark on each knee. I brushed clinging dirt off my already mud-stained jeans and continued through the forest.

As I moved forward, my mind shifted inward, rehashing Denny's accusation of Georgie as the likely killer. Denny based this claim on what he said was "the fact" that Georgie had been in the house alone before I arrived to find the body. But that wasn't a fact—Georgie was never alone in the house. Someone did go past her in the hallway. That wasn't based on just what Georgie claimed, but what I'd seen when Denny left me at the house.

When I'd first gotten to Grandpa's house, in the middle of that thunderstorm, I'd seen someone leave the house. I closed my eyes, to picture the dark figure that disappeared into the timberline. No matter how hard I tried, I couldn't put a specific person to the shape. It had been as dark as night. We were both bent, struggling into the wind, rain, and mud of the storm. But I had no doubt that person was the killer, who had probably taken Wilson's life just minutes earlier.

The thought stopped me cold. A hot coal formed in my stomach, threatening. I took a deep breath and tried to get control of the burning anger. I exhaled, blowing the hate away. I could not have it here, or now. I took in another breath, felt the positive energy from the forest-rich air, then released it and pushed the anger away. I opened my arms, tried to clear my mind. Only after I resolved to find the real thief and killer, to get justice for Wilson, was I ready to travel on.

Eyes on the dwindling path, I returned to my march. Light shafts shifted and wavered below as an occasional breeze rippled through the leaves above. The breeze was suffocated before reaching ground level. Here, the air was still and muggy.

I pushed damp hair from my eyes. Timing was beginning to come together in my mind. After my aborted chase after the killer, I'd gone into the house. This would have been about the same time that Georgie discovered the body in the no-no room and heard me stomping around, as she claimed.

I was surprised Georgie hadn't come running out of the room screaming after finding the body. She must have been afraid I was the killer, returning to the scene of the crime. Which explained why Georgie hid in the closet when I came into the room and discovered the body myself. And why she ran out of the room before I found her.

I nodded and kept moving forward, staying between the rows of cedar. The trail was less traveled here. I bit my lip as I considered. I might have caught Georgie, if Anna, and then later Nita, hadn't barged in. A flare of anger ignited when I remembered Nita already dressed for the meeting at Red Buffalo Hall and her obvious glee in Grandpa being accused of stealing the peace medal. I released a deep breath, pushing the anger down again.

Absently, I noted a lizard skitter into the brush. My thoughts moved on. Yep, the person I'd chased outside Grandpa's house had to have been the killer escaping. That left Georgie out because she was in the house. There was relief in that. She was a heartbreaker, but not a killer.

My eyes remained on my feet, to avoid another fall. The trail was overgrown and narrow. I had been sure Buck was the killer. He had fit so well—but it wasn't Buck. His reaction to hearing of his grandfather's death was too real. Buck was doing our People, the Tribe, wrong. He'd helped Gerald steal from his family, friends, and tribe members. But Buck couldn't fake that raw emotion. Buck wasn't the killer.

I shook my head. Who did that leave? The air was thick with the combined smell of still earth, vegetation, and trees. I pushed sweat-damp curls from my face.

The two oil boys obviously hadn't done it. They'd stayed outside, looking in through the windows. If they had entered, the house would have been a mess. But there was Anna. I had found her earring at the fracking office.

I could see a bit of light ahead in the distance. Maybe another mile to reach the end of the Parallel Forest.

Anna? How did she fit into this puzzle? Could she be the fracking boss or just in for a cut of the profits? For Denny's sake, I pushed her out of my mind . . . for now. That left Gerald.

Something scampered from the path and dived into deep brush. My feet moved as my mind kept processing possibilities.

Gerald. He seemed to be behind everything bad that had been going on. Gerald had gotten Buck to scout and steal—yes, it was stealing when you paid next to nothing for Kiowa family regalia and treasures from those who were barely hanging on financially. Especially if a nudge was added to any who resisted selling their family treasures. Gerald's TribalVision Gallery must be making quite a profit. Buy at a real steal, sell high.

I shuffled on, heard a low snort. My thoughts continued to flow.

Interesting that Gerald had returned my suitcase. I was sure he had taken it to search when I'd left it beside the truck in his gallery's parking lot. But why think *I* had the peace medal?

Bushes rustled. I wondered about the peace medal. Having all three of the largest Jefferson peace medals as a complete set must be worth a small fortune. Worth enough for Gerald to pay Buck a reward and give back to the Crow family the *Koitsenko* sash and lance. That's a big motive for murder.

I stopped to take a sip of water. I held it in my mouth and swished the water around before swallowing. And considered: Was Gerald willing to kill for the third Jefferson peace medal? I wasn't sure of the answer. Gerald was a thief, but did that make him a killer? I capped the canteen, slung it over my shoulder, and returned to the trail.

The tree canopy had let the rain through in places. The damp red dirt was forming a slippery claylike mud in spots. As I maneuvered around the slick clay, I wondered how Gerald had discovered the Kiowa peace medal. At some point, the precious peace medal must have been stored and forgotten. Who did Gerald work with inside the Complex? The thought brought me to an abrupt halt: Denny had said Anna oversaw the museum. Was that it? Anna and Gerald were working together? Was one a killer—or both?

A welcomed breeze broke through the stillness. It urged me onward.

There was no hard evidence pointing to the killer. Nothing indicated why Wilson had been killed. I didn't know if the death was over the peace medal or fracking or something else entirely—or if someone had thought it was my grandfather they were bashing over the head.

The path dwindled to an animal trail. I followed it. Bushes shook on one side, and the air had a thick, musky smell to it.

Grandpa would have the answers. I blew a breath out in relief. I sure was glad Grandpa had not been home. It could have been him—

All thoughts flew from my mind as I plunged to the ground. I had been too preoccupied with murder to notice an exposed root on the path. It brought me to my knees—again. My jeans were a mess from the mud of the storm earlier, and now red dirt was staining the knees.

I swung the canteen forward. The water was cool inside. I drank deeply. As I screwed the lid back on the canteen, the hair on my neck stood on end. I felt watched.

It was quieter here. Everything muffled except for the persistent buzz of those cicadas. So close I could feel the vibration—my phone!

I answered to hear Marcus immediately launch into a cheerful, "Yo, wanted to let you know the texturing with movement idea is working. I'm cooking a piece now that I think will actually add a nice touch to our intro."

The pure joy in Marcus's voice was a welcome light in this murky forest and my dark thoughts. I absorbed the positive vibes and told him, "Great news. I appreciate hearing it."

Marcus laughed. "Hate to admit it, I might be glad Richard started whining at the last minute . . . it looks *sooo* good." He sang out, "*Sooo* good!"

When he paused to catch his breath, I dived in. "How's the rest of the graphics doing?"

"We're moving along. By tonight all graphic elements should be completed." He quickly added, "You won't see the logo treatment. That won't be ready until tomorrow."

Something shuffled to the side. I looked about but saw nothing. Feeling lighter, I got to my feet and continued my trek, talking while I walked. "Sounds like everything is moving along. Good job, Marcus."

I could hear the smile in Marcus' voice. "Yeah, it came together. Tag-teaming the client with Bernie helped—a lot. Speaking of whom . . ." There was a shuffling noise as the phone was handed around.

I liked hearing that Marcus was happy working with Bernie and the client. It was their first time without me there, dictating all the moves.

Bernie's cheerful "Hey, hey, hey. How are things?" kept my positive vibe going. I picked up my pace as I told her, "Not bad. I'll be seeing my grandpa soon." My gaze went up through the thinning canopy to catch a glimpse of a granite pinnacle.

I turned the topic to the client and job at hand. "Sounds like Marcus is happy with how things are coming along. What do you think?"

Bernie would let me know if all was well, or not. I'd spent so many hours at the agency, and she was the one I saw the most in my daily life.

Bernie answered, "The client and Marcus are happy. We are slightly under budget. Who could ask for more?" I heard clicking as her hands flew across a keyboard, typing as she talked.

I told her, "Sounds too good to be true. I'm relieved you are there keeping things together." I had to add, "And watching the bottom line. Are we on schedule?"

"Let's see, we have a crew of three working through today, and one tonight on the keynote address, and all creative is in final reviews. You should see those as they finish through the night. I want to have as much in front of you for your approval before anything goes to the client." With an obvious smile in her voice, she added, "I know how you are."

Bernie and Marcus were in a good place. I was glad they had called to share their happiness with the show's progress.

She went on, "Tomorrow afternoon we'll have the client's first stage rehearsal. I'll be there to take notes, like you would—no worries. I kinda enjoy working directly with the client."

I sent a smile to her. "You're going to take over my job."

A giggle escaped before she answered, "Not possible. I'm efficient, but I don't have that final magic you sprinkle at the end." Bernie's voice turned serious. "Speaking of the end, you are going to be here for the final rehearsal and the show, right?"

A blue jay squawked. I looked up from watching my marching feet. I felt I had to watch them to avoid another fall. With my head up, I could see larger swatches of light filtering through the branches above. There was an end to the forest in sight.

I answered, "That's the plan."

Bernie let out a deep breath. "Good. We're doing fine, but . . ." Her voice wavered.

I stopped and gave Bernie my full attention. "But what, Bernie? What aren't you telling me?" Hair bristled on my neck.

"I've told you everything, it's just . . ." She hesitated, then finished in a rush: "Well, it's too quiet here. After all the uproar Thomas started this morning, the silence scares me. I much prefer his roar than this quiet." All keyboard tapping stopped. "This is scary quiet."

"Hey, don't worry about Thomas. He's my problem." My jaw tightened with the thought. I was going to face our partnership issues when I returned. "Your focus is the client. Keep Richard happy. *'Don't worry, be happy,'*" I sang at her in my cracked voice. The forced cheer left me feeling better. Maybe things could work out with Thomas.

Bernie said, "Yeah, easy for you to say. You're visiting family on a surprise vacation." Keyboard tapping resumed; Bernie was back at work.

Oh, Bernie, if you only knew nearly slipped out before I forced it back and instead said, "Yep, Bernie, I am having quite a family adventure."

I hung up, smiling for the few seconds it took to tuck the phone into my pocket. The tingle at the base of my skull was back. This time, I could hear it. The silence was screaming at me. It was scary quiet here too . . . until it wasn't.

There was a snort and a grunt before a massive brown mottled blur came barreling through the trees at me. I had no time to think. I ran. I zigged and I zagged. I kept putting trees between me and the bristling beast from hell behind me.

Chapter Twenty-Six

I had to stay on my feet. If I fell, the huge boar would be on me in an instant, its six-inch razor-sharp tusks ripping into me. Its hooves pounded the ground. Seized with sudden panic over falling, I looked at my feet. Immediately stumbled. Caught myself and righted. The curved tusks got closer; the boar's heaving breath louder. I put on a burst of speed.

The boar's grunts sounded gleeful and too close. It slobbered in anticipation of a fall. I kept moving, slapping low-hanging branches out of my face. Tried to think.

Wild boars are fast, aggressive, unpredictable, and smart. Bad characteristics to have in a nearly six-hundred-pound beast right behind you. The boar was too close for me to get up a tree safely. If I slowed, it would have me for lunch. The thought chilled me, kept my feet pounding.

The beast's breath sounded like laughter. It taunted me.

I scanned the ground ahead, spotted what I had to do and zigged. The boar's hot breath followed. It was getting closer. Fear spurred me on. I zagged, gained some space between me and the tusks. The beast grunted its frustration, shook its head and kept coming. Its split hooves spit up clods of red dirt behind us. I plowed ahead.

My breathing was coming in gasps. I was tiring. There was one chance. I couldn't think of anything else and wouldn't last much longer. I stole a backward glance; I shouldn't have. The boar smiled at me.

I faced forward, determined, heaving for breath.

One chance.

As I ran, I shifted the swinging canteen from my back and slipped the strap over my head. I grasped the strap firmly in my hand and timed my steps, willing myself not to look back at the slobbering boar. Looking would only slow me, and I knew the beast was on my heels. I could smell it now. It stank of death.

This had to work.

After two quick stutter steps, I made an abrupt U-turn, putting a tree between me and the rushing boar. As it slowed to follow my sudden turn, I swung the canteen, hitting the boar's exposed flank. It squealed from the unexpected attack and retreated a few feet, shaking its head in disbelief.

I took advantage of the boar's retreat to grab a solid-looking three-foot branch I had spotted while running. It had a good heft to it. I knew the canteen had not hurt the boar; its skin was like armor topped with wire bristle for hair. This branch wouldn't do much more against the boar's protective hide, but a well-placed hit on its most tender spot would . . . *could* . . . I shook my head. Might.

Had to.

I looked up in time to see the boar pawing the ground. Slobber swung from its sharp tusks. Its yellow eyes drilled into me. For a moment, I froze, staring into the boar's calculating eyes. There was a brain working behind its fury. This beast was hunting me.

The realization chilled me to the bone.

The boar never broke eye contact. It came at me full speed.

Its yellow eyes held me.

I calculated.

The boar claimed me as prey. It let loose a triumphant squeal as it charged at me. The screech rooted me to the spot. Goose bumps broke out across my body.

The beast lowered its head, prepared for a kill lunge. Its yellow eyes stayed on me, staring its cold satisfaction. Midstride, the boar shifted power to its rear legs for the takedown—of me.

I held.

Only at the last second, after the boar launched, did I break eye contact and step to the side, exposing the tree directly behind me. The boar was committed. It was midair, too late to stop. Flecks of spittle sprayed my forearm as it barreled past my sidestep and rammed into the tree.

The tree shook from the boar's mis-aimed charge. So did I.

The boar bounced off the tree. It shook its head, spraying snot and slime from nose and mouth. Before it could charge again, before I let fear stop me, I stepped forward into the best fastball swing of my life. Using the branch, I delivered a hit dead center on the boar's tender nose. Its beady eyes popped wide open; the beast screeched. Its knees buckled; first the front, then the back collapsed. The boar went to the ground with an abbreviated squeal-grunt.

Continuing my forward movement past the temporarily downed boar, I spotted the dented canteen and slung it over my shoulder. I ran on without thought, putting as much distance as possible between me and the boar. My hands shook, but I held the branch at the ready. I ran with the branch in hand way beyond the point where the boar was out of sight and hearing. I'm not sure when the branch slipped away.

Slowly the forest animals began to speak again. The birds were first to return, followed by squirrels and some other small forest floor–dwelling mammals that skittered from place to place. Still my heart pounded. Adrenaline pulsed through me, and my hands trembled. Finally, I stopped, leaned forward, and was sick.

I walked away from the mess, staggered, and stopped again, leaning on a tree. The rough bark felt good—real. I pulled water from the canteen, rinsed my mouth, and spit it out. I closed my eyes and tried to center myself. I listened. I could hear no signs of the boar. Just a forest at play again after a minor near-death disruption.

Seconds seemed like hours while I took a moment to gather myself.

Before moving, I looked about. I was surrounded by tree after tree, all aligned as if waiting for an order to march. No wind moved through the trees down here, though a gentle breeze moved the branches above, adding a rhythmic undertone to the forest melody. Light shafts shot in random display. I was no longer sure in which direction south lay. The trees closed in on me.

My heart quickened. I sucked in quick, shallow breaths and looked about wildly. I didn't know which way to go. My stomach churned, and I jumped at the snap of a twig.

Before panic won, I took control. Forced myself to deepen my breath, release it slowly, and repeat. The slow breathing gave me time to think, time to listen and feel comfortable in my surroundings. Time to remember my early lessons. Panic kills.

I got control. Heard the chatter around me. There was no sense of danger in the animal conversations. I used my shirt to wipe sweat from my face, scanned the ground, and found a relatively straight six-inch stick. I planted the stick in the center of a light shaft. The stick immediately cast its own shadow, letting me know where the sun and south were located.

I let out a deep breath of relief. Took another moment to listen before I headed south toward the Ghost Mountains again. This time, I stayed alert to the animal conversations around me. I would heed warning squawks or sudden silences. I would respect my surroundings.

After ten minutes of mindful marching south, sounds and light brightened. The canopy above thinned to reveal the ragged tops of the Ghost Mountains. Faces of the Ancient Ones could be seen in the shadows cast on the jagged gray rocks. It is said that the Ancient Ones' spirits dwelled within the mountains, providing wisdom and healing to those that seek. Medicine Creek has its beginning there, where the Ancient Spirits and their medicinal powers are the strongest.

One of our early Kiowa legends tells of a mother climbing to the top of a jagged peak with her sick child. The child died before reaching the healing source waters of Medicine Creek. Hearing the cries of the distressed mother, the Ancient Ones melded the mother holding her child into the rocks, bonding them together while freeing their spirits to windwalk above forever.

I easily spotted the mother-cradling-her-child rock formation from here. I was too far east, but not that far from the trail

I wanted. It was a relief to see that I would be out of the Parallel Forest soon. A deep breath escaped. It wouldn't be soon enough.

The sunlight felt refreshing when I broke free of the Parallel Forest into the rolling mixed grasses of the prairie. I stood for a moment, soaking in the fresh air on my face and the sun's heat on my body. Sounds were ratcheted up several octaves as other lively animal voices were added to the chorus. My senses celebrated the awakening.

I knew I should hurry, yet I felt compelled to experience my surroundings. The land demanded attention. This was Kiowa country as it had been for my ancestors—rough, wild, and harshly beautiful.

The prairie seemed to dance and sing. Its three grasses, each a different color and height, flowed in rhythm to the orchestra of animal sounds. It was easy to see how the Kiowa Grass Dance had emerged. A Grass Dancer's steps interlaced and wove a pattern of strength and flexibility across the arena floor while the long strands of the dancer's shawl replicated the soft flowing movement of the prairie grasses. It was hypnotic.

Free of the forest's canopy, I was able to look up and soak in the ragged peaks of the Ghost Mountains. An eagle's shrill call pierced the air as it soared in the blue sky above the jagged gray rocks that formed the faces of the Ancient Ones. The earlier thunderstorm had left water streaming from a gray-streaked, rock-formed forehead to a granite nose, bouncing from rock to rock as it traveled downhill toward a distant lake.

Some places on Earth are special. They have an energy that can be felt. This was such a place. The air around the Ghost Mountains buzzed with ancient power.

This place felt spiritual to me. It always had. If any place could be, this was my church.

In the early 1700s, the Kiowas had been forced from their home country around Yellowstone by the Sioux—who had been pushed from their eastern homeland by invading Europeans. After a long and difficult trek, the Kiowas found the Wichita Mountains and knew this land was meant to be home. *Daw'Kee*, the Creator showed them the truth of it.

Kiowa spiritual leaders could see that the mountains were ancient, gnawed low to the ground with age and bent with wisdom. But it was the naturally formed, round, orange-red cobblestones scattered around the Wichita Mountains that confirmed this was sacred land.

Round was the sacred shape of the Creator. Early Kiowas knew this from observing their surroundings: the rising sun was round; the shining moon was round. They could see that Mother Earth was round with every rounded horizon line. When twisters spun through, Kiowas recognized that the most powerful wind on Mother Earth was round. In daily life they saw the power of the circle; trees grew round, birds built round nests, and all animals slept curled in a circle.

To honor *Daw'Kee*, Kiowas lived in round tipis and arranged their homes in camps of circles, never in lines. The rare round cobblestones surrounding the Ghost Mountains were an obvious sign to the Kiowas that the search for a home was over. This was meant to be Kiowa country. The land had been touched by *Daw'Kee*, the Creator.

It always struck me how right the old Kiowa leaders had been about the land before me. The Wichita Mountains are ancient. They are among the oldest ranges on Earth, the oldest in North America. They were formed over five hundred million years ago. Through the ages, the Wichita Mountains' original chiseled peaks had been worn down to jagged hill tops and boulder-covered domes.

The sacred round cobblestones scattered through the area are found naturally in only four other places in the world. Unlike river-formed, slick round rocks, the cobblestone's unique pressure-pressed, rough, circular shapes were formed deep within the Earth. Early volcanic activity forced the round rocks out to the surface. Cobblestones are the only naturally formed round rocks that come from within Mother Earth.

I breathed in deeply. The air felt rich with nutrients for my spirit. I knew I needed to hurry, yet all urgency left me here in the hypnotic rhythm of the land. A distant bird's caw broke the trance.

Grandpa was waiting.

I moved through the grasses, finding an animal trail headed in the direction I wanted. With each step, I stayed alert, watching, listening, smelling, and feeling my surroundings. Not touching, but sensing for movements in the energy force around the sacred land.

It felt good to be here.

Thoughts of murder slipped away as I stayed attuned with the animals and land around me. I stayed watchful moving through the rolling prairie grass as it rose toward the tumbled boulder field that surrounded the Ghost Mountains. The boulder field was the final barrier to the stunted peaks above.

I stopped at the edge of the boulder field, taking a moment to turn and enjoy the view below. The prairie grasses of yellows and greens were splattered with vivid orange and reds of native wildflowers. Not far below, a herd of buffaloes grazed as they made slow progress toward a cottonwood and willow tree–shaded lake beyond.

My thoughts drifted to a game Grandpa had played with me as I got older. He and I would come out here alone—together. *The buffalo game.*

We would find a herd of buffaloes. Starting together, we would disappear into the grasses to see who could get closest to the herd without disturbing them—or getting trampled.

Grandpa always won. He moved with the wind through the slowly shifting grasses until he disappeared, only to suddenly materialize amid the herd, talking to the Grandfather Buffalo, always the oldest and biggest. After a short conversation, Grandpa would disappear again into the grasses, to emerge at my side minutes later. All before I even crawled beyond the herd's sentry bulls. Grandpa did this with no visible disturbance from the rest of the herd.

I moved my gaze from the buffalo herd below, up beyond the boulders to a jagged top, where I was sure Grandpa sat. Knowing him, he probably sensed my arrival. My lips moved upward into a smile at the thought of seeing Grandpa soon.

Above the boulder field was the false top of the peak. Infrequent hikers thought they had reached the highest point possible when they reached the flat top surrounded by four jagged peaks. My grandfather's grandmother, *Sawpole Gyah*, Owl Talker, had been the first to find the sacred ledge above, the closest point to *Daw'Kee*'s ear she could reach.

Sawpole Gyah was shown the passage to the secret ledge by an owl. In her first vision quest atop the partially covered ledge, she was told that this spot was sacred, a gift to her family forevermore. A powerful place for introspection, a place to find the Creator within, a place to seek answers. *Sawpole Gyah* was told her descendants would always find answers there. All I wanted was to find Grandpa there.

A chill down my back pulled me from my thoughts.

Instantly, I knew something was not right. Birds had quieted. No warning squawks yet, but something was wrong. There was a heavy silence in the immediate area.

I turned to see a buffalo bull the size of a Honda Accord walk casually along the timberline. He snapped low-hanging branches like match sticks. The huge buffalo was woolly, with a gray-dusty look to his massive brown coat, but the bull was large and powerful and . . . mad. He blew snot and heat from his nostrils to prove my point.

The old buffalo bull noticed me. He blew out another hot breath and aimed himself in my direction. He didn't saunter casually; he walked with purpose toward me.

I stood there in awe. Even at a distance, he was huge and so beautiful.

And getting closer. Quickly.

I tried to make eye contact, to talk to the buffalo as I had seen Grandpa do. But the old buffalo was not having any of it. He lowered his head and increased his speed toward me. Slime slid down his chin to his swinging goatee as he continued coming in my direction.

He was fast. Faster than expected.

At first, I slow-walked backward, watching the magnificent animal coming toward me. I knew the boulder field was in range. All I had to do was get up into the boulders to be safely out of reach. When the buffalo increased his speed and determination, I sped up my back-pedaling and aimed myself toward the closest boulders.

My eyes remained fixed on the oncoming old buffalo. I knew he was dangerous, could easily maim or kill me, but I had always been in awe of the magnificent animals. Buffaloes, like Kiowas, had been hunted to near extinction but still had found ways to survive. As a child, I pestered my great-aunts to tell me the early stories of Kiowa life entwined with the buffalo nation.

I glanced back to note my position to the boulder field. Still about a hundred yards away. I made an adjustment and kept backing toward the boulders. Once on them, I would be safe from the rushing buffalo. Its hooves would not find easy purchase on the boulders.

My eyes returned to the nearing old buffalo. Like in the red light, green light game of childhood, while my back had been turned, the buffalo had gotten much closer than expected. It startled me. My feet tangled. I stumbled and fell to my butt.

The old buffalo quickened its pace and shortened the gap between us. He snorted his delight.

The ground trembled. I joined in.

I scrambled to my knees and fast crawled toward the boulders. I dared a look over my shoulder as I got my feet under me. The buffalo was way too close. Dark eyes of coal bore down on me.

I sprinted up into the boulder field. I didn't stop. I moved from boulder to boulder, climbed upward until I finally felt safe. Then I turned to look back. The huge old buffalo bull glared up at me, snorting and stomping in a rage.

I was glad I was up on the boulders, beyond his reach. Down below in the prairie, the bull could reach speeds of thirty-five miles an hour. Fortunately, his hoofs had no grip on the granite surfaces I planned to stay on.

I wondered why the buffalo bull was up here rather than heading to the shady lake with the others in the herd. He was such a massive bull and so dusty colored, he must be very old; perhaps he had been vanquished from the herd by a younger, stronger bull. That would explain why the old buffalo had an attitude.

The pinnacle's false top was just a few boulder leaps away; then through the hidden tunnel to the ledge above and to Grandpa—

My thoughts were wrenched back to the present.

A human shriek pierced the air.

Chapter Twenty-Seven

It was followed by a second scream, which ended abruptly.

I turned about, slid back down the rock face. Leapt from one boulder to another. Low, intense snorting grunts came from below. My lungs burning, I came over the top of a lower ridge, glanced, and gasped. I could see the old buffalo bull's monstrous dark head and small beady eyes glaring toward a still figure below.

The man let loose another shriek, which only seemed to irritate the buffalo further. The buffalo bellowed, raised his tail, lowered his head, and charged. Gerald stood frozen, soundlessly opening and closing his mouth as the charging buffalo bore down on him.

Time seemed to move in slow motion as I quickly slid down the rocky ridge. Without thought, I hurdled from the boulders down into the path of the furious buffalo bull. My heart thundered. The old buffalo barreled onward.

I waved my hands, forced sounds out of frozen vocal chords, and jumped about. I thought I could turn the buffalo away from trampling the now rapidly back-pedaling Gerald.

I thought wrong.

Tremors ran through my body as the buffalo thundered on toward us. Hot spittle flew from its slobbering lips. It was so close, I choked on the thick, gamey, earth smell of the buffalo. The ground trembled under the buffalo's stampeding feet. He wouldn't stop.

Gerald and I were going to be trampled.

A bellowed order sounded from the side.

The old buffalo pulled up abruptly, leaving raised ridges of red dirt. He let out a protesting bellow that sprayed snot across my arm. I dared not move, as the buffalo's heaving breath was hot on my face. It stank of heat and rotted grasses. I stayed still. Not quite sure what to do next. Too in awe to be afraid, but too afraid to move.

Gerald ran toward the timberline. The buffalo's massive head turned, slinging drool, watching the retreating Gerald. I felt each of his exhaled angry breaths, snorts of frustration.

Another snort came from the side, just out of my sight. The old buffalo seemed to calm. His head rose and his tail swung from side to side, slapping flies. He shifted, turned to look where the other snorts had come from.

Involuntarily, my hand crept forward. The buffalo bull was so close to me, I could reach out. I tried to stop myself, but my hand took control. It reached. My fingers curled around the buffalo's matted fur, so thick. His head swung my way; the buffalo glared through a single black eye. My fingers let go of the coarse curls. My arm dropped to my side. I looked down, unable to face the buffalo.

Another bellow sounded. Closer. This one demanded immediate attention.

The old buffalo turned, shuffled a few steps to the side, and looked directly into my grandfather's deep brown eyes. Grandpa let out a soft snort before moving to a chant thanking the old buffalo bull. He told the buffalo what a beautiful beast he was, how much this simple old man appreciated that Grandfather Buffalo had found his wandering granddaughter. As Grandpa sang directly to the attentive buffalo, his hands flew in the old sign language. To me, Grandpa signaled *Away, now.*

I looked at the buffalo snorting a reply to my grandfather. It towered over Grandpa, yet the two seemed to communicate. Buffalo stomped his foot in response to Grandpa's snort. Were they talking?

I shook my head to clear it.

The two exchanged agreeable grunts. I stumbled backward, moving away from the conversation. It felt like I was intruding on old friends.

Grandfather Buffalo noticed me backing away. He turned his giant head to examine me again with a single eye. He considered, swished his tail, flicked a biting fly away from his rump, then turned his full attention back to Grandpa. I was dismissed.

I looked toward the timberline where I had last seen Gerald headed. He stood behind a tree, peering out. I trotted to him. He was bent at the waist, breathing hard when I arrived.

Between gasps Gerald got out, "A charging buffalo . . . who puts buffaloes where people are walking?" Gerald's sunburned scalp peeked through his yellow-blond strands. Then he straightened. "Geez, did you see the size of that thing!" His eyes were wide.

I remained silent. I was struggling to get my breath and hoped Gerald couldn't hear my pounding heart. I didn't want to admit how scared I'd been. I needed some time.

A nervous titter escaped from Gerald. "Your grandpa oughta take that show on the road." He stood there shaking his head. "Man, that was something . . ." He trailed off at my continued silence, his face bright red under streaks of sweat and dirt.

I wasn't sure I could control my voice yet, so I held it. Took in another deep breath and looked at Gerald, then beyond. My attention moved to the two old ones conversing in the distance. In the late afternoon glare, both seemed to have similar dust-colored manes. Shadows shifted, made it appear as if Grandpa put his arm around Grandfather Buffalo's shoulders to console him. I rubbed my eyes, cleared them. The two stood apart, snorting.

My silence made Gerald uncomfortable. He shuffled, kicked the dirt with the pointy toe of his ruined yellow snakeskin boot. "Guess I owe you a thanks." His eyes tried to catch mine.

I finally broke my silence. "Gerald, what are you doing here?" I made no attempt to hide my disapproval of his presence.

Gerald spotted a knee-high boulder and sat. "I decided on a hike." Now he avoided my eyes as he removed one of his battered snakeskin boots, dropped it to the ground, and rubbed his toes through paper-thin socks. A sigh escaped from him.

I didn't push for the truth, just let the silence grow. Most people felt an urge to fill the void. My gaze drifted from Gerald to where we had left Grandpa and the old buffalo. At a distance,

Grandpa seemed to be listening intently to Grandfather Buffalo. He offered encouraging nods during the exchange.

A loud moan brought my attention back to Gerald as he forced his tender foot into the narrow, pointy-toed boot. Foot jammed in place, Gerald lifted his head and made eye contact with me. "What's it to you where I go?"

I didn't speak at first. I let him watch my eyes slowly move from his pointy-toed, slick-soled cowboy boots up to his open collar with the once-yellow tie hanging torn and loose, then slowly over to binoculars with a cracked lens swinging from his shoulder. His eyes watched me take in his inappropriate hiking attire. I gave it a beat before I looked directly into Gerald's eyes, "You're not dressed for a hike out here. You—no, *we*—were nearly killed."

"This hike wasn't planned." His face twisted. As if he couldn't hold it in, he added, "The Crows were supposed to stick with you."

Carefully, I touched his broken binoculars. "You've been watching me." This explained my consistent feeling of being watched and how he had found me here.

Gerald returned a flat smile. "Yeah, so what? I'm here because you're here, and that darn Wilson stopped following you. I don't know what you did with him and his worthless grandson." Gerald eyed me closely. "Pretty good show, watching you and Buck. What did you say to get him to leave?" He tried to put warmth into his smile. It didn't work.

Instead of an answer, I followed with a question. "What do you want?"

This time Gerald's smile reached his cold blue eyes. "You know what: the peace medal." He watched for a response.

My gaze drifted through the timber back toward where we had left Grandpa and the old buffalo. Grandpa still seemed to be listening intensely to Grandfather Buffalo. The buffalo's pointed goatee seemed to quiver with indignation in the telling.

I came back to Gerald. "What makes you think I have the peace medal?"

"Wilson said so." Gerald's cold face changed to disgust; he dug his hands into his pockets. "Wilson was supposed to get your suitcases and the peace medal first thing this morning."

I thought of Wilson rushing out of the airport with both of my bags. He must have been disappointed when I caught up with him before he left in his truck. Their desire for my luggage sure explained my strange morning.

Gerald jangled loose change in his pockets.

I cocked my head at him. "You." The jangling stopped. I went on, "You locked me in the storage closet at McClung's." I remembered the man standing outside the storage closet, jingling coins in his pocket before trapping me inside it.

I watched Gerald thinking now while I went on, "At the time I thought it was Buck's grandfather, but it was you who trapped me in the storage closet."

The coin jangling started again, and a true smile lit Gerald's face. "That was pretty funny. I just thought of it, you know, spur of the moment . . . and it would have worked beautifully." Here the smile dropped, and his eyes went hard. "If that Crow clown had gotten your messenger bag to search . . . everything would have gone as planned. We'd have the medal already."

As if remembering, he added, "Of course, I would have returned the peace medal to the Kiowa Tribe once I had it."

I shook my head. "You and the Crows wasted your time. I don't have the peace medal."

"That's become painfully apparent." Gerald looked as if I'd disappointed him. "Wilson had bad info that led me to a wrong conclusion."

I threw this at him: "You offered Buck's grandfather the Crow family's *Koitsenko* sash and lance in exchange for the peace medal."

Gerald showed no surprise. "Sure, that's why Wilson stuck to you. How'd you shake him?"

Did that question mean Gerald didn't know that Wilson was dead? If he didn't know, he couldn't be the killer. Or was he only pretending to not know that Buck's grandfather was dead? I kept running into more questions than answers. I looked beyond Gerald to see that the buffalo had shifted position, blocking Grandpa from view.

Gerald went on, "When Wilson didn't show up with the medal, I went looking. Thought maybe you two made a deal—without me." At this he turned dead cold, blue eyes on me.

Chilled, I refused to let him know it. "I wouldn't give you the peace medal if I did have it." I faced Gerald to give him my best dirty look.

Gerald ignored my response and glowering look. "I saw you waving an envelope around and celebrating at Meers." His eyes locked on me. "I told Buck to get it from you. Instead, you sent him off crying."

This time I said nothing, just smiled at him. My eyes stayed hard.

Gerald's face distorted with anger. He moved toward me. "Where's the peace medal?"

I let anger carry me. Forgetting he might be a killer, I leaned into him to announce, *"I don't know."* We stood nose to nose. I was prepared: knees bent, fists balled.

He stepped back, clenched and unclenched his fists. "What were you waving around then?"

My nose curled as I declared the truth. "Junk mail with a note written on it."

He tried to stare me down, but I laughed at the attempt. Boiling emotions played across his face as I kept my eyes on his. Grandpa said the eyes would give away the next move. A body could feint, but the eyes told the tale.

He had another question for me: "Why are you out here?" His eyes slid from mine to look at our surroundings. Those eyes told me his heat was gone.

I wasn't ready to make nice. "I'm done answering your questions."

That seemed to amuse him. He nodded as if we had an agreement. "Yeah, you just go get the peace medal from your grandpa."

I took my eyes from Gerald to check on Grandpa. He was gone. They were gone.

Gerald didn't seem to notice my eyes scanning the prairie behind him. He went on unprompted, "May not be what I wanted at first, but I can work with it. Just bring the Jefferson peace medal to the Kiowa Complex tonight." As if thinking out loud, Gerald said, "Yeah, I'll announce the theft and its return. That will just about guarantee that I am the next curator of the Kiowa Museum." With a real smile, he added, "And that would raise the prestige of my gallery significantly. This will work."

I started shaking my head before Gerald was finished. "That is not happening, Gerald." I became more forceful. "Not when the People hear of what you and Buck have been up to—stealing regalia and artifacts from the poor—"

Gerald interrupted, "As I told you earlier, I purchase everything I sell in the gallery." He slowly enunciated, "I . . . am . . . not . . . a . . . thief." After a moment, he added, "I'm an opportunist. Always looking for the best deal." His salesman smile appeared.

I looked up into his dead eyes. "What kind of deal were you making for the peace medal?"

"I do pay a finder's fee for unique items—but I don't steal. I make fair offers. I have a receipt for everything in my shop." Gerald avoided giving a direct answer.

I scanned the horizon, looking for Grandpa.

Gerald tripped on a rock, splitting the sole from the snakeskin top of his boot. His boots were not made for hiking or, I suddenly realized, for running in the mud. And just like that, I knew he wasn't the figure I had seen running into the timberline at Grandpa's house. He couldn't be—not in those boots. He wasn't the killer.

But Gerald could still be behind it all.

I stopped searching for Grandpa and faced Gerald. "You expect me to believe you did not put Buck and his grandfather up to stealing the Kiowa's Jefferson peace medal to complete your set?"

"I don't care what you believe, but I can *honestly* say"—Gerald stopped to let a bit of a chuckle out—"I did not have those two Crow clowns steal the Kiowa Jefferson peace medal. I merely offered incentive—a finder's fee—to them." He continued with all trace of humor gone, "And that was after your grandfather's theft of the medal."

I couldn't resist responding to the taunt. "You know my grandfather did not—"

Gerald spoke over me. "Items like the Jefferson peace medal can be worth quite a small fortune to private buyers." He moved close. "Was that your grandfather's plan? To sell the peace medal himself?"

My fists clenched again. I should have left him to the charging buffalo.

Gerald chuckled before telling me, "Don't worry. I don't care—just show up with it tonight." Then his face turned wistful. "The art and items you have in your grandfather's house . . ." He smiled large and took a breath. "What I—*we*—could do . . ." He shook his head again. "Man, that stuff would give you enough to"—he stopped to think, then continued, "expand your business, or buy it outright . . . Never have to come here again . . . no questions. Think about it. Wilson said you had partner problems in your business."

It took no thought to answer him. "I am *not* interested in profiting from the rape of my heritage. You may be doing it legally, but you are stealing from people who have had everything else taken from them. Now you're purchasing their history as they struggle for existence."

My anger had no effect on him.

"I don't know what that fool Buck told you, but he greatly benefited from my finder fees. What he negotiated with people, how he got items . . . that's on him, not me."

Gerald dusted himself off. "I really have nothing more to say." He looked about, pulled a compass from his pocket, and determined north. Over his shoulder, he announced, "I need to get cleaned up before the meeting. That's in just a few hours." His loose boot sole flopped opened and closed with each departing step.

I stared at him and something he said struck me. *Cleaned up.* My brain locked on the thought, *cleaned up*. "Gerald, one more question."

He stopped, looked interested. "Go ahead."

"Was Buck your only go-between—the only one getting artifacts for you?"

Gerald looked at me, considered, then said, "That would be bad business. 'Course not. I would never rely on a single source." He seemed ready to stop there, took a step before turning back to confide, "In fact, Buck was small potatoes compared to my primary source."

"Who is your primary source?" The question burst out; I knew he would not answer.

"That I would rather not tell you. I do have a living to make . . . if by some chance I don't get the curator position." His face slid into his twisted smile. "So many treasures in that museum."

That was how he was going to make up for the loss of the peace medal. Gerald was going to raid the museum of all its forgotten treasures. I had to speak out against Gerald at the meeting.

Then another thought came to me. "Is it Anna?"

That stopped him. Gerald turned serious, eyed me angrily. "Stay out of my business. I'm giving you a pass because of the buffalo thing."

I returned his gaze. Watched for any tells in his eyes. He gave nothing away. Then, with a slight nod, he announced,

"Gotta go. I have a museum to save." He chuckled as he limped away.

I absently watched Gerald make his way toward the Parallel Forest. My mind kept coming back to *clean up*. What did it mean?

A distant hawk's screech pulled me back to reality. I looked to where I had left Grandpa and the buffalo. The prairie grasses waved in a breeze. There was no sign of the old buffalo or Grandpa.

Chapter Twenty-Eight

I moved quickly across the prairie and back up to the boulder field. I wasted no time scaling up the boulders, making it onto the flat top. Once there, I had to take a moment to walk to the edge, to look out at the horizon and the rolling land below. It was a beautiful sight. The wind was stronger here and had a refreshing coolness to it, a remnant of the earlier thunderstorm.

On the wind, I heard a faint heartbeat that slowly turned to a summoning note. I looked up to where the drumming was coming from. I couldn't see him from here—one of the advantages of the family ledge nestled in the jagged pinnacle above. But I knew Grandpa was on the ledge. No one else could make a drum talk like that.

I circled to a point where, twenty feet above me, two of the stunted pinnacle rock formations remained joined before separating several feet higher. Close to the mountainside, below the juncture, stood an old, gnarled oak tree—burnt by lightning on one side, flourishing with life on the other—surrounded by thick scrub brush.

The drum called me.

I dropped the dented canteen, emptied my pockets, removed my phone, earrings, and all other modern devices I had on me. I left the collection sitting near a blooming yucca plant. These items could not enter our sacred place.

I crawled up the scree to the scrub brush surrounding the old oak tree. Struggling not to slide back down, I circled the brush until I found signs of a rabbit's run burrowing through nature's barbed wall. There I bent and crawled through the scrub opening to reach the lightning-struck tree. The oak's silver-white, grooved bark with branches full of green leaves contrasted sharply with the opposite side's streaked, jagged black-and-white trunk with twisted charcoal limbs. The marked oak was key to reaching the ledge above.

I stood, brushed brambles from my shirt, jeans, and wild curls.

The drum's tempo increased.

Using the tree, I climbed up, limb by limb, to reach the granite wall's groove, created by the separation of the pinnacles. The climb was much more difficult than I remembered; too many hours at a desk had taken a toll on my fitness. I eyeballed the distance and made a leap from tree to mountainside.

The drum's summons was louder, more insistent here.

I nodded my answer, in beat.

Seated in the granite groove, I planted both feet on one pillar's wall and my back to the other. The fit was tight, but that made this easier, at first. With bent knees and my back wedged against the opposing wall, I pushed myself upward, slowly, between the two rough rock walls of the slot. I slid my feet up a few inches, then pushed, scooted my backside upward until leveled with my planted feet. Then rested. After each upward push, I rested.

Always, the drum called.

I leveraged through the squat climb, a few long feet, to reach the hidden ledge above. My out-of-shape knees, back, and lungs complained with each upward thrust. Strained thighs quivered.

With every push, the drum urged me on.

As I climbed, the gap in the separating pillars widened. At the point where the separation in the formation was too far apart for my wedge-climb to continue, I emerged onto a hidden ledge that ended in a hollow carved into the east-facing pinnacle. I flopped onto the ledge, rolled to my back, looked up into the now clear blue sky. I needed a minute to catch my breath. But I couldn't take it.

The drum made demands.

I rolled to my knees and pushed up, squinting through the afternoon's glare toward the shadowed entry of the hollow. There in the opening was Grandpa's hazy form. He sat crossed-legged in front of a small fire with billowing smoke. The fire outlined him while the veil of smoke blurred his lines. His hair looked like ribbons of blue and gray, flowing loose in the breeze.

Grandpa put the hand drum aside. He reached into his spirit bag—a red-dyed deerskin pouch that held the special medicines needed for one seeking answers. He sprinkled the fire with dried herbs that made it pop, spark, and crackle. Wisps of smoke snaked upward. Grandpa chanted softly. I could not make out his words, but the pungent scent reached me.

I entered properly from the east—in honor of our rising sun—and moved quietly inward to sit across from my grandfather. I did not speak. I sat with my eyes lowered while Grandpa fanned me in the purifying smoke. I breathed in deeply, cleansed my thoughts, exhaled all negative energy. I tried to place myself in a positive state, struggled to be patient.

I raised my eyes to look over at Grandpa. I knew not to speak—yet.

He had his ceremonial eagle-feather prayer fan. Made not from the expected black and white feathers of the bald eagle, but the cherished brown eagle feathers. Kiowas valued the brown tail feathers of this, the fastest and most courageous and cunning of birds. The brown eagle flew the highest of all eagles and was able to take precious words directly to *Daw'Kee*'s ear.

Grandpa looked upward, chanted while fanning the special-blend smoke toward me.

"Breathe, Granddaughter."

On command, I took a deep breath. The mixture smelled of earth—rich, ripe, and sharp. I held the breath, pulled it deep into my soul.

In his clipped rhythmic voice, Grandpa told me, "Breathe deep of life's breath. We share this breath with all our relatives of yesterday, today, and into the many tomorrows." He fanned more potent smoke my way. "We all share Mother Earth's breath; it circles the world." He said this in Kiowa, then repeated it in English, as he had always done for us as children.

Grandpa tossed another handful of mixed herbs onto the fire. I inhaled deeply, held the breath, thought of all that have shared this life-giving breath—from eight legs to two. For a moment, I pictured Wilson, who had taken his last breath only hours ago. In my mind's eye, he rode a blue spirit pony with a mane braided in red ribbons that flowed behind on the wind. I released the image and breath back to the world as

I whispered, "All my relations . . ."—the Kiowa formal closing of prayers, sending good thoughts out to all my relations that share Mother Earth, and directing extra energy toward the Crow family.

I took another breath in deeply and held it. Sparks rode the wind upward. I followed one up until it disappeared into the ribbons of rising smoke. I thought of following it further.

Grandpa pulled me back.

"Granddaughter, it took you a long time to arrive."

Frustration flared. "If you had picked me up at the airport—"

I was silenced with a fan full of smoke that left me coughing. Grandpa nodded in agreement with someone only he saw before he spoke again. "Grandchild, your quest demanded you find your way from the start." He gave me an all-knowing smile. "As you have done."

Grandpa silenced my protest with a wave of his eagle fan and another deep breath of spirit medicine smoke. As I held the shared breath, Grandpa fanned my head with his eagle feathers. His fan touched the top of my scalp, at the start of my head's natural spiral, where it is said our spirit enters and exits. With each feathered touch, my day flashed through my mind. Too quick to grasp. Yet telling . . .

Frustrations floated away. A peace settled.

Through the veil of smoke, Grandpa said, "You were slow, even with Grandfather Buffalo moving you along."

A smile erupted across my face. *"I touched a buffalo!"* My eyes glazed in memory of the stolen touch.

"Granddaughter," Grandpa gently scolded, "you further annoyed Grandfather Buffalo on your shared day of change."

I cocked my head at Grandpa. "Day of change. What do you mean?" Blue flames danced.

I wanted to get right to the Jefferson peace medal, fracking, and the murder, but tradition demanded that prayers and talk be completed before getting to business. Anything else would be rude. And rudeness in the Kiowa world was a harsh offense, usually resulting in a shutdown of all communications. I'd seen this treatment dished out by others. Grandpa had never done it, but this was a risk I could not take, especially now—and here.

Grandpa considered before answering. "It is the circle of life. It is time for Grandfather Buffalo's next adventure. I told him he should be proud of the bull he sired—this one is the best of him, ready to lead his people into tomorrow." Grandpa settled on his blanket.

"*Haw*, yes," I nodded my head in agreement. "I thought Grandfather Buffalo must have been pushed from his herd. He was pretty angry."

"We don't all respond well to change—at first." Grandpa eyed me through the haze. "But when accepted, change leads to growth in this life's journey."

"Is that how Grandfather Buffalo sees being pushed from his herd . . . as positive change?"

"He will." Looking intently at me, Grandpa continued, "Then, if we are lucky, we see change is an opportunity for further growth and learning." He held my eyes. "*Keah kam daw awnee aim ohm ah.* Life is forever changing."

The fire twirled upward, sending smoke into a widening gray whirlwind.

With each word, I seemed to hear more than the four words "*life is forever changing.*" I felt them vibrate in the air.

Staying in English, Grandpa emphasized, "Granddaughter, for you I want a long life with much change."

The smoke seemed to circle Grandpa; then, in a whirl, it spun out, released to the sky above. He stopped speaking, though I knew he was not finished. This was a time to let silence grow into more.

I thought of changes. Those coming.

After a long pause, Grandpa raised his fan to push more smoke my way. "While Grandfather Buffalo was a bit amused by the annoying gnat that is my grandchild"—here Grandpa's voice deepened—"don't do it again. It is disrespectful . . . until invited."

Before I could respond to *invited*, I started coughing from Grandpa's blend of quest smoke, fueled with cedar, sage, and something else.

I could hold it in no longer. "Grandpa," I coughed out, "we gotta go."

Grandpa looked at me. His gaze seemed to focus on me, then beyond. "I can't leave, Granddaughter. I must complete the circle. I shall remain."

Grandpa fanned another billowing cloud of smoke my way. I tried not to breathe deeply. I turned toward the hollow's opening and strained for a breath of smoke-free air. I wanted to clear my mind, to explain to Grandpa that he must come with me, now.

I finally found my voice. "You don't understand. The Tribal Council thinks you stole the Jefferson peace medal from the Kiowa Museum."

"I did."

My head jerked up. "What—why?"

I had seen Grandpa take it, but *steal*? Not him—not without a reason.

"For you. For the Kiowa People. It was being sent away." He reached into his pouch for more herbs to feed the fire.

I tried to gather scattered thoughts. "What? I don't understand. Why would you take it for me?" Grandpa's form shifted with the smoke. I felt confused by him and . . . the smoke. It filled the hollow, engulfed Grandpa and me.

His words came through the haze. "It is time. You must protect our heritage. You are the chosen guardian of our sacred stories." His eyes looked beyond me.

I started to follow his vision. I shook my head, cleared it. "Grandpa, I can't protect it. The Jefferson peace medal was safe in the Kiowa Museum."

His eyes found mine. "Granddaughter, you know better than that. Our treasures are walking out of that museum's front door. It is time for you to protect our heritage." The fire snapped and crackled.

I took a slow breath before I disappointed him. "Grandpa, I don't live here. I cannot take on the responsibility." I hated saying the words, but my work was fifteen hundred miles away.

Grandpa left my words unanswered.

The silence lengthened.

My eyes drifted to the ledge's floor, where we sat. Here a deep spiral had been carved into the granite floor from generations of truth seekers within my family. On my first quest, I'd joined the link of ancestors seeking answers through vision quests. At the start, we each took a rock and carved our route from the center of the universe outward to the open unknown, in search of life's path. The life spiral was etched deep into the granite floor by the many generations that had sat on this ledge, seeking their truth.

Guilt made me break the silence. "I don't have time for a four-day quest." I rose.

Grandpa stood and came to me. Using large swooping motions, he smoked first the soles of my feet, then up my legs. He struck my heart four times and chanted a prayer to the Ancient Ones. His dark chocolate eyes melted into mine. Grandpa took a deep breath in, held it for several beats, then blew it directly into my face. Involuntarily, I inhaled.

He smiled at me, then announced, "It has been said. So it is."

He returned to the fire and placed his eagle-feather fan into a plain cedar box. From a fold in the blanket, Grandpa picked up a turtle-shell rattle by its antler handle. He stood with his face and arms raised to *Daw'Kee* in silent conversation with the Creator. Grandpa announced the talk's end with four short shakes of his rattle.

He came to where I stood. "It is your calling." Grandpa accented each of the four words with a thrust of his old rattle. He chanted to the Ancient Ones to give me wisdom and guidance, to help keep my feet on the true road. After the chanting, he shook the rattle over me in each of the four directions. At the end of the fourth shake of the old rattle, Grandpa announced, "Your quest started with today's rising sun and will end with unexpected awareness at the close of the fourth day." With another shake of the turtle-shell rattle, he finished, "It is said. So it will be."

I blew a deep breath out in frustration. "This is not the time." I seemed to lose focus, then regained it and pushed on.

"Grandpa, they will think you stole the Jefferson peace medal for money and killed your old school friend to—"

Grandpa's gaze seemed to go in and out of focus. He wasn't hearing how serious the situation was. I took in another deep breath to start over. My lungs filled with more of the potent smoke; I hacked and coughed. My head seemed to spin, then slowed and settled.

Clearing my throat, I croaked out. "I meant to tell you earlier . . ." I hesitated, started again, "Grandpa, Mr.—" I abruptly stopped. Here of all places, I could not utter the dead man's name and hold his spirit back from riding the wind and beyond.

I tried again. "Buck Crow's grandfa—"

This time Grandpa cut me off. "Yes. I felt him go." He lowered his head, shaking it and the rattle. "I feared it would be so. He was chased by an evil wind."

I used my eyes to plead. "Grandpa, don't you see? Everyone is going to think you stole the peace medal and killed Buck's grandfather to get away with it."

Grandpa put the turtle-shell rattle aside and picked up his hand drum. "I would never do such things." A faint thrum vibrated in the air.

"Grandpa, I know that, but . . ."

The drum drew my attention.

"The People know me. They know my heart." Grandpa's words rang true.

The drum spoke in a steady beat.

My mind seemed to float; my attention drifted. I could hear Grandpa's true heart. He was right. Grandpa was innocent. I knew the truth of it. The People would feel it and know it too.

I drifted with the floating drum beats. Until a tug of logic pulled me back.

"But the police don't know you, and, Grandpa, they have security footage of you taking the peace medal."

Grandpa bent his head to the drum. They conversed.

The drum's tempo melded our heart beats. My head nodded in time with the drum. Grandpa would understand now. We were in tune. He spoke a single word: "So."

The rhythm broke.

I felt confused. Why was this not getting through to him? I tried again. "You must go with me to Red Buffalo Hall. We can bring the peace medal back—"

Grandpa never lifted his head from the talking drum. He just stated, in beat, "*Hawnay,*" and then repeated in English, "No."

The drum agreed.

After a few more beats, Grandpa lifted his eyes to me. "You are the next sacred story keeper. It has been said."

As his drum sang to the wind, fear pulled my thoughts together. He shouldn't make that statement—not here. I wasn't ready, might never be ready. He had to hear me. "Grandpa, I can't be . . . I live in California."

Grandpa pulled his focus to me. He smiled deeply into my eyes and used my name. "*Ahn Tsah Hye-gyah-daw*, She Knows the Way. You will find the way."

I felt the warmth of his smile flow through me. Made me believe. . . .

Grandpa tilted his head, as if listening to a distant voice. His focus shifted back to me. "You must go to the meeting. Your quest started and continues beyond this ledge." He nodded in agreement with the unheard speaker, seemed to look through me, then came back and looked directly at me. "Granddaughter, breathe deep and believe in yourself. Exhale all doubts."

My breaths matched his drum. He continued, "Inhale deeply and hold. Grandchild, you have many gifts to share with our People."

Here he confused me.

The drum tempo increased, banging out each name as Grandpa continued. "*Tsah Hye-gyah-daw* the new guardian of sacred stories; daughter of Joseph Sawpole; granddaughter of James Sawpole, keeper of the sacred stories; descendant of *Sawpole Gyah*, who spoke to owls and took their name. Granddaughter, you come from a family that has shared their gifts with the People through the generations. It is your time now." The drum beat came to a rapid close.

His eyes locked on mine. "Breathe out, Granddaughter. It is time."

I let out the breath I forgot I had been holding.

"I gave you the Jefferson peace medal, and you know who killed my old school friend. Let the truth be known to all." Thunder boomed in the distance.

Grandpa stood before me. "Now go. Continue your quest. Go to the meeting. Speak your heart, and truth will flow." He looked deeply into my eyes.

My mind cleared for a moment of comprehension and panic. "Wait, Grandpa, I don't have the medal and I really don't know who the killer is." I ignored his vision quest remarks. There was no time to sit and contemplate life right now.

"Granddaughter, you have the answers you seek." He grasped my forehead, and a yellow light exploded in my mind's eye. "They are within you."

Grandpa turned back to the fire, his gaze focused inward as he continued drumming and chanting. He was done talking. I would get nothing more from him.

My eyes misted from the smoke. Yeah, the smoke.

Chapter Twenty-Nine

The drum pounded. I felt it in my bones. Its irresistible rhythm caught me, moved me off the ledge.

With his drum, Grandpa pushed me out, down the pillar slot and to the lightning-struck oak. A sunray reflected off my phone's screen. The glint caught my eye; my body followed. I gathered the items I had left before going up to the ledge. I thrust the phone into a back pocket, then reached for and shook the dented canteen. A gurgle answered. The canteen still held water. I drank deeply.

I knew nothing, but I didn't seem to care. The answers would come.

The drum spoke lightly on the wind. It urged me down the boulder field. I slipped and slid, on the soles of my shoes and the seat of my jeans, downward at a speed I would never have ventured in my daredevil youth. Yet I slid to a safe halt at the start of the rolling prairie grasses. Birds sang in delight of life. Here, I took a moment. Listened to the distant drumming on the wind. It spoke of urgency. I slowed.

The prairie grass glinted gold in the lowering sun while a slight breeze moved the grass tops in a circular surface wave.

I watched the prairie grass's shifting rhythms as my thoughts moved in and out of focus. Had a life been taken because of fracking or because of the peace medal? If I could understand that, I could make sense of this whole mess. I would know what to do. Like the grass tops, my thoughts swirled in surface circles, not exposing the hidden answers below.

An animal trail through the prairie grass revealed itself. I followed it toward the Parallel Forest. Grasshoppers catapulted from the trail while male cicadas belted out high-pitched mating songs. Thoughts seemed to flow freely, from fracking to the Jefferson peace medal, to the dead man, to cleaning up . . . cleaned up—

A sharp snap brought me to an abrupt halt.

Grandfather Buffalo, about twenty feet ahead, blocked my passage to the Parallel Forest. My eyes rose to meet the graying hulk. I stayed a respectful distance away, eyeing the surrounding area. I spotted a nearby scrub oak with a branch at the necessary height for a quick scramble up if Grandfather Buffalo held a grudge.

We locked eyes.

The air buzzed.

I felt a connection.

A chant burst from me. I told the beautiful, old, bearded buffalo that I was sorry for disturbing his day. I had feared for the safety of the out-of-place man. I told him that Gerald knew no better. And to please forgive my intrusion—I did not intend insult to such a wise one.

Grandfather Buffalo turned his head to eye me better. He took several rapid steps in my direction. I held. I didn't sense attack in his eyes or body. His tufted tail swished from side to side. He halted a couple feet away and blew a deep gust of hot breath out. His life breath pushed into my face, blew a limp curl off my forehead. I smothered a choking cough, forced the aborted cough and hot buffalo breath in, mixed with a deep breath of my own making. Grandfather Buffalo's eyes stared, held mine. I saw depth in his rich, coal-colored eyes.

I coughed out, "*Ah ho, Thone*—thank you, Grandfather," and slowly backed away.

Grandfather Buffalo side-eyed me, then stepped to a nearby scrub oak and casually rubbed an itch on his shoulder and down his back. The tree leaned away from the massive beast. The buffalo gave his itch a final rub, shrugged, snorted, and with an over-the-shoulder glance at me, moved on.

I waited until the old buffalo was clear of the area before I stepped forward to continue into the Parallel Forest. As I came to the now bent scrub oak, I noticed a tuft of coarse buffalo hair stuck to the bark. Instinctually, I moved to the tree and removed the gift from Grandfather Buffalo. I raised the tuft of hair to the four directions, giving thanks for the spirit medicine.

I looked off into the direction of the departing buffalo and whispered a heartfelt "*Ah ho*—thank you," for his parting gifts.

Grandfather Buffalo had chosen me. A warmth filled me.

Like many Plains Indian Tribes, the Kiowas felt that at different junctures in life—if deserved—a spirit animal would choose to assist someone through life's journey, as a guide. It was an honor when one of the wise, older relatives—be it one that slithered, walked, or flew—offered to be a mentor, a guiding force toward achieving life's potential, in balance.

Grandfather Buffalo, the guardian of his people, had chosen to be my spirit animal, my teacher. This was an honor, and as my grandfather would say, this was powerful medicine to think upon. This type of spirit medicine was intended to be placed in a medicine bag worn on the body as a constant reminder of the traits needed to embrace in life on a day-to-day basis. I no longer wore my leather medicine bundle around my neck. It had brought too many inquiring eyes and questions, especially in business attire. I did keep my medicine bundle close to me. It was in a zipped pocket within my usually ever-present messenger bag . . . which I couldn't quite place right now. But it had to be around . . . I always had it with me. It must be at Grandpa's house with my suitcase.

I tucked the tuft of hair securely in my jeans change pocket. I intended to add Grandfather Buffalo's gift to my medicine bundle, once I located my messenger bag.

Maybe it was time to cleanse my white deerskin medicine bundle and wear it again. The thought felt right.

Grandfather Buffalo's gift carried me safely through the dark Parallel Forest directly to the front of Denny's truck. I dug the key out of a pocket before climbing behind the wheel. The old truck coughed, stuttered, and sputtered as it shook into life. My mind cleared as I left the Wildlife Refuge behind and drove past the old Meer's store down State Highway 58 toward Carnegie, the heart of Kiowa country.

The Kiowa Tribe of Oklahoma and its Tribal Complex were headquartered in Carnegie. Red Buffalo Hall hung off one side of the government offices, always available for large gatherings of the People. Tonight's meeting would be small, just the seven legislators, a couple of museum personnel, and maybe a few Tribe members.

I floated down the road and through my mind.

The Wichita jagged mountain tops transitioned to rolling ranch foothills with tumbled boulders peeking through here and there, to peanut-rich plowed fields just outside of Carnegie. Thick plumes of dust and twenty-foot peanut dust twisters were common during the harvest of the underground crop. Most avoided the area during harvest time. The peanut dust clouds were unbearable.

Unbearable also was the thought that kept seeping in. Was Denny right? Did Georgie kill Buck's grandfather? I shoved the doubt down for the final time. No, the facts didn't change. Georgie was in the house while I chased the killer during the thunderstorm. Suddenly the image of her new Nikes flashed in my mind's eye. No way those white sneakers had been out in that rain and mud. It wasn't Georgie.

I mulled the thought of Buck as the killer. I could see him killing someone in a blind fury, but not his grandfather. In my heart, I knew Buck didn't do it. His shock at learning of the death was too real. I remembered his cries, and I shivered in the heat. Yeah, his cries were too heart-wrenchingly real.

And Gerald? He was cold-hearted enough. My lips squeezed tight at the thought of the Kiowa art and regalia he'd purchased for dollars and sold for hundreds of thousands. I shook my head. Like Georgie's white sneakers, Gerald's flimsy snakeskin boots proved he wasn't the killer. Wearing those boots, Gerald could never have escaped through the mud to the timbers.

The road stretched between neatly farmed fields for miles, and I thought of those oil boys. But I tossed them from mind—those two were trouble, but they hadn't committed this killing. If they had entered the house, they would have brought the storm's mess with them, not to mention the stench of oil.

It couldn't be avoided any longer. Despite Denny's objections, Anna had to be considered as the killer. She'd overseen the reviewing of the stored museum boxes. She could have found the peace medal and arranged for its theft and sale with Gerald. But then Wilson got in her way.

Outside, an occasional structure broke the monotony of neatly plowed fields. But I remained focused.

I liked Anna. She projected strength and sincerity. I understood why Denny didn't want to think it was her. But it wasn't just the peace medal that incriminated Anna. There was the fracking. Anna, in some way, was involved with fracking on Indian land. I had her earring as proof of that.

A farmer drove his tractor across the highway, from one dirt road to another.

Mentally, I slapped my forehead. I hadn't asked Grandpa about Anna, fracking, or Jimmy Creek Spring. I had expected him to be going to the meeting with me. I'd thought we had plenty of time for answers.

I tightened my grip on the steering wheel. The truth was, my trek to Grandpa had been a bust. Grandpa hadn't provided the answers that I had hoped for and needed. Now I had to face the meeting at Red Buffalo Hall alone, with no Grandpa, no answers, and—worst yet—no Jefferson peace medal.

Carnegie Peanut Factory was closed for the day. A few cars lingered in front of its Goober House, where you could buy fresh peanuts by the pail.

I wasn't sure what to do next. I would be arriving at the Complex soon.

There really was only one thing left to do.

Time to get answers directly from the source.

Anna had mentioned several times she wanted to see Grandpa before the meeting. I was sure she would be in her office at the Complex. I glanced at my watch. Plenty of time to see Anna before the eight o'clock meeting.

On Main Street, I made a left at Carnegie's four-corner stop sign. I traveled a bit farther before turning into the Kiowa Complex parking lot. Gravel crunched under the truck's tires as I drove to the back of the Complex offices where a few office doors opened to the parking lot. A plume of gravel dust trailed.

Visitors for legislators usually came into the complex from the front, weaved through the halls passing through various gatekeepers to a central receptionist that announced and escorted all visitors to appropriate offices. Since the legislators' offices were along the back wall, several had second doors exiting directly into the parking lot. Over a decade of service entitled Anna to one of these much-desired offices.

I parked a row away, facing the offices' back doors. A continuous *beep, beep, beep* drew my attention down the opposite side toward Red Buffalo Hall. A truck backed to the Hall's doorway. A young woman signaled *Stop*, then shouted it. The truck's tailgate was dropped, and several young Kiowas appeared to carry chairs through the opened double doors.

A small woman dodged a chair leg as she came out yapping at a large Kiowa man. The man leaned low to hear her berate him. I rolled my window down to catch a breeze and to eavesdrop. Nita's voice carried to my open window. "We will need one more load. Do not—are you listening? Do not let them all go to pick up more chairs. Those three there need to stay and start—Are you listening?" Nita banged on a clipboard.

The man stooped low to face Nita. With patience I could only dream of, he told her, "Yes. We will be set up and sound tested by seven thirty." He rose to his full height, prepared to escape, when she called him back.

Nita stretched her neck to look up at the patient man. "Corky, that's less than thirty minutes. Be sure you're operatin' on white man's time." She didn't wait for his reply. Nita stepped away, absorbed in her clipboard. Corky remained in place watching his workers. Nita looked up, saw the still man. She stepped back and banged on Corky's shoulder with her pen. "You and another go get 'em all set up. Go on . . . Now." She watched as the man moved to the opened doors.

Satisfied, Nita turned her attention back to her clipboard. The pen went to her mouth for a nibble as she thought. She glanced up, caught me watching her, and smiled. Gave me a nod and practically danced through the double doors after Corky and others to boss around. She was in her element.

My eyes drifted back to the office doors. I wasn't sure which was Anna's, but I was determined to find it and her. Time to get answers.

I watched windows for signs of life. After a few minutes, it was obvious only one office had movement behind its shades. I knocked on its door.

Anna opened the office door wide, with a warm smile and a greeting. "James, I am so glad you got here early. We need—" The smile froze. Anna looked around and over me. The smile withered as she realized James was not beside me.

I watched her carefully. "Anna, what is it you need to discuss with my grandfather?" Stale air escaped from the office building.

Anna remained holding the door, her eyes moving past me to scan the parking lot in hopes of spotting James. Resigned, Anna's eyes returned to me. She ignored my question and countered with her own. "Where's James?" She swung the door inward, narrowing the opening.

"Taking care of business." I had no other answer.

Anna positioned the partially closed door as a shield. Conflicting emotions flooded her face as she struggled to speak. "I thought—hoped James's business would be here." Irritation slipped into her tone. "This meeting is all about him." She moved to close the door.

The sun was low on the horizon. A faint breeze teased.

I struggled to keep my voice and temper controlled. "Not sure I agree with that." I leaned toward Anna. "But I would like to hear more about the peace medal theft."

Anna sounded surprised. "That was news to me too." She lowered her voice. "I thought you were going to see James, get answers. What happened?" She rested her free hand on her hip.

"Grandpa left me with more questions than answers."

This brought a small laugh from Anna. I waited for more, but nothing came.

I eyed her. "Some of my questions deal with you."

For an instant Anna's face showed surprise. She quickly took control. "I really don't have time." The door started to close. "I just snuck in here to change. I was quite a mess from running around this afternoon."

Anna had looked a mess when I last saw her at Meers, but I couldn't remember if she had been a muddy mess. I looked at her closely now. Only then did I notice that Anna was in a fresh dress with calf-high, beaded white leather moccasin boots. Her hair was once again in control, pulled tight in a single braid down her back. A simple dark blue dress was complemented by a silver sun-disk necklace. She looked like a powerful leader.

Anna stood in the doorway, poised to leave. "Well, I need to check on Nita." She shook her head. "Truth be told that woman runs this place. Just wish it was with a gentler touch." A single earring disk swung.

She waited for me to step away, so the door would not be closed in my face.

I didn't move. "You know my grandfather summoned me to help." I waited.

Anna stayed silent, but her eyes asked questions.

I said, "Anna, there are things we should share." Mentally, I sent supportive thoughts and energy to her. Tried to show she could trust me.

She bit her lip. We remained in the doorway—the door had not closed, yet.

An engine roared to life. The truck was off for another load.

"Why did you want to see James?" I asked softly.

Her face twisted in the struggle to stay silent. Finally, Anna lowered her eyes from mine. "James called me to meet."

I didn't push, kept my voice low. "Did he say why?" Gravel crunched in the background.

Anna looked across the parking lot, toward the Red Buffalo Hall's open doors. "He just said he wanted to talk, and left a message on my answering machine." Her gaze came back to me. "James asked—*demanded*, really—I come early this morning to discuss . . . a problem." Anna changed her wording at the end.

I moved closer to her. "Is that what he said? A *problem*?" Background noise faded away. I focused on Anna.

She shifted, avoided making eye contact. "That's all he said." Anna cocked her head to the side, as if a thought had just occurred to her. "You can check with Nita; she heard the message too."

On a hunch, I said, "But you talked to James before he left that last message."

This brought her eyes to mine. She looked deep into me and seemed to make a decision. "We talked briefly. You know how James is—doesn't like to talk on the phone. So he came here to the Complex." She kept her focus on me.

I whispered, "Why?"

Anna rubbed a bare earlobe. "First, over fear that the museum was being emptied." The rest came out easier once she started: "A couple had an old painting he had done; James insisted that they should not have it. I reminded him I had one similar." She looked to me for support. "It's got to be hard to keep track of all the paintings he's done through the years." Her eyes waited for me to confirm. I couldn't.

A slight smile lifted my lips. Grandpa knew each of his paintings. He would know if one he gave the museum ended up with a collector. He often recreated the same painting, but the first time he did a painting, he marked the original with a blooming yucca plant to symbolize strength, endurance, and hope.

Anna continued her story. "James insisted only one had the bloom." She shook her head. "Not sure what he meant . . . He can be cryptic."

This I knew all too well. Answers often came in the form of more questions when dealing with Grandpa.

Once started, Anna seemed to need to tell her story. "We were to meet to discuss possible museum thefts . . ." She floundered for a beat before continuing, "And another issue, when James left a 'come now' demand on my voicemail." She remained partially hidden by the door in her office's doorway. Her hand held the doorknob so tightly her knuckles were white. "James's voice sounded urgent . . . important." She looked at me now. "Then this peace medal theft came to light . . ." She just ended there, staring off into the distance.

I didn't move or make a sound. I stood watching her, waiting for more. The beeping truck returned with more chairs.

In a distracted voice, Anna continued, "James has never asked me for anything." She seemed to return to herself. "Your grandfather has always helped me. He is a good man."

This I already knew.

Anna made sure I was listening. "When I started serving the People, he guided me. He is . . . has always been my sounding board, someone to discuss the old ways with, and the new." She locked eyes with me. "He helped me find a way to braid the two together to find the middle road." She smiled with an inner thought.

I nodded. Grandpa much preferred the role of mentor to leader.

As it has been with generations of children listening to an elder, I urged Anna to continue her story by saying, *"Haw."* More than a simple yes, this *haw* assured the storyteller of an interest in hearing more.

Anna stepped from behind the door. "James is my . . . guide stone." She focused on me. "Do you know what a guide stone is?" She didn't wait for my affirming *haw*, but continued, explaining, "It's a Kiowa compass. In the old days, travelers would find stone or wood markers on trails from village to village, like highway signs. Guide stones showed where you were headed while always noting true north." Anna swung the door open wider. "James kept me true."

I held her gaze, but I gave her the silence to continue.

Anna broke eye contact. "I feel bad. He came to see me . . . on another issue." The door swung inward again. "I didn't get to see him; he left before I arrived. Later the security footage came out, and the peace medal theft was exposed." She shook her head. "I know James did not steal the peace medal." She stopped, thought, and added, "Not without a good reason."

I continued to watch her. Anna was back to using the door as a shield. She confused me. She came across as very sincere, yet avoided giving full answers.

Anna glanced at her watch. "Oh my, I really have to check on things." She moved to close the door, to bring an end to our conversation.

But I wasn't done yet. I said, "Beautiful necklace."

Anna's hand touched the silver disks at her neck. "Yes, it's one of a kind." Unconsciously, her other hand moved to rub a bare earlobe. Then her hands dropped to the door. "Well, I really . . . "Her voice faded away as she watched me pull the silver disk from my pocket. I rubbed the last of the mud off and handed it to her. "Is this yours?"

A smile broke out. "Yes." She reached for the offered earring, telling me, "My son made the necklace and earrings—one of his first sets." Anna poked the earring into her earlobe.

"It would have broken my heart if I had lost it." She gave me the Kiowa thank-you: *"Ah ho."*

I remained in the doorway, preventing Anna from closing the door. Using my chin, I pointed at the earring. "I found your earring at that wildcat fracking operations back behind my grandpa's Jimmy Creek land." My eyes stayed on her. "You know, the place that's stealing my grandpa's spring water."

This froze her.

I couldn't help myself: condemnation spewed. "You're working with fracking against your own People. You're jeopardizing the lives and health of people, animals, land"—my voice came out hard—"for money. How could you?" My eyes bored into her.

Anna's jaw tightened. She spoke in a low, intense voice. "I hate them. More than you could know. This is just the latest battle Indians must fight. We've seen land grabs in Oklahoma before, but this time they're trying to wring the last drop of oil from Mother Earth, no matter the cost." Her face twisted. "And the agencies sworn to protect our land, our People, are now the state and federal agencies doing everything they can to facilitate the oil scums. I needed to talk with James—" There she stopped.

Her words seemed truthful, but her actions . . . I wasn't sure.

A chime rang. Anna pulled her phone out. She glanced at the screen, read a text, then looked back at me. "I have no more to say and no more time." She shifted to close the door, and then stopped to whisper, "Talk to James. He will tell you. I'm a good guy." She looked over her shoulder toward the front of the office, then back to me. "That's all I can say." The door closed, followed by a resounding snap of its dead bolt.

I stared at the closed door, thinking . . . Anna had never spoken of the dead man.

Slowly, I wandered back to the truck, deep in thought. It wasn't that she avoided voicing Wilson's name; she'd just never thought of him or the body. The killing had never entered Anna's mind.

Wilson didn't concern her.

I slid into the truck. Still thinking. Then knowing.

Anna hadn't killed Wilson—she'd never mentioned the dead man. Anna wasn't worried about Wilson, dead or alive.

The day's heat lingered. The truck's interior was hot. Sweat beaded on my forehead.

I thought back to Anna's arrival at Grandpa's house. She had been worried . . . and wet. I recalled water dripping from her as she sat on the couch. Even then, she hadn't been worried about a dead man in the other room. She'd been concerned about Grandpa missing an early morning meeting with her.

I rolled both windows down. Cooler air rushed in.

Anna could be up to something with fracking, but I was sure she did not know there had been a dead man in Grandpa's no-no room.

Anna didn't do it.

I was back to square one, with the meeting starting in fifteen minutes.

Chapter Thirty

I wiped sweat off my brow.

Anna, Gerald, Buck, and Georgie: none of them did it. Was I wrong about the frackers? No, those two were fools, not killers.

I released a big sigh and sank deep into the old truck seat. My mind stayed on *who*. Who benefited by the killing . . . by the theft? With a start I remembered, it all started with the theft, or Grandpa's prevention of a theft—

My phone's muffled ring broke through my thoughts. My spirits lifted. It would be Bernie. I pulled the phone out of my back pocket, ready to hear her upbeat voice. I was ready to tell her everything. Truth was, I needed to talk.

Without looking at the screen, I answered, "I am so glad you called." A smile started.

Clouds of dust followed sounds of tires crunching across gravel.

"Really?" boomed from the phone.

I dropped the phone when I heard Thomas's baritone instead of the expected uplifting lilt of Bernie's voice. An ultra-fake-sweet voice rose from the truck's seat. "I am so pleased to hear that." I got the phone back to my ear in time to catch,

"Just as I hope you will be pleased to hear my news." I felt his self-satisfied grin.

My jaw clenched. News from Thomas was not going to be good.

I tried to interrupt. "Thomas, I don't—"

He continued, with a note of glee. "Richard and I . . . did you choke? Yes, our client Richard and I decided a drink would calm the nerves. You know, big show coming up and all. Perfect time to get to know each other."

I pleaded, "Thomas, no. Not now! Not drinks before the company's IPO." This was the SEC-enforced quiet period for a company going public. Weeks in advance, no one associated with the organization could talk about the company—anywhere.

At least it had just been the two of them.

My pleas landed on deaf ears. Thomas said, "Hey, Richard, I got Mae on the line. Here you go." Glasses tinkled, dishes clanked, and voices cut in and out as the phone shifted from one hand to another.

Richard, sounding slightly confused, came on the line. "Hey there, Mae. Your family emergency sorted out?"

I stuttered, "Not yet." I went on to explain, "A family emergency is the only thing that could keep me from the office right now. I intend to return on a red-eye tomorrow night."

Thomas was in the background, ordering drinks for the table. As if it would help, I pressed the phone closer to my ear, strained to pull the background noise in. Was Thomas ordering drinks for more than two? *Please, no.*

Richard cleared his throat. "I have to say, when you left abruptly, I had my doubts . . . Well, I got mad." He paused to let his words sink in.

I wanted to defend myself, but I held back. I had to let him voice his concerns. I needed to listen.

The background noise increased. It sounded like a party was starting on his end.

Richard lowered his voice. "This is a big thing. We are going public." His voice slowly rose in volume. "You came highly recommended. Jack said you doubled their IPO expectations by honing his company's story. That's why I went with such a small agency."

A knot formed in my stomach. I felt sick. Still, I forced myself to remain quiet.

Thomas led a cheer in the background. He was with a group.

Richard released a long, slow breath. I felt his exasperation. This was not good. I prepared for the worst.

Richard seemed to gather himself before finishing what he needed to say. "I gotta admit your work these last six months has been . . . well, you clarified the business for us . . . and—he let out an unexpected guffaw—"we started the damn thing."

The knot in my stomach loosened. This was beginning to sound better. A breeze came through the windows. Another set of cheers erupted in the faraway background. That worried me.

Richard's voice rose with excitement. "That Marcus, his visuals are on point while being stunning, and your Bernie . . . well, I want her. She got everyone toeing the line and . . . learning their lines." He let out a laugh—music to my ears. Then he continued, "Your team easily made up for your absence. And frankly, I liked seeing the depth."

I started to breathe again. Another breeze blew through. Outside, dust settled.

Voices rose and laughter increased on Richard's end. The place must be getting busy with the after-work crowd.

Richard lowered his voice. I strained to hear his words over the bar's background clatter. "But your partner, he makes me un—

I sucked a breath in, held onto it. In the background, Thomas called out, "Richard, pre-celebration bubbles." I heard a loud pop, followed by louder cheers. Thomas let out a wickedly loud laugh.

Close behind Richard, glasses clinked in celebration.

He returned to the phone. "This is getting out of hand. We have rehearsals to do tomorrow." Richard hissed into the phone, "We're in the last of our quiet period. If anyone talks, the IPO is over. Millions of dollars lost."

Thomas called out another cheer. Glasses clinked, one clanked.

Richard in a low, tight voice announced, "I have got to go."

My bubble of joy popped in an instant. I sat sweating in the truck with an ear pressed to the phone. Nothing. No connection.

Thomas out drinking with my client was bad enough, but partying with the executives days before the planned IPO was a disaster. All it took was one overheard, drunken comment about the company. The agency insurance wouldn't cover that blunder.

My fingers raked my hair, breaking through tangled curls. The tiny pricks of pain felt deserved.

I could lose my business—the agency, everything.

Reality hit hard. I choked back a sob.

There was nothing I could do about Thomas with my client . . . my business and my professional future laid on the line.

I stared into the darkening horizon. Emotions whirled.

I could do nothing to help Grandpa, and I had no idea how to explain Grandpa's theft of the peace medal or where it was now.

I shook my head, damp curls flopping around. I pushed them back with a clenched fist.

Why had I left Grandpa up on the vision quest ledge? I should have convinced him to come down with me. At least if Grandpa was here, he could explain why he took the Jefferson peace medal. Tell the legislators his suspicions about happenings at the Kiowa Museum. The People knew Grandpa; they trusted him. They would have listened to him.

I banged on the steering wheel.

Through the windshield, dusk settled in. Scattered clouds turned charcoal against the purple sky. I watched the changing sky, yet saw nothing.

Grandpa had said I know who the murderer is. But how does he think I know that—when I don't even know where the Jefferson peace medal is?

My staring eyes welled with tears.

Grandpa claimed that he'd given the peace medal to me. Yeah, just when did that happen?

"The answers will come." That's what Grandpa said. A wild laugh escaped. How did I believe his gibberish?

My fingers pulled at my tangle of curls. I needed answers now.

And I had none.

Chapter Thirty-One

A crunch of gravel under tires raised dust trails that caught my eye. Cars were coming in, parking close to Red Buffalo Hall's opened double doors. A stream of cars.

I should have known by the number of chairs going in, but I'd been so absorbed, I hadn't seen what was happening in front of my eyes. I'd thought it would be the legislators and museum personnel. Not this. This was a Tribe summoning. I slid out of the truck and stood next to its open door, staring at cars parked around Red Buffalo Hall's doorway. People gathered in small groups were chatting. I couldn't make out the words, but there was a buzz of anticipation.

The moccasin telegraph, the Kiowas' informal communication network, had been busy. And by the amount of younger Kiowas joining the crowd, there had been texting, lots of texting.

I wasn't ready for this.

Denny, face shining with fresh sweat, rushed over. "Been hopin' to find you."

I squinted into the sinking sun to watch the growing crowd gather outside Red Buffalo Hall's doorway.

Denny craned to look beyond me into the truck's cab, then turned a puzzled face to me. "Where's Grandpa?"

Through the glare, I tracked a small woman flitting from one group to another, increasing the chatter at each perch. Small groups merged, became larger groups. The air seemed to vibrate. Discontent brewed.

Denny repeated, louder, "Mud, where is Grandpa?"

"Grandpa refused to come." My attention stayed on the gathering crowd. Groups dissolved, reformed, and finally moved through the doorway into Red Buffalo Hall.

Still I watched. Spotted the woman fly to a newly arrived group. My eyes lingered.

Denny laughed. This pulled my attention from the birdlike woman to him. "What—"

He stopped laughing and grasped my shoulder. "Kinda what we should've expected." His eyes shone. "It is Grandpa." He followed with another laugh.

The laugh annoyed me. I pulled away, trying to gather my scattered thoughts. "No, I expected Grandpa to come. That he would want to be here." Denny should realize the importance of Grandpa speaking tonight—now.

Movement beyond Denny drew my attention. My eyes returned to the small woman silhouetted by the setting sun. Her back remained to me as she went from a large group, waited, and then slipped to the far side of the building, away from the hall's crowd. There she melded with growing shadows.

I remembered Grandpa's comment about artifacts walking out the museum's front door.

I turned to Denny. "Where's Buck? He can explain what Gerald's been doing with family artifacts." My voice rose with excitement. “Buck can tell the legislators that Gerald intended to steal the Jefferson peace medal and will take treasures right out of the museum.” For a moment I felt relief. This could work. I mustered a smile. “That will keep Gerald from being appointed as curator to the Kiowa Museum and give us time . . .” I trailed off, watched Denny shake his head.

“I don’t know where Buck is.”

Before I could ask more, Denny put his hand up in the universal stop gesture. Then he explained, “After we left you at the Wildlife Refuge, I took Buck to his grandfather’s body. We stayed there quite a while.” Denny’s eyes became distant, then returned. “I left Buck alone for just a bit, and then, next thing I know, that van started up.” Denny half laughed. “I barely caught Buck before he got to the road. Bad hand and all, he was coming here.” Denny finished, leaned against his truck.

This surprised me. “Why did Buck want to come here?” I had expected him to stay with the body and call the authorities.

Denny took in a deep breath and explained, “Buck thinks all bad things, including the killing of his grandfather, are Gerald’s doing.” He pushed off the truck and turned to me. “Buck claims Gerald poisoned his mind and others’.” Denny shook his head. “Buck worked himself up and blames all his troubles on Gerald.”

The sky slowly darkened, and the few working outside lights popped on. I scanned the parking lot. A mad Buck on the loose worried me. Examples of Buck’s violent temper came way too easily to mind. “I hope you talked him out of it.”

“Tried but failed. I agreed to drive him here, then lost him.” Denny shook his thick black mane. “Buck jumped out of the van before I had it parked. I haven’t seen him since.”

I glanced back at the Hall's doorway. Currently, Buck was nowhere in sight. Neither was the small woman.

Denny stepped into my view. "Mud, listen. It's okay. I lost Buck. You're here." His face lit up. "We don't need Buck for the meeting."

I was not sure what Denny was talking about. For the first time in my life, I wanted Buck.

Denny gave my shoulder a squeeze. "You may not have Grandpa, but you got the peace medal from him. We'll go in and use that to . . ." He watched my face, and this time his voice trailed away. He stared, knowing but unbelieving. Finally, he asked, "Where's the Jefferson peace medal?"

I couldn't look at him when I answered. "Grandpa didn't have it."

Amplified voices came from Red Buffalo Hall. Stragglers hurried. The meeting was starting. First there would be a prayer. All Kiowa events start with a blessing. That would take a while.

"What did he say about the peace medal?" Denny waited.

I admitted, "Grandpa said I have it." I leaned back on the truck. The metal still held the day's heat.

Denny didn't hesitate. "Then you do. Grandpa's not wrong about these things."

"Really? Cause I've got nothing—no medal and no idea where to look or what to do." I looked away from Denny—I had to. I didn't want to see his thoughts. Or show my fear.

A familiar darting movement in the distance caught my eye. Nita parted from Gerald and entered Red Buffalo Hall. The amplified blessing ended.

Denny pulled me square to him. "Mud, look at me. What are we going to do?" I gazed back at him. My mind seemed to be moving slowly. Denny was talking, but I wasn't listening, I was trying to connect dots.

Denny shook me. "Geez, Mud, focus . . . will ya? What are we going to do?" He let go of my shoulders, looked at where I stared. Red Buffalo Hall's double metal doors remained open. A few dawdlers lingered outside. Legislators were making introductory remarks inside.

At the airport—I'd seen it at the beginning, if I had only looked. Slowly things came into focus. Then blurred. I wasn't sure how it all connected. But I knew the first step.

"We're going to the meeting."

The answers would come. I hoped.

Denny continued to stare at the entrance to Red Buffalo Hall. He didn't look convinced.

I thought of Grandpa seeking truth on the ledge. Me, seeking Grandpa. And his words: *"You know who killed my old school friend."*

Maybe.

I pushed Denny aside. Peered into the truck, looked on the seat and floorboard. Found nothing.

I continued the search while I asked, "Have you seen my messenger bag? That green bag, I had. . . ." I leaned low to look under the driver's seat.

Denny's brow wrinkled. "Lime green?"

I looked over my shoulder at him. "Yeah." Hopeful.

His face twisted in thought. "Think I saw it last on the ground at the Refuge."

I shoved the driver's door closed, moved to the other side, and muttered, "Yeah, it dropped in the puddle." I opened the passenger door. "But I picked it up and . . ." I pulled the passenger's seat forward to reveal my messenger bag jammed against a crowbar and the cab wall. "Yes!" I pulled the bag out and shoved the seat back into position.

Denny stepped in behind me to watch. Carefully, I pulled my laptop out of my messenger bag and laid it on the other seat. Hot breath blew down my neck. I pushed at Denny with my shoulder. "You're breathing on me." Denny shifted to the side. A welcomed breeze slipped in.

I reached into the bag, pulled out show files, notes, and handfuls of miscellaneous papers and envelopes. I tossed another handful of papers onto the truck's seat. Denny reached across, grabbed some antibiotic moisture wipes lying among my bag's innards. He ripped a package open.

I pawed through the items on the seat. Searching. Hoping.

Sickening, perfumed wetness smacked my face and moved upward. I shoved Denny's hands away. "What are you doing?"

Denny continued, mama cat–like, wiping at my face. "Mud, you are a mess. If we're going in, well . . . you're definitely living up to your name." He took another swipe at my face.

I turned away from Denny to grab the messenger bag again. This time I completely upended it, to shake everything out of it. The last of the junk mail spilled out, but not what I wanted. My stomach knotted.

Hope sunk.

It was gone.

A faint memory stirred. I leaned across the seat into the truck.

Maybe.

I reached between the seat and console. Sent silent pleas upward. Ran my fingers between the console and seat pan. Found nothing I wanted to find.

A final push farther beneath . . . a fleeting touch of a hard edge. Yes. I pulled the cardboard express mailer out from its nest, smiled at where I had scrawled Grandpa's *"I am where you seek"* note in large letters across the envelope's middle. That seemed a lifetime ago.

I would need this.

I tucked the mailer in the back of my pants. It was too large for a pocket, but it would be safe in the small of my back. I emerged from the truck and announced, "Let's go."

Denny didn't move. He placed a wipe in my hand. "Mud, you can't go yet." He gave me a hard look and commanded, "Wipe."

Frustrated, I did a dutiful swipe at my face with the provided wipe. As I wadded it to toss, I caught a glimpse of the slightly used wipe. I returned it to my face and scrubbed until the wipe was useless. Denny handed me another. I promptly muddied it, but had removed enough dirt from my face and hands to pass his inspection.

Denny began his mama-cat routine again, this time trying to push my wild tangles into shape. I slapped his hands away. "There is no hope for my hair. This is as good as it . . . I get."

Denny gave my hair one final pat and smiled deep into my eyes. "And that's plenty good enough."

We turned together to go to the meeting.

I stopped, turned back, grabbed my messenger bag. This time I went directly to its inner zipped pocket. I removed the white deerskin medicine bundle; the leather was stiff from disuse. I opened its top, slipped in Grandfather Buffalo's gift and pulled the leather pouch closed. I held the medicine bag in my hand for a moment, squeezed it. Without hesitation, I lowered my head and hung the bundle around my neck. It nestled comfortably between my breasts—out of sight, yet a constant presence. It felt warm.

Denny kicked at the gravel, raising dust. "So, what are we doing?"

I looked at my cousin. "Seeking truth."

His face cycled through a mix of emotions. None expressed confidence.

"Tell me you got an idea . . ." Denny left it hanging: a question, a hope.

"I got an idea . . . I think."

Only one side of the double metal doors remained open. Light and a steady thrum spilled from the doorway.

We headed toward the light.

Chapter Thirty-Two

Red Buffalo Hall was built to hold indoor Powwows, large gatherings, and basketball games. The cavernous gym-like structure hummed with excitement. Accordion walls were pushed open to accommodate the unexpectedly large crowd for the meeting already in progress.

People grabbed extra folding chairs leaning along the back wall. As space became available, it was claimed. A young official attempted to form the scattered groups into seated rows. That wasn't going well.

As Denny and I entered, we were assaulted by Gerald's voice ricocheting from the cavernous walls. "I have a master's in fine arts. My credentials are beyond . . ."

The crowd's loud hum settled to an occasional buzz. Gerald stood on a raised stage, addressing a table of seven legislators to one side, with the audience in front. A mural filled the wall directly behind the stage. A large buffalo head, haloed in red to signify being in a spiritual state, was centered between two eagle prayer feathers. Grandpa had designed it, but many hands had painted it.

Gerald stood center stage with the mural directly behind him. The red of his latest set of snakeskin boots, as had been the case with the yellow pair before, matched the red accents in his tie. He was the perfect pretend cowboy once again. I would bet Gerald knew that red was a spiritual color for the Kiowas and had deliberately chosen to wear it tonight to manipulate emotions.

I watched him closely. He wasn't the killer, but he was an instigator. As Buck had claimed, "Gerald poisoned my mind and others'." I wondered what other minds Gerald had poisoned.

Anna was seated at the table with the legislators. Her eyes searched the crowd. I knew she still hoped for Grandpa's arrival. She spotted Denny and me. Her eyes found mine, held, and questioned. When I shook my head, she seemed to deflate into her seat. She gave a half-hearted nod, bit her lip, and looked toward the still-talking Gerald.

". . . no one can care for your treasures better," boomed across the heads of the assembled crowd. Most continued visiting their neighbors, admiring an outfit, ignoring Gerald.

My eyes slid from Anna to an obviously fuming Nita seated in the front row directly below the stage. Her body barely contained the anger vibrating within. She sat board rigid, posture perfect, hands formed in tight fists that clasped a purse trapped at her lap. Her lips were as one in a straight white line, and her eyes were blowtorches aimed at Gerald. One foot rapidly tapped up and down. Gerald's intent to be the Kiowa Museum curator seemed to be news to the bossy little woman. And not good news.

It surprised me that Gerald's plan had gotten past the know-everything Nita.

One of the legislators voiced agreement with Gerald. "I have been saying, we need to take care of what is in our museum now, before it is too late." Gerald and several others nodded back, with an occasional *haw* ringing out from the rustling crowd. The audience was getting interested. Attention shifted to the show on stage.

Anna leaned into her microphone. "Ernest is right—we all know it. But we don't need to rush into a decision of this magnitude tonight." She looked at the head of the table. "This was a special calling for another matter." The mic squawked its support.

Several legislators nodded in agreement. A pair at the corner of the table leaned together to whisper.

Gerald appealed to the legislators. "Nooo, you don't need to make a decision today." The legislators turned to listen. "But . . . well, I hate to say this, but you all gotta know." Gerald tried to look apologetic but couldn't pull it off. "Your people are just not trained to handle such valuable items."

Heads nodded agreement around the table. Discussions broke out in clusters throughout the crowd. Complaints were muttered.

Nita burst from her seat. "Trained. I been taking classes for years. No one notices, but look at my certificates." She threw her purse at the stage. It fell short and slid under the stage's curtained barrier.

Her tirade reached the ears of a few. Several at the table murmured to each other and turned to watch Nita. A tribal police officer stood across stage; he watched the audience with crossed arms. The small woman's antics, so close to the stage's front, went unseen by him.

On stage, Gerald continued his sales pitch with a slick smile for the legislators. "One of the advantages of going with me as curator is that I do want you to be back in charge of your museum as soon as possible." He upped his smile voltage to share it with the crowd. "So, I will offer professional-level training to your staff. Get them all up and ready in no time." Gerald stood between the legislators and Nita, blocking the angry woman from their view.

Interest buzzed.

Nita vibrated with anger. Only those close by noticed the small woman full of heat.

She got louder, "I got certificates! I should be in charge." Nita stomped her foot from below the stage. "Don't you hear me?"

A giggle slipped from someone seated near her. Nita turned to find the offender. The giggle stopped abruptly.

Gerald moved from the legislators to address the audience. His eyes noted yet skimmed past the quivering Nita. He boomed into the microphone, "You'll get professional training and one day—a day I will welcome—the Tribe will manage the museum again." In a lower voice, he added, "After a thorough inventory and when your treasures can be assured of continued proper care."

He turned his gaze from the audience, let it fall to Nita, and gave her a smile that actually engaged his eyes. He intentionally poked the beast.

Nita shook with rage; her face flooded a bright red. Making gasping sounds, her mouth flapped open and closed.

From the table above, Anna commented, "Gerald is only the first we should talk with—"

A middle-aged legislator shook his head and leaned into his mounted microphone. "We need to do something about this now. Who knows what all is being lost?"

The crowd bustled. One voice noted loudly, "Why is there a basketball on display in the museum instead of my family's headdress?"

"Riverside won state championship that year. What did your great-grandfather win?" someone replied. Some laughed, but most moaned and shut down the heckler.

Nita's voice came out in a near shriek. "We don't need another person outside the tribe coming to tell us what to do." She marched up the stage steps, her screech having silenced the grumbling crowd. All eyes followed her to the stage. She stomped over to face the legislators. "We have been doing just fine without any *Hanpokos* interference in our government and our museum." A few at the table smiled at the Kiowa word for the conquering Americans while several others nodded in agreement with Nita. Many in the audience whispered to confirm the word's meaning.

Hands on hips Nita stated, "Kiowas need to take care of Kiowa things."

This brought more head nods around the table. The audience loudly agreed. Encouraged, Nita moved to where Gerald stood on stage. She reached for his handheld microphone.

Gerald slid away from Nita to face the audience. He lifted the mic. "Can you really say that the museum is doing well, Nita, really?" She stood with her hand stretched upward grasping at where the mic had been.

As one, the audience looked at Nita. She stared daggers at Gerald. The question hung in the air. Gerald moved to the side, putting Nita center stage. She swayed, undecided between moving to the legislators' table or to Gerald and the microphone.

Gerald's next words rooted Nita in place: "I mean, we're all here tonight because of the loss of a priceless treasure." He dramatically hung his head and shook it slowly. "Under you, the emblem of first contact between our people has been lost." He let his words sink in.

The crowd became restless. Most had not heard the details of a theft.

Nita took determined steps toward Gerald, her face twisted in anger. This was news she had hoped to spread in her own way.

Gerald lifted his head to look at Nita. "The Jefferson peace medal is gone. Lost under your care." He returned to the surprised audience. "Who knows what else has gone missing?"

Gerald may not have been a cowboy, but he knew how to milk a crowd. The audience's low rumble rose in volume and intensity.

Many Tribe members donated family artifacts to the Kiowa Museum to ensure precious items stayed visible and available to Kiowas and others with an interest in the Tribe. In earlier days, the Tribe and the People had lost precious artifacts to museums or private collectors who then hid the historical treasures from view.

Nita paused mid-stride toward Gerald. Her face seemed to spin through rage, fear, cunning, and back to fury. Her eyes never left her prey.

Gerald enjoyed the crowd's reaction; he sent a sly smirk at Nita. I had a feeling Gerald knew what else had gone missing under Nita's watch.

He stepped forward, near the very front of the stage. "Under my supervision such carelessness will not happen again." Gerald looked earnestly out at the gathered Kiowas. "I honor Kiowa treasures." Gerald once more lowered his head and did the slow head shake routine. "How, *who* . . . leaves a priceless relic on a desk in a hallway . . ."

These words moved Nita. She turned eyes full of hot hatred on Gerald and got closer to him, unnoticed.

Gerald raised his head to look at the legislators and finished, ". . . for anyone to come in and take?" He gave a more dramatic, slow head shake.

While in the throes of his performance, Nita grabbed for Gerald's handheld microphone. He spotted the clawlike hand and pulled back. The sound system screamed.

Nita's "I . . . tell . . ." came through mounted speakers as Gerald reclaimed the mic with a resulting screech that forced hands to ears. Yet Nita held on.

The tribal officer stayed in place, unsure what to do.

On tiptoe, Nita hissed into Gerald's ear. His eyes widened. Nita grinned. Gerald released the microphone, and Nita stumbled back at the sudden loss of resistance. The sound system screeched its protest.

We all watched.

Nita regained her footing. Gerald moved to the side as the officer talked into his radio.

The mic shook in Nita's hand, causing another resounding squeal through the speakers. She double-handed the mic and silenced its complaints. For a moment Nita stood looking out at the audience, surprised, unsure how she'd ended up holding the microphone. Then she became aware, and her eyes burned with resentment, desire . . . triumph.

She stepped forward to the front of the stage, searching the audience. Her eyes landed on me. She smiled.

Nita's cold smile scared me. It reminded me of the boar.

She grasped the mic firmly in a single hand while her other hand rose slowly. My eyes locked on it. Microseconds seemed like long, slow minutes as I watched the hand come up to extend outward.

The Hall was eerily quiet.

Ignoring the Kiowa chin-pointing custom, Nita pointed with her finger, as the early invaders did when they rounded up our ancestors to be tossed into pits for months, or placed on death trains headed east, or forced onto reservation lands to starve, as they say Kicking Bird did when he gave up our last three war chiefs, our ancestors' last hope for a free life in Kiowa country.

Eyes turned to follow her crooked finger.

Nita's shrill voice screeched out from the captured mic, bouncing off the walls. "James Sawpole took our Jefferson peace medal."

The bent finger pointed to me.

"She has it."

Chapter Thirty-Three

I stood, frozen, like in a dream—no, a nightmare. I was unable to talk or move. All eyes from the legislators' table rested on me. The crowd's unified gaze focused on me. There was no escape.

Chatter erupted. Voices rose and lowered. All questioning, all yammering, all aimed at me.

Above the turmoil Nita's bitter voice continued, "Nothing was ever taken before. But you will see that James Sawpole just walked in and took."

This got the crowd's attention. Questions were silenced. Nita smiled as she claimed, "He's probably been stealing from us for years."

Whispers started.

The tribal police officer moved to the legislators' table; he was joined by another.

I shook my head in silent denial and looked to the legislators sitting above, onstage; none would meet my eyes.

The crowd's whispers became louder.

Triumphant at spitting out her bile, Nita continued, "Things are good just the way they are at the museum. We don't need others in charge of us again. Just tell James to give back the medal and answer for his crimes."

"Haw" and "Yes" were shouted from the crowd.

The sibilant *S* in "crimes" caught my ear; it released my frozen mind. I moved to the front of the auditorium, stood below, looking up at Nita and the legislators on the stage above. In a voice projected to be heard, I began: "You all know my grandfather, James Sawpole. He is an honorable man."

Murmurs of agreement came from those around. Anna nodded. "*Haw*, yes."

Encouraged, I took a breath to say more, but was cut off.

Nita's amplified voice rang out, "Honorable men don't steal from the tribe." She looked to someone off stage. "Show them."

Lights dimmed in the front of the Hall. The crowd murmured interest. Many shifted in their seats for better positions.

A light rolled across the stage, landed on a screen that I had not noticed on the other side of the seated legislators. A flicker appeared on the screen, followed by blurred black-and-white footage of Grandpa going to a hallway desk, looking about, then down at the desktop.

I'd seen it before, but the projected image held me.

Silence descended as people watched Grandpa go off screen, then return to the desk. He leaned in to take the Jefferson peace medal off the desktop. He held the medal reverently in his hands before again reaching to the desk. Grandpa gathered available materials, wrapped and slid the peace medal into a white cardboard mailer. He sealed the envelope. The screen faded to black as he walked out of the frame with the envelope in hand.

In the stunned silence, Nita's voice sounded, "He's always been full of himself—now you all saw it. James Sawpole stole our Jefferson peace medal." Lights came on to shine down on a gloating Nita.

Her words ignited the crowd. Questions rose from all around. "Where's Sawpole . . . lost the peace medal . . . well, what else is gone . . . or going to disappear . . . tonight?" Questions moved to anger.

One officer used his radio to make a call. The other huddled with two legislators.

My blood ran cold.

The crowd noise increased. One voice rose above others: "Anna, is it true? Is this why we were called?"

Anna shook her head. "Frankly, I don't know who drummed you all in. This was to be a private meeting with the legislators and—"

"And the People, if it's about theft of our heritage . . ." sounded out from someone in the grumbling crowd.

A chorus of *"Haws"* joined shouts of "Yes, we should know."

A single voice loudly asked, "Did James Sawpole steal the peace medal?"

Denny's voice answered, strong and clear: "My grandfather did *not* steal the peace medal."

Ernest Crabapple, a legislator, shook his head. He leaned into his mic. "Not what it looks like from where I'm sitting."

Many voiced agreement with Ernest.

I tried to make eye contact with Anna, but her eyes flicked away.

Gerald must have wrestled the mic back from Nita. He announced, "That treasure should never have been out of its case. That's the first problem." He still hoped to get control of the museum.

Nita glared at him and pulled the mic back. The two fought for it as they spewed hate at each other. A muffled ". . . nothing . . . change . . . everything. . . ." sputtered across the speakers. Gerald released his hold on the microphone, glowering at Nita, and stepped away.

Nita turned to the audience with hatred in her voice. "James thinks he can walk in and take what he wants."

Denny came to the bottom of the stage and stood at my side. He gave me a questioning look.

From behind me, I heard someone mutter, "Where is James?" Then repeated louder, "Where is James Sawpole?" Chairs scraped aside as people turned to look about.

Not wanting to, I moved up the steps to the stage, past a profusely sweating Gerald.

Someone in the crowd called out, "Let's hear from James."

Nita added more fuel to the fire. "Where is James Sawpole? He needs to account for this theft." Her smile deepened as the din increased.

Many chanted, "Where's James?"

As Gerald slid down the stage steps, I took center stage and, heart pounding, announced, "I am Mae Sawpole."

The legislators murmured. One conferred with both officers. The crowd bustled; complaints became louder. No one listened.

From below, Denny urged me on. I spoke over the commotion and tried again. "I'm Mud. James Sawpole's granddaughter." Still louder I added, "James is not available."

That got some attention. Heads swiveled toward me from the legislator's table. The crowd settled; some hushed others close by.

Georgie stood at the back of the auditorium. She didn't look at me. I saw her head move slowly as she scanned the crowd. Not finding what she sought, she slipped out a side door.

I pulled my focus back to the legislators. One had turned his mic on to ask a question. "What do you mean, 'not available'?" He looked around the table, noted the *haws*. Encouraged, the legislator finished by pounding a fist on the table. "This is important business." The legislators and crowd agreed loudly.

I ran my fingers through the curls that Denny had tried to control. I raised my voice above the clamor. "James knows this is important." I struggled to find an explanation. In my silence, the audience got restless. I spoke up again. "He sent me to explain. As our . . . our next story keeper."

Someone loudly announced, "Just what we need, another light-eyed Kiowa . . ." followed by a laugh and a louder, "Worse, she's a curly-headed Indian." More joined in. Laughter surrounded me, bounced off the walls.

Words stuck in my throat. The laughter haunted me. The taunts silenced me.

I faced the people and culture I knew, had grown up with, and loved. I'd been rejected for my outward appearance not being enough. My bloodline, heart, and soul disregarded. I lowered my eyes.

A faint tapping began. And then Nita's contempt blared out through the Hall. "There's nothing to explain. Pictures don't lie." She gained power from the spotlight.

I couldn't let Nita's amplified hate go unanswered. I forced my head up and got words out. "Those pictures aren't telling the whole story."

The tribal officers whispered together.

The hubbub increased.

No one listened.

The steady tap got louder.

Another "Where is James?" call came from the crowd. The question was picked up and repeated.

I forced myself to the front of the stage, to talk to the People. I told them the truth. "James is where he needs to be." I tried to make them understand through my eyes, my voice. But they were too angry, hurt, and confused to listen.

From the crowd below, Denny offered an encouraging nod.

Someone shouted, "Forget Sawpole—where's the Jefferson peace medal?" This started an avalanche of questions and accusations.

Several legislators yelled questions at the same time. I looked wildly at them, not sure whom to answer, what more to say, what to do. A cold feeling slowly engulfed me. This was a mistake.

The crowd's demands increased, rising in volume.

My phone called from my back pocket just as both tribal officers moved toward me. The tapping became louder. A steady beat in an orchestra of discord.

Nita stood holding the microphone, watching the chaos with a look of vicious satisfaction.

Denny moved to the stage steps, but before ascending, he stopped and looked back. I followed his eyes to an old Kiowa grandmother, bent with years, the source of the steady beat. She used a cane to walk slowly from the back of the auditorium to the front. As she walked, her cane tapped the steady drum of a heartbeat.

Slowly, one after another, the legislators noticed the old woman with snow-white hair move to the front of the Hall. They shushed one another as each turned to watch the elder. Denny went to help. The old woman noted the offer with a slight nod but continued her slow march to the front unassisted. She tapped a strong, steady beat.

The crowd quieted as one after another watched the grandmother hobble to the front of the Hall, below the stage. She planted her cane, faced the crowd, and slowly looked out, seeming to make eye contact with each individual as she scanned the faces before her. The steady heartbeat continued. Someone in the audience had started his hand drum in unison with the elder's beat. The old woman took her time looking into the hearts of those around her.

The People waited.

Without a word, the old one raised her beaded cane. Heads moved upward with the cane. The old woman banged the cane down in four loud beats that brought complete silence in the Hall. In a shaky voice she announced, "My children." She paused, gathering strength. "I have seen many things in my many years. As my eyes fail, much comes into focus." A faint drum beat resumed with her words. "It's clear to me, this Kiowa girl"—to my ears and heart she seemed to emphasize "this Kiowa girl," and I stood straighter as she continued—"Mud has a calling. James sees it. I see it. Plain as day to all with opened eyes." The old grandmother stared out at the crowd, daring any to contradict her. None did.

The drum beat on.

Satisfied, the grandmother continued, "Mud has a story to tell." She looked out at the audience. "Let her speak." She banged the cane once more for emphasis, turned to look up at me. "We are ready to listen, grandchild."

I swallowed. I'd lost my words.

Nita chuckled into the mic. The evil laughter echoed around the Hall.

The grandmother kept her eyes on me. She leaned on her cane. "*Koyh mie-tone*, Kiowa girl. You, too, open your eyes to see what is before you."

I breathed in deeply and struggled to settle. Eyes were riveted on me, waiting.

My mind went blank. My eyes skipped wildly around until I landed on Denny. He nodded and breathed out support, confidence, and belief in me. I took it in. Closing my eyes, I felt the positive energy flow. I opened my eyes to Anna. Her focus was locked on me. It, too, offered support.

The old grandmother waited for me to speak. Still, no words came.

Then I turned to look at Nita. Her face was frozen in a satisfied look of glee that came from deep within her. Her delight sparked memories.

I saw it in a flash. I was enlightened.

Somehow, my medicine bag was clutched in one hand. Breathing deeply, I held and then released my medicine bag and breath, in unison. My pounding heart settled into a steady beat.

Awareness lit me from within. Its glow warmed me. Surrounded me. Showed the way.

Looking deeply into the waiting grandmother's eyes, I told her, "*Ah ho, Ti-gui-day*. Thank you, Grandmother." I lifted my head and smiled again to everyone, a sea of faces in a mixture of shades from light to dark—*all my relations.*

I centered myself. Closed my eyes and felt the light within.

Truth came.

I took center stage. I started again.

This time properly.

Chapter Thirty-Four

I stated my true name: *Ahn Tsah Hye-gyah-daw*, She Knows the Way.

I introduced myself formally, noting my seven generations—the Kiowa Way.

Then I brought it back to James Sawpole, my grandfather, our sacred storyteller.

The grandmother nodded her approval. The audience listened.

I found Denny, held his eyes for a moment, then continued. "Many know me as the story keeper's curly-headed grandkid." I grabbed a handful of my unruly curls, released them, and they sprang wild. Faces grinned up at me.

"I followed James, my grandfather, around everywhere. He couldn't get away from me." I smiled remembering. "I would watch from a distance when he sat—squatted, really—with the Old Ones in a circle, all squatting together, passing stories from one to another."

Many in the crowd nodded as they remembered too.

"Grandpa would find me crawling closer and closer as the stories went on. He finally gave in and let me be his shadow." My eyes glazed with the distant memory.

Several *haws* sounded. Then I spoke from my heart. "Grandpa taught me a lot about the Kiowas—our culture and our history. But most important, he showed me how to be Kiowa." I touched my chest where my medicine bundle and heart lay. A warmth generated from within.

A few heads nodded. The old grandmother took a seat in the front row as the crowd settled. They were ready for a story.

Like all Kiowa tellings, I started at the beginning.

My chin pointed toward the front of the Kiowa Complex. "At twelve, I watched with such pride when the Jefferson peace medal was returned to us." I smiled out at the crowd, shared my joy. "I remember my grandfather cleansing and blessing the Jefferson peace medal before presenting it to the museum for us, for all, and others who care about our history, to see the emblem of first contact."

The legislators leaned forward, listening. The audience stayed silent. Waiting to hear more.

Nita broke the moment. "Enough of this. You're not answering our questions."

I hesitated.

An initial gasp of surprise at Nita's rudeness for interrupting burst from the crowd, then turned to a few murmurs of agreement.

The elder kept her eyes on me. I felt her strength. I stepped to the front of the stage, looked out at the People, and waited.

When attention returned, I leaned toward the audience. "My grandfather, James Sawpole, our tribe historian and sacred story keeper, would never take treasures to be sold and hidden away for privileged eyes only."

I saw agreement.

Nita burst in again. "Then where is James and our peace medal—now?"

Her interruption did not disturb my flow. I turned to her. "James is where he needs to be."

She stared back in disbelief, then frustration. She'd expected more.

Before Nita found additional hate to spew, I turned to the audience. "James Sawpole sent me—the one he trained as the next sacred story keeper—to explain, to keep our history safe." I took a beat, then announced, "To speak the truth."

I felt the rightness of my words. They pulsed with life.

Nita's voice sounded harsh across the speakers. "Safe, *hawnay*, that's why we lost one of our most precious treasures."

The truth started with Nita.

I shifted to face the small woman. "Nita, under you we have lost many of our treasures to Gerald and your greed."

Gasps slipped out, then a hush settled through the crowd, broken only by Nita's sputtered, "How can you—"

I turned from her and spoke directly to the People. "You saw part of the story on that security footage. What you don't see is what matters most." I saw questions in the upraised faces. "James came to the Complex to talk to Anna because he was worried about thefts in the museum."

Nita announced, "I heard of no such thing." She gave the People a sincere look.

This brought loud whispers.

I waited.

Anna stood. "It is true. James said a gift he gave the museum fifty years ago came back to him in the hands of tourists. He came to talk." Her words silenced the crowd and Nita.

I nodded my thanks to Anna and turned back to the People. "James saw the Jefferson peace medal on a desk in the hallway—"

Again, Nita interrupted. "I was cleaning it, caring for our artifacts like I do all the time."

I waited her out, let her go silent before I continued. "You saw James, our story keeper, look around and see the Jefferson peace medal." I said it again, voicing my shock, "The Jefferson peace medal—given to the Kiowa from Lewis and Clark. The emblem of our first contact—sitting in the midst of shipping materials." I let the crowd feel the moment before I went on. "You saw James slide the precious treasure into its intended shipping package and escape with it."

Nita couldn't stop herself. "Yes, just as I've been saying, James is a thief." She looked about for support.

I ignored the interruption to tease the audience, "It's what you don't see that matters."

Nita let out an amplified snort.

Faces stayed turned to me. Questioning. The grandmother leaned forward on her cane and waited for more.

I explained, "We don't see cleaning materials. Just shipping materials." Here, I stopped and paused for a beat.

Slowly, eyes showed awareness. Whispers spread the meaning to others.

Anna signaled the nearest tribal officer. He moved to her.

"Nita was getting the Kiowa peace medal ready for Gerald." I spoke above gasps and loud murmurs. "He had the other two mounted in a setting custom-built for all three of the largest Jefferson peace medals. I saw it at his gallery, today."

Whispers erupted into angry voices. Heads swiveled, looking first for Gerald and then, not finding him, back to Nita. She sputtered incoherent protests into the mic.

Georgie stood along the side wall of the Hall, examining the crowd. Again, she slid out a side door.

I continued, "Gerald has been getting Kiowa artifacts and selling to private collectors at a huge profit. It may have started with Buck Crow and needy Kiowa families in the area or with Nita and forgotten treasures in the museum."

"Lies, lies! She is telling lies." Nita's denials bounced from the walls, ending in an amplified screech from the sound system.

Two legislators close to Anna shifted to talk with her and the officers. Many in the audience whispered stories of neighbors' recent losses.

Nita screamed out a final accusation, "James stole the peace medal. You all saw it!"

I waited. Slowly, the rustling settled, and faces turned back to me. I told the People, "Our story keeper gave me the Jefferson peace medal to protect." I pulled the mailer from its nest at my back. Raised the white envelope above my head.

Eyes followed the sealed envelope upward.

A fleeting uncertainty came and went. I had no doubt. With a single tug, I ripped the top tab across the cardboard mailer to open it. Lowered the mailer to peek inside.

I pulled the Jefferson peace medal from the envelope. In the light, the silver disk glistened. The etched Indian and American hands, clasped in peace and friendship, sparkled. Nita had polished the medal. The shine caught her eyes. She stared at the medal, speechless.

Then I walked to the table, made eye contact with the man sitting at its head, the Tribe chairman. He rose, and I placed the peace medal in his cupped hands.

From her seat below, the old grandmother nodded her approval.

I kept the envelope in hand as I walked toward Nita. Talking directly to her now, I said, "When you heard James's message to meet with Anna about the museum, you knew your secret was out."

Silence descended once again.

Nita's eyes looked about wildly. She squeezed the forgotten mic, causing a steady feedback hum.

I confronted her. "Is that what you told Gerald at the airport? That James took the peace medal and suspected you had been stealing from the museum?"

She retreated to the edge of the stage. Looked about wildly.

I followed. "I remembered seeing you two talking at the airport. A pretend cowboy in yellow boots and tie talking to a small Kiowa woman in the back. Buck's grandfather saw you together too. He knew you wanted the peace medal for a big payoff from Gerald." I shook my head. "Unfortunately, he wanted it too."

Nita stepped back to center stage. She patted her hair into place before speaking into the microphone. "You're just trying to help James get away with murder." Nita let the microphone drop to her waist as she enjoyed the crowd's shocked silence.

I stepped forward, seized the microphone to ask Nita, "Who said anything about murder?"

Nita realized her mistake. Her eyes widened. Panic flashed across her face.

I continued, "Nita is right. She is not just guilty of thefts." I stepped closer to her, wanting her to feel the truth of my words. "Nita is also guilty of murder."

She shrieked, "What? How can you say such a thing?" Spittle flew from her lips.

I kept my focus on her. "You said it yourself. You accused me of helping James get away with murder." I drummed it at her. "You didn't say theft—you said murder. No one else said anything about murd—"

Buck burst on stage. "You . . . you killed my grandfather." He towered over the small woman.

Before I could react, Denny was there. He moved to Buck and captured him in an unexpected bear hug that pinned Buck's arms to his sides. Slow to react, one of the officers stood to the side with offers of help.

Nita watched Buck struggle to break Denny's hold. She turned to look at me, then to the stunned audience, her eyes making rapid calculations.

Before her denials could start, I went on with my accusations. "No one showed up at my grandpa's house in muddy clothes like the killer would have after running through the thunderstorm and into the back timber."

This made her relax. Nita thought her cover was in place.

I leaned close to her. "But someone did show up, unexpected, all dressed up in new clothes and ready for this meeting—hours in advance." The microphone made sure my words were heard by all.

Nita shook her head, moving away from me.

My phone buzzed in my back pocket. I ignored it. There was no time for worries over my agency.

The People watched as if a play were unfolding on stage. They waited for the next act in silence. Even the tribal officers stood watching the story come out.

I didn't let Nita get far. I followed her with mic in hand. "You even tried to get into James's workroom." I shook my head, remembering Nita's insistence on going into the no-no room. "You knew what was in there"—our eyes locked—"because you killed Buck Crow's grandfather."

No one seemed to move or breathe. All eyes stayed focused on the small woman.

Nita stared at me, then slowly let a crooked smile out. "Yes . . . yes, I killed him."

Gasps went up. Denny held onto a violently struggling Buck. The officer took hold of one arm.

Nita appealed to the audience. "Wilson deserved it. He . . . he. . . ." She clenched her jaw, anger building as she remembered the insult. "Wilson turned his back on me." Her eyes flashed hot. "He disregarded me." Disbelief played across her face and voice. "Turned his back on me!" She stomped her foot.

Still, everyone remained silent, watching.

Nita went on, telling her story. "I had that buffalo jawbone." She looked at her hand for a moment. "We'd been talking about it earlier. Wilson . . ."

She saw me cringe at the use of the dead man's name. Nita's face twisted into a smile as she looked directly into me. "Such a silly superstition—never name the dead." She sang out, "Wilson, Wilson, Wilson."

A collective gasp echoed through the Hall. They were learning of a death and seeing the true Nita for the first time. A cry went up. Several called out, "Stop! . . . *Hawnay*, no . . ."

One alert, older man moved to a side door and propped it open. Others followed suit giving any trapped spirit means to escape.

Buck lunged for her. Denny and the officer held him back. A faint, resin-laden, sweet smell wafted through the Hall. Somewhere a cedar bundle burned. Its scent seemed to settle the crowd and Buck.

Nita turned to the legislators. Bitterness leaked into her voice. "We were waiting for James. He took the peace medal"—her nose curled—"and Wilson and me, we both had reasons to want it." She smiled at no one.

Anna signaled to the officers. They moved behind Nita.

"Wilson picked up that buffalo jawbone first." Nita's eyes focused elsewhere. "He told me that he remembered James making it when they were boys. James brought down a buffalo calf with it."

Nita let loose a haunting laugh. "That's when Wilson put that jawbone down, right next to my hand." Her gaze went downward as if seeing the jawbone on the table top.

The Hall was quiet, absorbed in the unfolding story. Buck no longer struggled for release. He made no sounds as tears ran down his face.

The grandmother listened.

Nita wrinkled her nose. "Wilson . . . you know how he always cleared his throat." She cleared her own before going on, "Anyways, he finally choked out that he didn't care that no one ever showed him how to make a buffalo jawbone club when he was a boy."

Nita seemed to forget all others; she looked at me. "That made me laugh. You know, Wilson still cared, after all these years." Nita laughed again, thinking about it. "Cared about who made a buffalo jawbone club." She looked through me. Another chuckle escaped as she moved toward the legislators with her story. Her eyes went dreamy with a distant look. "I picked it up, just to feel it." She seemed to hold the buffalo jawbone again. "It felt good in my hand. Kinda had a life in it." She looked directly at Anna, unseeing. "A warmth."

No one breathed.

Coming back to herself, Nita turned to me. "That stuck-up Wilson said I should go. He was getting the peace medal from you." She gave me a look full of hate. Then her body shook with the remembered insult. "Wilson talked to me as if—as, as if I was of no consequence." She shook her head. "Wilson just up and turned his back on me . . . *on me*." Her voice rose at the end.

Nita and I locked eyes. Glee filled her face. I felt sick.

"Bet he was surprised." Nita eyes lit up with the memory. "I let that buffalo jawbone do the talking for me. And by god, Wilson listened then."

Chapter Thirty-Five

Shocked silence filled the Hall, followed by an explosion of sound and action. The two tribal officers stepped forward and took Nita's elbows to escort her off the stage. Before leaving, Nita turned to her audience with a final triumphant smile.

Buck watched them leave, his body slumped in Denny's arms. A legislator dragged his chair over. Denny shoved Buck into the chair. In a voice that carried, Buck repeated, "I thought it was Gerald. I was sure." His face dropped into dirty hands.

Anna was surrounded by people demanding answers. Gerald was nowhere to be seen. He had disappeared.

I caught a glimpse of the old grandmother's back as she left the Hall. For a moment, I stood in the center of the universe, in balance. I breathed in deeply. All was good and right. Then from behind, Denny shoved me. My breath burst loose. Balance lost, I plunged to my bruised knees.

"Mud . . . Mud, man, I am so sorry. I didn't think you would fall over." Denny tried and failed to smother a laugh. He reached a hand out. I grabbed it and let him pull me up. Denny said, "Gotta say, I really thought it was Georgie." He looked around, making sure no one overheard.

The crowd broke into groups talking, questioning, demanding answers. Changes to the museum would be coming.

Still grasping his hand, I told Denny, "Naw, I forgot to tell you. Georgie had new white sneakers."

He squeezed and released my hand. "Well, if you had said that, I would have known it was Nita." Denny's eyes twinkled. "Tell me how it all came together, Storyteller."

"Well, you heard most of it on stage." I moved us away from the lingering few before explaining, "Gerald told me he had a source better than Buck for Kiowa artifacts." I looked over to Denny. "That's what got me thinking about Anna. You said she oversaw the museum and its storage." Denny nodded his understanding. I didn't voice that I still had unanswered questions about Anna.

I went on, "Nita probably started selling to Gerald when he first got into town. You could see, she thought she deserved better in life." I shook my head. "She really did not care about Kiowa artifacts except for what she could get for them."

Anna heard the last bit about Nita. She joined and put her hand on my shoulder. "My mistake." She shook her head. "I delegated going through those stored items to Nita. It's no excuse—I take responsibility." She added, eyeing Denny, "There's just so much work to do."

Anna turned to me. "I heard you say Nita was going to take the peace medal to sell to Gerald."

I nodded. "Somehow Gerald got the other two peace medals." I stopped Denny before he interrupted. "I don't know how he got them. Something the police will check." I made sure this satisfied him before informing Anna, "There are two more Jefferson peace medals at Gerald's gallery. The Kiowa's Jefferson peace medal completed the original set of the three large medals given during the Lewis and Clark Expedition. The set is worth quite a bit."

The phone in my pocket shot me with a few short buzzes. I had messages waiting. They scared me. I pushed thoughts of the agency from my mind. I wasn't ready to come down from this high yet. Reality could wait—for a little longer.

I got back to my story. "Nita planned on cashing in with the peace medal. Gerald was willing to pay big money for it. She had the peace medal out and ready to go when Grandpa stumbled on it. Grandpa sent it to me, which set off a race between Nita and Buck's grandfather to find the medal first."

Denny set his jaw. "Buck's grandfather wanted the peace medal to get his family's *Koitsenko* sash and lance back. He didn't think much about Nita or what he stepped into the middle of until it was too late. It ended with a bash for him."

I lowered my eyes. "I hope it was fast and painless, and he is off riding the wind." As one we uttered, "All My Relations."

Denny wasn't satisfied. "What about Gerald? Looks like he gets to walk around free and clear." He threw his hands up in frustration. "What about the two other peace medals and all the Kiowa artifacts and regalia?" He looked crushed. "Lost . . . forever."

Anna stepped to Denny and pulled him in a hug. She held him for a beat and released him with a smile. "The legislators will deal with Gerald when we find him. We've already started talking." Anna stepped back, shook her head. "I hate thinking of all we've lost. We may never know the full extent and will probably never get things back." She grasped Denny's shoulder. "But we can try. And you, young man, can help." Her earrings danced.

Denny slowly nodded, "Yeah, yeah. It's time for me to give back."

Anna hugged Denny again. "You will make a great legislator. We need more youth."

I stopped listening and watched the two. Denny was so excited. Anna seemed sincere, delighted at strengthening the tribe with another strong mind and voice. Yet I couldn't forget Anna's earring had been at the fracking office steps. I worried but held my tongue. For now.

My phone nagged, reminded me of waiting bad news. I sighed loudly and could delay no more. I called to Denny and Anna, "Excuse me. I hate to, but I need to check my messages." I don't think either noticed me shuffle a few feet away to face the messages on my phone. Denny and Anna were deep in discussions on immediate needs and election strategies.

I took in a deep breath. I was as ready as I could be.

I pressed "Voicemail" and put the phone to my ear. Immediately, I pulled it away. Music blasted. Richard shouted over a background of club noise. I barely understood his repeated, "Hang on, hang on, let me step out here."

I tightened my hold on the phone, prepared for the worst. I dreaded hearing that the IPO was over and the agency was responsible for the millions lost.

Laughter roared.

I looked at the phone to verify that I was still listening to Richard's message, then returned it to my ear. "Oh, Mae, it was priceless. Bernie came stomping in here. Reminded my senior executives of the rules and regulations around initial public offerings. She straight up told all the executives that this was the quiet period and it was forbidden by law for them to be in a bar, talking about the company. That Bernie—did a drill sergeant routine and marched every one of them out the door." He ended with more laughter.

Bernie! My spirits lifted.

Richard choked out, "I really do want her!" and ended the call.

I held the phone, staring at it, when it announced another call. I answered to Bernie's laughter. "Hey, Mae, you listen to your messages yet?"

"Bernie, yes. Yes! I can't believe you marched Richard's executive team out of a bar." A silly grin took over my face.

Bernie huffed into the line. "I got wind of my guys off drinking at a public bar before the show rehearsal tomorrow. I went and got them and told them to go home and *prepare*."

"Richard says you did more than that. He thinks you saved the company."

"He's such a cutie." My eyebrows went up. Bernie had never called a client a cutie before. Was there something more in her voice?

Bernie broke into laughter again. "The absolute best thing was watching Thomas, speechless when everyone left with me. I sure hope Richard had enough sense to shake Thomas and go home too."

"Bernie, you are priceless."

"Yeah, I've been meaning to talk to you about that. I want a raise."

"We'll talk." And I meant it.

I smiled as I pushed the phone into my back pocket. Tomorrow Denny and I would deal with those oil boys. Tomorrow I would face the problems with my business partner. Now, it was time to enjoy the moment.

Author's Note

Although this is a work of fiction, the Kiowa customs and oral traditions shared are real. I share the information on the Kiowa culture intentionally. It is my hope that by adding a touch of Kiowa to my stories, it will keep the culture alive. I do this with nothing but respect for the culture my grandfather and his brother and sisters instilled within me.

—Ah Ho

Acknowledgments

I would not be the person or writer I am today without the help of so many people through life. My parents were my first cheerleaders; a father that supported his family to make sure they had more opportunities than he ever had and my mother, who took me to the library, instilled a love for reading and truly believed I could reach for the stars. Thank you.

I started writing this novel while taking courses through UCSD Creative Writing Extension program. Carolyn Wheat was my first instructor and the one I absolutely needed to get my words onto paper. I cannot thank Carolyn and my fellow students enough for reading my first tries and urging me to stay with the story. I miss you all and our weekly discussions!

Carolyn is the best teacher I've ever had. Thank you so much for your help through Novel I, II, III and beyond.

The following people kept me writing: Miki Webb with her constant glow of positive energy, Jill Norman who made me believe I actually had a story that others may want to read and Greg Norman, partner in all my wild endeavors. They gave me the encouragement I needed to believe in myself and keep writing. Thank you so much!

I was lucky to get an agent, Elizabeth Trupin-Pulli, who liked my story enough to find the right home for it and the perfect editor for me in Sara J. Henry. This has been an amazing experience, made even better by the team at Crooked Lane. Thank you all.

Last but by no means least, I want to thank my family. My son Lucas delighted me when he read a near final draft and announced, "I liked it." I still have the text!

My book would not have happened without Lanie telling me to follow my heart and then keeping the home fires burning while I did. All I have done, has been through your love and support.

—Ah ho!